HAPPY ENDINGS

G.A.HAUSER

Happy Endings

HAPPY ENDINGS

Copyright © G.A. Hauser, 2011

Cover design by Colt St. John

Cover photography by Dennis Dean

Edited By Stacey Rhodes

ISBN Trade paperback: 978-1-4636-4581-6

The G.A. Hauser Collection LLC

WARNING

This book contains material that maybe offensive to some: graphic language, homosexual relations, adult situations. Please store your books carefully where they cannot be accessed by underage readers.

First The G.A. Hauser Collection LLC publication:
October 2011

G.A. HAUSER

About the Photographer
DENNIS DEAN
www.dennisdean.com

Award-winning Photographer Dennis Dean continues to make his mark as an internationally known photographer. He is credited for his creative abilities, strong composition, and dramatic lighting. Dennis specializes in state of the art digital photography for fitness, fashion, and fine art.

Dennis published his first art book, "Within Reach" to rave reviews which led to his work being showcased in a plethora of art publications, fitness magazines, calendars, greeting cards, as well as countless exhibitions, including two in London at the Adonis Art Gallery.

Dennis' travels have spanned the globe. He has photographed from Central America and the Caribbean to Scandinavia, throughout Western and Eastern Europe and Russia. His work has been featured in several issues in the travel magazine, Passport.

He is the Creative Director and Photographer of Five Star Monkey's Ruff Riders and Live Free Be Strong brands. He is also the Editorial Photographer for Mark Magazine, having shot countless covers and fashion layouts.

Dennis is proud to be working with Managing Partner Mario Careaga on making the Dennis Dean Galleries a success. This ideal space located in Wilton Manors, Florida allows them to showcase their photo works, along with other incredible artists from around-the-world. It also includes an area for Dennis to use as his studio to produce eye-catching images in his photo sessions.

To make a photo shoot appointment with Dennis or to take a tour of the gallery, please contact dennisdeangalleries@me.com.

Happy Endings

Visit, www.dennisdean.com.

Dennis Dean Galleries

Dennis Dean g a l l e r i e s

Happy Endings

Prologue

Seventeen-year-old Kelsey 'Kellie' Hamilton gripped the sides of the massage table with both hands, face up, his head thrust back on the padding as he choked on his climax. "Oh my God! Oh my God!"

"You like that?" JC Corbett asked, rubbing Kellie's cock with his oily hand.

He blinked staring at the white cum puddle on his stomach. The sheet wasn't covering him any longer, drawn down to his knees by JC. "Are all massages like that?"

"No. Just the good ones." JC smiled wickedly.

Chapter 1

Ten years later...

Kellie folded the sheet so it wrapped around Lenny's right thigh. A canvas belt around Kellie's waist had a pocket to hold his massage oil. He pumped more into his palm and worked on the back of Lenny's left leg.

Wind chime music mingled with the soft new age sounds in the background. Though the CDs he bought for his clients were cliché—humpback whales singing, waves on the beach, harp and flute music—he found anything else playing while giving a massage was intrusive, and usually got complaints.

The scents of his different essential oils were pleasant to him. He mixed his own for each client depending on their requests. Some wanted to just unwind, others needed deep tissue therapy for aches and pains.

Lenny Silverman, sixty-five years old, all five foot four inches of him, had been a regular customer for two years.

"You have the hands of a saint," Lenny moaned as he spoke.

Kellie chuckled. Lenny usually got more vocal when Kellie kneaded Lenny's ass and upper thighs. "Saint Kelsey Hamilton, that's me."

"I wish you weren't one."

He knew exactly what Lenny meant. "Behave. You're in a perfect position to get a spanking." Kellie used the sheet to cover Lenny's bottom as he moved lower down his left leg.

"Why is it I never need Viagra with you?"

"Because there's no pressure to perform." Kellie bent Lenny's knee and rubbed his feet and toes, squirting more oil onto fingers. Though Lenny was in his mid-sixties, he was a regular at the gym and very well manicured, right down to his toenails. Lenny was retired from the entertainment business. A man of many talents, Lenny acted, wrote, produced and directed hundreds of shows.

"Tell my wife that."

"Which one? You've had several." Kellie placed Lenny's left leg down gently, adjusting the sheet so he could work on his right.

"You get me hotter than any of them."

"You're straight, Lenny. Or at least that's what you appear to be. Why am I getting you hot...again?"

"Again? You've made me get an erection twice a week for nearly two years."

Kellie smiled and stood at the foot of the massage table, holding both Lenny's ankles and tugging his legs as he swung them gently to loosen him up. Lenny moaned.

Walking around to the side of the table, Kellie straightened out the sheet and caressed Lenny's back affectionately. "Okay, Mr. Silverman...Time to scoot down and roll over." Kellie held up the sheet so Lenny's modesty was preserved. He heard him shift on the table and waited for him to settle. Once he had, Kellie lowered the sheet again, seeing the usual tented protrusion and ignoring it. He lowered the face rest and took off the ring pillow to set aside. After he adjusted the cushion under Lenny's knees, Kellie folded the sheet down to his waist and pumped more oil into his hands. Lenny wanted a pure relaxation massage, head to toe.

When he glanced at Lenny's face, he noticed Lenny staring at him. He smiled, picking Lenny's arm up off the table to attend his fingers.

"You should get a portfolio of headshots done."

Kellie said shyly, "I don't want to be an actor."

"How could you not? All the beautiful boys in West Hollywood want to be one."

"Lenny...you know how many times you've said that to me?" Kellie worked Lenny's forearm.

"I've got the connections, you've got the looks."

Kellie noticed Lenny's 'pup tent' get taller. "I don't want to be an actor. I like what I do."

"Touching men."

"Massaging men *and* women." Kellie rested Lenny's limp knuckles against himself and worked his biceps and shoulder. Though he didn't look, Kellie could feel Lenny's gaze on him. In the quiet that followed, Kellie set Lenny's arm back down and stood behind him to massage his chest, running his palms over the gray hair covering it after he added more oil.

Lenny groaned, closing his eyes. His cock kept moving as Kellie ran his fingers over his chest and down his stomach to where the sheet was folded.

"Keep going."

"You are persistent." He did not keep going and began working on Lenny's left arm.

A disapproving sound came out of Lenny.

"If you want that type of massage, you need to see someone else, Len."

"I don't want anyone else." Lenny pressed his fingers into Kellie's hip as Kellie rested Lenny's hand on himself to massage his forearm.

It was fun banter, and Kellie didn't mind. He met Lenny's eyes and gave him a wink.

After Lenny was gone, Kellie scrubbed his hands, stripped off the sheets and placed fresh ones on the table. Then he tidied up the room and checked the time. He limited his work to three or four appointments a day. It was enough and left him time to work out and do other things he enjoyed. With his arms loaded with laundry, Kellie headed behind the spa area of the gym to exchange the dirty sheets for freshly laundered ones.

"Hi, Chelsea," Kellie greeted another massage therapist as she was doing the same.

"I had no idea you needed sheets. I would have brought you some."

"No big deal. I had to bring down the dirty ones anyway." He picked up a few fresh towels as well.

"How's your Wednesday going so far?"

"Good. Just finished Lenny. I have Neal next," he said, "How's life in general going for you?"

"Eh. So-so." She made a face, gathering up the pile of clean linens to carry with her.

She and Kellie started heading back to the massage area to fit their tables with fresh sheets. "Yeah. Life's like that."

She rolled her eyes comically. "We need to exchange massages soon. I'm dying."

"Sounds good. Anytime. Catch ya later."

"Okay."

After Kellie fixed up his table so it was ready for his next client, he stopped at the men's room to relieve himself. When he stood at the sink to wash his hands, he checked out his appearance. He removed the rubber band from his short ponytail and coiled it around his hair again to keep it off his face while he worked. A few strands fell around his jaw, too short to tuck behind his ears. He wore a loose fitted, off-white cotton sleeveless shirt, matching baggie jersey yoga pants—without briefs—and flip-flop sandals which he removed once he began working.

He met his own blue eyes in the mirror and sighed. The yearning for coffee to keep him alert was strong, but too much caffeine screwed up his system. He tried hard to eat only organic fruit and vegetables, and no meat.

"Right." He motivated himself to keep going, making his way to the waiting area by the receptionist. Neal was waiting, reading a magazine. Neal was thirty-five, nicely built, mildly receding hairline, average height, and worked in construction.

"Neal?"

Neal looked up, tossed his magazine on the rack and followed Kellie to his room.

"How are you?"

"Sore." Neal rubbed his shoulder, moving his arm around to indicate he was in pain.

"Okay, buddy. Just get ready and I'll be in in a minute." Kellie closed the door behind Neal, heading to the staff room to mix up the right oil to ease Neal's pain. As he inhaled the scents of peppermint, ginger, and cinnamon, he heard the noise of many conversations around him. The salon was upscale-Hollywood-elite with a sauna, Jacuzzi, juice bar, lap pool, facials...the works.

The clientele tended to be mostly L.A.'s *almost* A-list with a few wannabe reality stars tossed in for good measure.

The oil smelled more like an herbal tea than a massage lotion, but Kellie was convinced these essential oil recipes worked.

He sank the plastic bottle into his utility belt holder and headed back to his room. Leaning his ear on the door, he knocked lightly.

"Yeah," Neal said.

Kellie entered the room, seeing Neal lying face down in the ring face-rest, the sheet at his mid-back. As he straightened out the sheet, Kellie asked, "The shoulder again?"

"Yes. It's fucking killing me."

"Okay, babe." Kellie made sure Neal was comfortable with pillows under his ankles and the music at a low level. Before he greased up his hands, Kellie stood at the head of the table and ran his palms from Neal's shoulders to his ass.

"Oh, God, Kel…I don't know what I would do without you."

Kellie smiled to himself. He loved his job.

Chapter 2

Kellie finished his yoga class, making sure he not only took care of others, but babied himself as well. By evening the club was packed with clients, talking excitedly about the latest celebrity gossip and who was sleeping with whom.

Wearing her head-set, Lynn, the receptionist, caught up to Kellie as he left the yoga class to go change.

"Natalie Cushman called for an appointment. I said I didn't know if you were done for the day or not."

Kellie checked his watch. "What time can she get here?"

"Six-thirty."

"Sure."

Lynn nodded and headed back to her desk.

Once Kellie was in the locker room to change back into his massage outfit, he located his phone and dialed.

"Hey."

"Hey, Scott. I just got a late client."

"Okay."

"Did you plan on anything for dinner?"

"No. I...uh...actually I have a late job as well."

Kellie sighed and leaned on the locker behind him as men came and went, some checking him out overtly. "Okay."

"I've got an airport run and then I'm supposed to take some guys out for their bachelor party."

He and Scott Baldwin had only just begun dating, and already their two work schedules clashed. "Bachelor party? On a Wednesday night?"

"They're from Denver and are here through the weekend."

Kellie blinked. "They booked you as their chauffeur all week?"

"No. Not all week. Why do you sound so pissed? Don't be possessive."

That comment did piss Kellie off. "Possessive? Are you kidding me?" He felt like hanging up.

"We'll figure something out. I have to go."

"Bye." Kellie disconnected the phone and began undressing for a quick shower. He knew Scott would be a player. The first time Kellie met him, Scott boasted about having a three-way sexual bout with Keith O'Leary and Carl Bronson of *Forever Young*. Kellie didn't believe a word of it, but Scott said it was before the two superstars came out of the closet, or were huge celebrities. It should have been a warning to Kellie to steer clear, but Kellie always tried to see the best in people, sometimes to his peril.

"Hey, sweetheart," Mike, an older client said as he touched Kellie on the shoulder.

Kellie perked up and smiled. "Hi, Mike."

"I have an appointment with you tomorrow."

"I know. I'm looking forward to it." Kellie slung his towel over his shoulder.

"Not as much as I am." Mike waved as he walked away.

Kellie headed to the shower for a quick rinse before Natalie showed up. He was trying not to be angry at Scott because then Natalie's session wouldn't be perfect. Kellie wanted to give one hundred percent to his clients. He'd do nothing less.

Natalie Cushman was one of Kellie's favorites. She worked for Adam Lewis, L.A.'s top talent agent and had the best gossip to share. Bright dyed red hair, black at the roots, multiple tattoos and piercing, Natalie was someone Kellie would love to socialize with. He was drawn to her upbeat nature and energy. Nothing frazzled her.

Kellie greeted her at the lounge where she was drinking a juice smoothie. He held out his arms to her for a hug. "Natalie…"

She skipped towards him and gave him a one arm hug and Hollywood air kisses on each cheek. "So glad you can squeeze me in. I'm dyin!" She chugged the rest of her smoothie, making a face and crying, "Brain freeze!"

"You didn't have to do that." He held her hand once she tossed out the cup and they walked to his private room. "Where do you ache?"

"All over. I need to get laid."

"Can't help you with that." He gave her hand a squeeze and bumped hips with her.

"I know. You're not my type."

"Oh?" He stood at the entry to the room as she sat on the chair inside and began unlacing her black Doc Martin boots.

"I like big ole bears with beards." She winked.

"Natalie Cushman!" He feigned a feminine gesture, something he rarely did. "You never told me that before."

"Did you ask?" She tucked her socks into her shoes.

"I don't remember. We usually catch up on all the good gossip from Adam's clients."

"Shh. Agent-client privilege." She held her finger to her lips.

"Okay, Nat. Get ready, face down and I'll be right back... The usual?"

"Yes, please."

He threw her a kiss and shut the door behind him. When his phone vibrated in his pocket he took it out, hoping it was Scott. It wasn't. It was Tyson Hopper, his best friend and one of the personal trainers who worked here at the spa. Tyson was asking him if he was free for drinks later. He texted him, '*yes, after this client.*'

'*sweet*' was Tyson's reply.

Kellie continued on his way to mix the oil for Natalie. Once he had, he called through the door, "You ready?"

"Yup."

He entered, closing the door behind him, straightening the sheet over Natalie's back, and adjusting the pillow for her legs. While she relaxed, Kellie heated up the massage stones, which he knew Natalie liked, and stood close to her, running his hands down her back to get her ready. "Breathe, babe."

She inhaled and blew out a breath through the donut hole in the face rest.

"Just for relaxation?" He brushed back the wisps of hair from her neck that hadn't been attached in her hairclip.

"Back, shoulders, you know the drill."

"So? Are you seeing any bears?" Kellie folded the sheet down to her waist, admiring all the artwork on her skin.

"Yup. I got me a bear. Just met him so I haven't fucked him yet."

He could hear the smile in her voice. "Good girl." He rubbed the oil into his hands and began smoothing down her back.

"He's a big ole' tattooed biker. So opposite from the men I see on the job."

"I can imagine." Kellie framed Natalie's spine with his palms and ran them down either side to her hips.

"Gotta tell you the latest."

"Tell me."

16

"Mark Richfield had this crazy masquerade party and all the guests stripped and jumped in the pool."

"Sorry I missed it."

"Me too. Adam was talking to Carl about it over the phone. He didn't know I was eavesdropping, laughing my ass off."

At the name drop of one of the night-time soap stars, Kellie thought of Scott. "Hey...would you know if those guys from *Forever Young* had a three-way with their chauffeur ages ago?"

"Carl and Keith?"

"Yes." Kellie began working Natalie's right shoulder, feeling where she was knotted up.

"I don't know. Why? I wouldn't doubt it. I heard all sorts of shit about them."

"So...you think they would be the type to ask a driver to come to bed with them?"

"Definitely. Why? You want me to see if I can get you a date with them?"

"No. Just the guy I started seeing recently said he played with them when he was their chauffeur."

"Oh."

"Yeah. Oh." Kellie loosened Natalie's arm from the sheet and shook it out, letting it hang beside the table, then began working her back deeper.

"I'd tend to believe him."

"Yeah. I thought so too." Kellie blew out a breath and tried not to let it bother him. He and Scott certainly weren't a couple, and had only had sex once.

"Oh! Let me tell you the latest on Alex! You're gonna die!"

Kellie laughed and shook his head. "Go for it."

~

Before Kellie left for the day, he stopped by the front desk to see what Lynn had scheduled for him for tomorrow. Two new names were penciled into his Thursday—Tessa and Monty.

17

Someone placed their arm around his shoulder for a hug, standing alongside him. Kellie gave Tyson a smile and kiss on the cheek.

"You ready for some drinks, girl?" Tyson asked.

"Hell yeah."

"Come with me. Time to catch up." Tyson held Kellie's hand and they walked out of the salon together. Though summer was waning as October crept in, it was still mild in temperature, and sunny. "Fubars?"

"Too loud. Can't catch up there." Kellie waved to someone he knew as they walked by. "Let's go to the Abbey."

"We'll never get an outdoor table."

"We might. It's only Tuesday."

"I keep forgetting," Tyson said, "You were off for the last two. I was working." Tyson rolled his eyes. "Is it Friday yet? Is it Friday yet?"

Kellie knocked into him playfully. He liked Tyson. The man was easy to talk to, and there was no sexual tension. Tyson liked his men to be slightly feminine and slender, while Kellie wanted a masculine macho man to enjoy. The sleeveless dress shirt Tyson wore showed off his sculpted shoulders and arms, and his mocha skin gleamed in the evening sunlight.

"Take this out," Tyson said as he tugged the rubber band from Kellie's hair. "You're not working now." He handed over the little elastic to Kellie.

"Thanks. I should have dried it after the shower. Now it's going to be all wavy." He put the band around his wrist.

"I'd kill for that hair." Tyson's hair was cut in a shaved style, with sharp angles near his forehead and sideburn.

"Fergie does killer weaves."

"My hair's too short for weaves. Are you walking us to your car or…?" Tyson asked.

18

"No. I was walking us to the bar. You're kidding, right?" Kellie pointed to the area in front of them. "It's just down that way, and there's never any parking."

"I spent eight hours training and working out. I'm so friggin tired."

Kellie pouted out his lower lip in exaggeration. "Aw. Let me carry you."

When Tyson hopped onto Kellie's back for a ride, Kellie was surprised but started laughing. He hoisted Tyson higher on his back, held his legs, and felt Tyson rest his head on him.

"You do realize how stupid this looks." Kellie caught the odd stares from passersby.

"I would have driven us." Tyson yawned.

"Are you going to sleep back there?"

"Yeah. Wake me when we arrive."

Kellie shook his head in amazement and wondered if anyone in his life was sane.

Chapter 3

Kellie didn't hear from Scott all night. And he didn't contact him, either. Another potential relationship, gone before it got started. Kellie had no idea if it was him, or the way of the world. Were they all disposable now? Tick the 'wrong' box and onto the next?

He hadn't gotten very attached to the handsome chauffeur and was glad for it.

As he got ready for his day ahead, Kellie washed his dish from breakfast and made sure his apartment in West Torrance was neat. No, it wasn't where he wanted to be in life, but after losing his house to a foreclosure, losing his job in real estate and finally getting a good job after massage school, Kellie forced himself to keep a positive attitude.

Once he was in his Prius and on his way to work, Kellie let go of his stress. He and Tyson had chatted all night over cocktails. It did help to share some of his concerns with a good friend, but it didn't make any of his problems go away.

His routine—which wasn't necessarily in the same order every day—consisted of a one hour workout, yoga class, and working with his clients. Kellie loved pumping weights and nothing was better for his ego at the moment than having men ogle his muscular body. If he was into the sex for sex alone scene, he'd be fucking someone every night. *Been there. Done that, not doing it anymore.*

The novelty of meaningless orgasms had *cum* and gone.

I'm twenty-seven. I want something more.

Though he swore he would not think about his past failures in both love and his career, it had caused self-doubt and anxiety in Kellie.

Using the pulley system to work his arms and chest, Kellie made sure his posture was correct, staring at his exposed abs from his midriff shirt in the mirror.

Tyson came up behind him, watching him. "You should go heavier. That weight is flying up and down."

"How much?" Kellie lowered the cable.

Tyson adjusted it. "Try ten."

There wasn't another trainer Kellie trusted as much as Tyson. Tyson knew Kellie wanted to be strong, big, and muscular. From behind, Tyson touched Kellie's shoulders, watching him pull the heavy plates up. "Slow down."

Kellie nodded, tasting the sweat from his top lip. When Kellie was deep inside his head thinking, he did have a tendency to whip through the repetitions too quickly.

"Better." Tyson ran his hand down Kellie's low back to the globes of his ass.

"You'll give me a hard-on." Kellie did the final few reps, needing to turn around and work the other side of his body.

"So? You give everyone you massage one. Turn-about is fair play."

Kellie released the handgrip and slowly spun around. He and Tyson were face to face, smiling at each other. "You haven't had a massage in ages."

"Not with you."

"Oh?"

"I get so hot from you I go crazy. And you never give me a happy ending."

Seeing the smile in Tyson's dark eyes, Kellie laughed. "No happy endings. You're right."

Tyson tilted his head seductively as he walked off. "When you do, let me know."

Kellie thought about his own experience when he was seventeen, getting his first massage. Happy ending indeed. JC not only used his hands to make Kellie come, he sucked him off regularly after the massages. For ten years Kellie had assumed that was part of the release. Get your back rubbed, get your cock sucked. It wasn't until he lost his job in real estate and became board certified in massage therapy that he realized a blowjob was *not* normal.

After checking the time, Kellie wrapped up his workout and headed to shower before his first client. The club wasn't an overt meat market, but because of its West Hollywood locale and the gorgeous clientele, temptation lurked. Kellie resisted.

Not only was he more focused on finding a 'suitable' partner, but hooking up where he worked would give him the raunchy reputation he avoided like the plague. The owners of this pricy salon would not be happy with employees having multiple casual sex partners on the job. It was an unwritten rule that Kellie agreed with.

And his license in the state of California didn't allow him to sexually touch his clients. Though some men were forward, like Lenny, Kellie didn't have a desire to gratify his clients that way. He didn't think he ever would.

In his outfit of loose fitting black, cotton jersey yoga pants with a drawstring waist, and sleeveless black t-shirt, Kellie made sure the room was ready for his first client of the day, Mike.

Mike Murphy, the aspiring actor with a few bit parts already in the works. Twenty-three, and what Kellie would call 'petite', Mike was all of five foot six inches tall, and slender.

Kellie walked in his bare feet to call Mike in from the waiting area and found him sitting reading a *People* magazine with the mega-star Alexander Richfield on the cover. The headline read, '*Alex in Love*'. Kellie had already gotten the inside scoop from Natalie on Alex's affair with an LAPD police lieutenant twenty years his senior. Rumor was it was doomed. Time would tell.

Since Mike was completely absorbed in his celebrity gossip mag, Kellie was able to walk right up to stand in front of him. He laughed and said, "Mikey?"

Mike looked up and smiled broadly. "You always look so fucking edible."

"Thank you." Kellie peeked into the magazine. "Catching up on pretty Alex?"

"Yeah. Lucky older fucker is nailing him." Mike tossed the magazine onto the rack.

As they walked back to Kellie's room, Kellie asked, "You'd like to fuck Alex?"

"Wouldn't you?"

"No, he's too young and too androgynous." Kellie gestured for Mike to enter the cozy room.

Mike immediately took off his shirt, draping it on a chair. "Shut up. You wouldn't fuck him if he offered?"

"Why do you seem so shocked?"

"Because he's become every gay man and straight woman's sexual fantasy."

Kellie figured Mike would strip naked while he watched. It wasn't protocol. "Not mine. Okay, babe. See you in a bit."

"You don't have to leave." Mike took off his shoes and socks, about to yank down his pants.

"I have to mix your oils. Just relaxation today?"

Mike dragged his lower half of clothing off and sported a semi-erection as he dropped his items over the chair. "Yup."

"Be right back." Kellie stepped out, trying to get his mind into work mode. It wasn't easy when everyone you worked with was nude.

~

Typically, between clients, Kellie took a yoga class, ate a lunch of salad and miso soup in the employee lounge, and checked his voicemail messages. During that time of day he was updated by Lynn as to his appointments for the week, which were accumulating quickly. If Kellie chose, he could work five or six clients a day, seven days a week, but even though he would love the money at this point in his life, he decided the work would not only tax him physically, it would burn him out.

Chelsea noticed him and sat with him at the table, setting down a shot of wheatgrass juice and a protein power bar. Working in a healthy environment rubbed off on all the employees. Kellie didn't want to say it was mandatory for the staff to be perfect specimens of humanity, but it seemed that way. The application process, even for someone like Kellie who was 'self-employed' inside the club, was brutal. The elite/snobbish culture of the salon would accept nothing less. Kellie didn't buy into the tacky attitude, but he needed to make good money.

His vegetarian-green-planet-loving ways fit right in with the owners. All Kellie had to do was mention he drove a Prius and the light turned on in the owner's eyes.

"Hey, Kellie."

"Hey, Chel." Kellie drank the last of his miso soup from his mug.

"Word behind the scenes is they're hiring another manager."

"Oh? What happened to Lindsey?"

"She had an affair with a client."

"So?"

"In the sauna…"

"Oh." Kellie chuckled.

"I told her to wait 'til it closed."

"She did it during business hours?" Kellie choked in his laugh.

"That's the gossip. So? Out she goes." Chelsea peeled back the wrapper of her protein bar.

"It's not easy resisting. There's so much testosterone and estrogen floating around in here all the time."

"I know. Hey, we can date people, just not have sex here in the club." She bit the bar and chewed like it was leather.

"True. Just a smidgen of self-control can go a long way."

"I know. And the massage therapists have it the hardest…" Chelsea laughed at herself. "Pardon the pun."

"I know. Mike Murphy was my last client." Kellie made a face of pleasure. "He may be short but he's perfectly formed. Everywhere."

"Mm." Chelsea wriggled in her seat. "Do they tell you if they're gay or not right off the bat?"

"Sometimes. Or they just flirt. I don't know the preference of each client. And with someone like Lenny, who's married and still gets wood…" Kellie shrugged, finishing his salad.

"Lenny's a perv."

"Nah. He's all right." Kellie stood, rinsing his bowl at the sink and checking the time. "I have a new client. I should go and make sure the room is ready."

"Okay. See ya later."

Kellie smoothed his hand over the sheet to flatten it, turned on the music, and checked his stone warmer. Everything was perfect so he walked to the waiting area to see if his client had shown up yet. There were nearly a dozen people hanging out as they waited for their manicures, facials, and training sessions. Before Kellie called out the name of his client, he played a game with himself. Could he tell who the newbie was?

Since the name of the client was 'Monty', Kellie assumed it was a man. But then again, who knew? Monica could be nicknamed Monty...no? No. Kellie's gaze rested on one man in particular.

Big, buff, dark hair, clean-shaven, wearing a short-sleeved t-shirt exposing tattoos on both of his shoulders. Maybe mid to late thirties, and not the usual pretentious clientele Kellie had come to expect. With his hopes high, Kellie called out Monty's name, staring directly at this masculine stud.

Immediately Monty raised his head from his *Men's Fitness* magazine. The look was a mixture of surprise and... disappointment? Kellie didn't know and felt a nervous pit in his stomach. Monty tossed the magazine on a chair and stood, approaching Kellie. The height of his new client impressed him.

"Hi. I'm Kellie." He reached for a handshake. His clasp was received but nothing was said. "Right this way." Kellie led the way to his room, wondering what was going on. He gestured for Monty to enter before him. Monty did, still looking uncomfortable. "Is there something wrong?"

Monty rubbed his forehead before speaking. He seemed to just notice Kellie's certificates on the wall. "Kelsey." Monty had spotted his name.

"Yes?"

Monty spun around and said, "When the receptionist asked if I wanted to make an appointment with Kellie, I thought she meant..."

"A woman?" From Monty's expression, Kellie assumed that was exactly what it was. "It's okay. Let's go see if Chelsea is available."

"No. No..." Monty stopped him. "It's okay."

26

"You sure? I won't be offended." *Straight boy*. Kellie waited another moment, just to be certain this truly was 'okay'.

Without answering him, Monty sat down on the chair and began taking off his shoes.

"Okay. See you in a bit. Start face down."

Monty nodded, not looking happy.

As Kellie closed the door, he shook his head. His photo was in the lounge area with his name and occupation; it was on the website as well. If a client didn't pay attention, and had a preference, that wasn't his fault.

Kellie figured he'd have this guy one time, then refer him to Chelsea. He had a mixture of straight and gay male clients. What did this guy think he was going to do? Seduce him?

It angered Kellie. He was a professional and any aspersions cast on his reputation hurt, be they imaginary or not. He mixed oils, taking his time, making sure the guy had enough of a chance to hide under the sheets and not be seen naked.

Kellie imagined Monty would be so paranoid and homophobic he'd wear his pants. With an effort Kellie refocused his thoughts to a more positive place and stood outside the door, listening. He heard no movement and knocked.

"Come in."

Kellie opened the door, seeing Monty under the sheet, his head in the face rest. He straightened out the sheet, observing that Monty was naked underneath. Once he had him comfortable, he began touching Monty's back gently, through the linen. "What do you want in specific today?"

"Just an overall relaxation massage."

"Have you ever had one before?"

"Yes."

"Okay." Kellie folded the sheet to Monty's hips, staring at the tattoo on his left shoulder. A US Navy SEALs insignia—an eagle holding an anchor, pistol, and a trident. It was Kellie's turn

27

to get a hard-on. Monty wasn't extremely cut like so many of the men in the gym—starved of carbs and fats to show off all their ripples and lines—but Monty was fucking *built*. Powerful-looking incredibly strong.

Calm down. Be professional. This is the kind of guy who will screw you if you fuck up—and not in a good way.

Kellie pumped oil into his hands and stood at the front of the table, smoothing his palms down Monty's back to his hips. Monty let out a long slow breath, as if he had indeed done this before and knew to remember to breathe—something Kellie had to remind other clients of constantly.

"Let me know how the pressure is."

"I like it deep."

A surge of heat raced through Kellie's groin at the comment. "Okay." *So do I...shit, I would love you deep.* In what felt like a complete role reversal, Kellie was the one growing excited. Sure he'd had handsome men lying nude on the table before—some offering to allow Kellie a touch or taste—but Kellie continued to decline for so many reasons.

Suddenly placed with a man he assumed was straight, who wanted a woman to touch him, Kellie remained professional, but his fantasy took wing.

I'm going to enjoy this. Kellie made long sweeping caresses down either side of Monty's spine, loosening him up and getting him used to his touch. As he made his way to the other side of the table, he saw another tattoo on the man's right shoulder. In a scrolling black script it said, '*The only easy day was yesterday*'.

Kellie preferred his clients not speak during their sessions, but left that decision up to each individual. Some used the hour to an hour and a half to rant or gossip. Each to his own. But Kellie had a feeling Monty would be stone silent. Who knew what the man had experienced. No one but a Navy SEAL would get that tattoo.

"You doing okay?" Kellie asked, to make sure.

"Yes."

The way it was said, Kellie decided not to ask again. It wasn't irritation, but it was as if the question was stupid. What could Kellie do to this man he hadn't already been through. He'd seen documentaries of the training. Very few men could endure that.

Kellie untucked Monty's right arm from the sheet, letting it drop limply over the side of the table. He used more oil and began going deeper, probing for the tight muscles. He certainly found them. Under Monty's tanned skin was tension. *Poor baby.*

Kellie began applying harder pressure to the area between Monty's shoulder blade and spine, where a series of knots were located. Using his elbow and forearm, Kellie tried to get them to release, helping Monty let go of pain and stress. While he pressed into Monty's back with his arm, he caught scent of his cologne or aftershave. The scent was soon going to be overpowered by Kellie's peppermint and eucalyptus oil.

He leaned down and took a quick sniff before it disappeared. The rush to Kellie's cock was completely inappropriate. He knew better. *Stop getting off on this guy. Stop it.*

Kellie squeezed Monty's trapezius, giving it a good work over.

He wasn't into uniforms—didn't go ga-ga over strippers who wore police or firemen get ups. Being a laid back vegetarian, Kellie had the impression most men in the service, be it military or paramilitary, had relatively big egos and narcissistic tendencies. There was nothing Kellie liked less. So while many men drooled over the boys in blue and khaki, Kellie preferred more holistically inclined creatures who liked hiking and whale watching.

Getting a suddenly flash of irony, Kellie imagined Monty had hiked around the planet, and seen more marine mammals than he could in a lifetime.

Happy Endings

What is it like to be you?

Kellie could only wonder. Under his hands, Monty took a few slow deep breaths. Using the timing of those exhales, Kellie pushed harder as Monty blew out. "How's the pressure?"

"Go deeper."

Kellie's cock was getting downright hard. In his flimsy yoga pants, he could see the fabric tenting. He wasn't wearing anything underneath. There usually wasn't a need. Until now.

Kellie checked on the message stones to see if they were warm. He picked one up and rubbed oil on it. With the stone, Kellie was able to work deeper into Monty's sore muscles.

A low masculine groan emerged from Monty.

Kellie couldn't get his body under control and it was embarrassing him. As he leaned over Monty to press into his upper back with the stone, Kellie's stiff cock brushed Monty's right arm, the one that was dangling over the table. Monty didn't react, and Kellie backed up quickly. He didn't panic, simply dropped the stone back into the warming pot and continued.

This guy is going to think I am getting off on him. I am *getting off on him!*

Stop getting off!

Maintaining a smattering of self control, Kellie replaced Monty's arm back on the table and stood at the head. He pumped more oil into his hands and again smoothed down the length of Monty's torso to his hips. As he reached the sheet which was folded on Monty's ass, Kellie glanced down. His extended dick was trying to brush against Monty's head as he lay face down in the face rest's donut cushion. If Monty's eyes were open, all he could see at the moment was Kellie's bare feet through the ring.

Kellie kept his massage on track though he was becoming a mass of nerves. The one guy who'd thought he was getting a woman therapist because he must hate queers, was going to be the one to make an accusation to cause Kellie to lose his job. But no matter what, Kellie could not make his dick obey him. It had decided to behave like a spoiled child and there was little Kellie could do while he continued to touch this macho warrior.

Biting his lip, seeing his dick creating a damp stain in the fabric, Kellie knew after he worked Monty's top half and moved to his legs, both his cock and the massage were going to get even harder.

Once Kellie finished working Monty's left arm, ogling the Navy SEALs tattoo, he began massaging Monty's low back. Again Monty let out a low moan—pleasure, release, something nice.

Kellie took a deep breath for courage and began folding the sheet around one of Monty's legs to expose the other. Once he had gingerly tucked the fabric between Monty's legs under his nuts, Kellie pumped more oil into his palm, staring at the long muscular limb in agony. The man was all legs, perfection once again. Kellie smoothed the oil down the back of it and began squeezing that hunk of man-flesh, losing his mind as he did. His dick was now a constant flag mast protruding from his groin and there was nothing Kellie could do about it.

With his probing fingers he moved the sheet so he could dig into the area of Monty's hip, where nerve endings created tension. Though his thoughts were naughty, his technique remained flawless. Training kicked in.

The globes of Monty's ass were impeccable. Powerful men tended to have ideal proportions. Kellie could only imagine how intense the training was for Monty. But whatever this man had learned about keeping fit was working.

Monty was not in his twenties. Kellie could see that. He knew the difference a decade made. This type of man only improved as he aged. Kellie had no doubt Monty was his ideal.

Kneading that fine ass was the agony and the ecstasy. Kellie was doing just what this man dreaded. *This is why he wanted a woman! You moron! Calm the hell down!*

But Kellie couldn't.

This must have happened to Monty before. Kellie never thought he'd be in this position. It had never happened to Kellie previously. Never!

Stop rubbing his butt. Stop rubbing his butt!

As he wedge his fingers into the hip flexor, feeling Monty respond by tightening, meaning, he was in pain, Kellie used a circular motion to loosen up the muscles. He watched Monty's gluts tense and release as he took another deep breath.

The fantasy took wing for Kellie as he imagined what he would do to Monty if Monty had been his lover. First order of business would be to devour this tight fucking ass.

Kellie worked his way down Monty's amazing left leg to his foot, bending Monty's knee and using more oil to give his toes and arch a good rubbing. Another low moan competed with the sound of ocean waves from the CD. Kellie smiled to himself. He rested the left foot down and stood near Monty's right, redirecting the sheet to wrap the leg he had finished and expose the one he had not. Seeing some of Monty's ass crack nearly made Kellie swoon. Though he was not taking liberties and doing what he did with every person he massaged, Kellie was struggling hard with his attraction.

He finished manipulating the sheet, again using oil to lubricate their contact. He rubbed that fabulous leg to the heel and again went for the hip flexor and low back before he headed to Monty's foot.

"How sore are you there?" The reaction of pain from Monty when Kellie pushed into his hip was strong.

"Sore." He sounded groggy, which was normal.

Kellie used his thumbs to spin tiny circles around that tender area. A dab more of oil and Kellie dug into the flexor, making Monty clench his ass cheeks delightfully. "Too much?"

"No. Go for it."

God! Do you say all the right things? Kellie's cock seeped into the tented jersey fabric again. With his elbow, Kellie pressed into the hollow of Monty's hip, holding it there. "Breathe."

Monty inhaled before exhaling, seemingly trying to let go of the tight muscle Kellie was manipulating. Kellie released the pressure and rubbed from Monty's gluts to his low back in an arcing motion. He continued down Monty's leg the same way as he had his other—to his foot, bending his knee and paying special attention to each toe. He rubbed his calf and noticed a long scar from a gash needing stitches, healed and no longer pink.

Kellie was tender with it, seeing how bad the injury had been.

He finished massaging his legs and untucked the sheet, covering Monty's lower half. Standing beside him, Kellie raised the sheet like a blind and said, "Okay. Scoot down and turn over."

The sound of rustling ensued and Kellie imagined Monty doing as he'd asked. Once the noise of movement stopped, Kellie replaced the sheet, seeing Monty's handsome face with impressions of the ring pillow on his cheeks. Kellie folded the sheet at Monty's shoulders and removed the donut cushion, lowering the face rest.

No hard-on. Monty was not excited by his touch. If this had been any other man, Kellie would have been relieved. But seeing Monty completely uninterested sexually was disappointing. Kellie rolled up a stool and sat down behind Monty's head. He removed two heated stones and rubbed oil on them. With a stone in each hand he worked under Monty's shoulders and up his neck.

33

Monty's lips parted as he sighed. "God, that feels good."

Kellie perked up. "I'm glad."

"Never had anyone use those."

"They've been around, just gaining in popularity." Kellie stared down at Monty's eyelashes. They were dark brown, like his eyebrows and hair. It appeared Monty's eyes were either closed or he was looking down at the far wall with Kellie's certificates on it. After giving Monty's shoulders and neck a good massage with the stones, Kellie tossed them back into the heater and continued with his hands. He folded the sheet to just above Monty's nipples and massaged his chest. Soft hair covered the center only, dark and alluring.

Kellie reached over Monty to use both hands. As he stood, stretching down Monty's torso, Kellie nudged the sheet down to his hips.

He walked beside Monty, folding the sheet to just above Monty's pubic hair. When he dared to glance at him, Kellie found Monty staring.

Those bright blue eyes studying Kellie made him nervous. He took a peek at his yoga pants. *Yup, still hard.*

Continuing to keep professional and do what he did with all the other clients who requested a relaxation massage, Kellie didn't look at Monty again. Instead, he massaged Monty's abdomen and his chest, back to his arms again. Taking the right one, he rested Monty's hand on his own hip, pumped more oil and then worked Monty's fingers. His hands were callused from hard work. Maybe from firing guns. Kellie could only guess.

He tucked that hand away under the sheet and kept in contact with Monty as he walked around him to do the same to the other side. He thought he felt Monty's stare but didn't check to see if he was actually watching. Doing the same on both sides, Kellie finished Monty's arms and brought the sheet back up to Monty's chest. Running his fingers down Monty's hip to his legs, Kellie stood at the base of the table and raised Monty's heels up, loosening his legs. He still had a few minutes to go, so he washed his hands at the sink, then sat down again on the stool behind Monty's head. Cupping Monty's head in his hands, Kellie pulled slight tension so his spine opened up, then used his fingertips to massage into Monty's scalp.

"*Ooh*," Monty crooned. "That is fucking amazing."

Kellie's cock certainly thought so. It was flopping around in his loose fitted pants like a fish out of water.

He licked his lips at the expression of pleasure on Monty's face—his furrowed brows, his parted lips…begging to be kissed.

Of course Monty was probably frequently kissed. Kellie figured the guy was either married and didn't wear his ring, because many people took off their jewelry for the gym and spa, or Monty had a runway model girlfriend. Either way, Kellie would never see him again after this. *Lucky Chelsea.*

Kellie rested both his hands on Monty's head holding it for a moment, trying to finish off the session on a strong sense of bonding, which is exactly what Kellie felt. "There ya go, handsome."

Monty let out a long low moan and said, "Thank you."

"Take your time getting up. I'll bring you a glass of water." Kellie left the room, closing the door behind him. He stopped short and asked himself, "Did I just call him handsome?" *No. No. No…* Kellie scolded himself silently heading to the staff room to remove his canvas belt and stop at the men's room. He closed himself into the bathroom, and checked out his pants. "Go down, you pathetic cock!" Kellie reached inside his pants and squeezed his dick. He was so stimulated he could jack off. *Think! Think of grandma! Climate change, anything!*

Kellie washed his hands and face, letting the cool water refresh him. With both palms on the sink, staring at his reflection in the mirror, he shook his head. "He's going to complain. I perved all over the guy."

Did I? No. I just gave him a massage. I got a hard-on, so sue me. All the guys I rub do.

But not Monty.

He threw up his hands in frustration and left the bathroom to get Monty that promised water. The door to his massage room was open. When he looked in, Kellie found it empty. Finally his stiff cock deflated. He set the glass aside as he removed the sheets and cleaned up the room.

Chapter 4

After his last appointment Kellie fanned through the forms Lynn required new members and clients complete. He removed Monty's and read it over. He was right about his age. The guy was thirty-eight. No one was listed as an emergency contact. No medical history had been filled out. Just basic facts. Name, address, date of birth, and cell phone. That was it.

Kellie replaced the paperwork as Lynn returned to her desk after an errand. "Can I help you find something, Kellie?"

"Did you get a complaint about me today?"

"No. Why?"

"Did that guy named Monty Gresham complain about me?"

Lynn appeared confused. "What did you do?"

"Nothing. He just thought I was going to be a woman and was surprised when he found out I was a man."

"He made another appointment."

Kellie nodded. "With Chelsea?"

"No. With you."

"With me?" Kellie rushed to look at the appointment book.

"Here." She pointed to her handwriting.

"Oh my God."

"Why would he make another appointment with you if he was going to complain?"

Kellie was confused. "I don't know. Never mind." He shook his head and walked to the juice bar where Tyson was laughing with a client.

"Hey, Kel."

"Hi, Tyson." Kellie ordered a berry smoothie.

"Talk to you later," the client waved at Tyson and walked off.

Tyson brushed his side against Kellie's. "So? What's shakin', hot stuff?"

"I had a very strange session with a client."

"Oh? Another happy ending not met?"

"Yeah. Mine." Kellie handed the woman who made his drink a five. "Keep the change."

"Thanks, Kellie."

Tyson held Kellie's arm and sat with him on a love seat. The area was cozy like a lounge or living room where people could chat as they drank the beverages. Mirrors lined the wall behind them, and from where they were they could see nearly all the aerobic workout equipment and some of the waiting area.

"So? He got you hard for a change?"

"Yes. He was so incredible I was in heat."

"Did you exchange numbers?"

Kellie stirred the thick shake with a straw and sipped it. "I don't think he's gay. When he first realized I was a man, he kind of freaked."

"Come on." Tyson made a face of disbelief. "What did he think you were going to do? Turn him?"

"If I were straight, he'd have turned me." Kellie took another drink. "I was fucking erect the whole time. That's never happened."

"You better point him out next time. Err. There won't be a next time, will there?"

"That's the weird part. He made another appointment with me."

"Ooo! This is so juicy! So? Did he get a nice pup tent for you?"

"Nope. Nothing. I was the only one in the room sporting wood."

Tyson reached for Kellie's drink. Kellie handed it to him.

"He had Navy SEALs tattoos on each shoulder. Fuck." Kellie felt his cock respond and nudged it, trying to get it to behave. Tyson handed him his drink back after taking a sip.

"I didn't think those jarheads did anything for you."

"Neither did I. How wrong could I be?" Kellie slouched in the chair while Tyson leaned his head on his shoulder. "Do we look lazy?"

"We can take a break. Screw 'em."

Kellie shared his drink with Tyson as they both stared into the depths of the busy workout area. A week felt like forever to wait to get to see Monty again. But pining after a straight man was setting himself up for disappointment.

Chapter 5

Friday afternoon, his workout done, Kellie's first appointment was with another new client, Georgia. The room was ready and he checked his watch. One of the benefits of working with a large financially stable health club was the perks. Kellie was given a free membership, with all the extras, as well as the use of Lynn's receptionist skills of arranging his appointments and collecting his fees. Not to mention, they did the laundry as well.

He looked into the lounge area. No one was waiting. Kellie walked behind the counter to where Lynn was standing, flipping through a *Glamour* magazine. Kellie leaned next to her to read with her. "My client is late."

"Yup."

Lynn turned towards Kellie and sniffed his shoulder. "You always smell good."

"I smell like my oils. I get sick of it by the evening and stick my nose into my coffee beans at home."

"You're so funny, Kel." She turned a page. The spa didn't get busy until late afternoon when the masses got off work.

Kellie noticed a cologne ad in the magazine. "Mm. *Dangereux*...that's my favorite." Kellie peeled back the flap and caught a whiff of the scent. He rubbed his wrist on it and stuck it to his nose. "I imagine Mark Richfield smells like this all the time."

"You think he's cute?"

"I can appreciate his good looks, but I like a more masculine guy." As Kellie spoke those words, someone entered the club.

Monty, holding a gym bag, wearing workout shorts and a threadbare US Navy t-shirt, approached the counter to scan his key-ring membership card.

Kellie stood upright, blinking, not knowing how to react.

"Hi," Lynn said, smiling.

"Hi." Monty met Kellie's stare, then continued walking.

"He's a member?" Kellie watched Monty's ass as he walked away.

"He's got a free pass from the owner. Think he's gay?"

"No. I don't know. Do you?"

"I don't know. Some straight guys wear skimpy outfits because they get hot in here."

"Yeah." Kellie watched Monty walking away until he couldn't see him any longer. "Damn. Now that man is my type." Kellie nudged his crotch.

"Got wood?"

"Yes. Wow."

Lynn giggled and elbowed Kellie. "I bet that's your one o'clock."

Kellie smiled at a heavy-set woman in her forties, looking rushed.

"I'm so sorry I'm late. My name is Georgia. I had to take my son to the doctor. Nothing too serious, but he's always complaining about a sore back."

"You should arrange for Kellie to see him." Lynn checked the appointment off in her book.

"Do you massage young men? My son is fifteen."

"Sure. Come this way, Georgia." Kellie glanced back at Lynn.

Lynn mouthed, 'Wood gone?'

Kellie replied silently, 'Yes!' seeing her giggle. He directed Georgia to his massage room.

"He's really a smart boy," Georgia said, "I want him to go to college, but he's not interested. My ex...well." She blew out a breath. "He's not encouraging him at all."

Kellie opened the door and gestured for Georgia to enter.

"And I have a son from a previous marriage. He's got ADD so badly, I don't think he'll get a job." She set her purse on the floor near a chair.

Kellie made a sound of sympathy. "What are we doing today?"

"I don't know." Georgia sat in the chair like a sack of grain. "I need something!" She laughed.

"Why don't I just give you a relaxing massage? How does that sound?"

"Like heaven."

"Is this your first time?"

"Yes. I'm a little nervous. A friend bought a gift certificate for me."

"How nice."

"She said you were amazing."

"Thank you. I'll try my best. Just undress to what you are the most comfortable wearing and lie face down under the sheet."

"Okay."

Kellie smiled sweetly and closed the door. He headed to mix oils for Georgia and grew distracted thinking about Monty working out somewhere in the building. Wouldn't it be nice to watch him unobserved? *Stop becoming obsessed.*

It wasn't easy to do. Not many men gave Kellie that strong of a reaction. But typically it was an unattainable straight stud. How many times had Kellie been through that?

Kellie paused to think about it. "Never!"

"Huh?" One of the employees asked over her fruit juice.

"Nothing. Just talking to myself."

An hour later, Kellie was exhausted. More mentally than physically. Georgia's nerves caused her to chatter non-stop for an hour. Not only did she use the session as a body massage, she also used it as a counseling session, complaining about her two sons and her ex, and asking advice.

It wasn't uncommon. Kellie preferred quiet sessions, but each client did what they wished. *They* were paying him.

As he wrapped up the massage, touching Georgia's hair lightly, Kellie was glad he had a yoga class afterwards.

Georgia said, "I seriously don't know what to do. I should make my ex live with him. I can't control either boy any longer."

"Mm hm."

"But my youngest is doing well in school. So I can't complain. He's got all sorts of hobbies. He's not on the computer all day like most boys his age."

"Mm hm." Kellie stood up straight. "Okay, sweetie. You just take your time in getting up."

"Thank you, Kellie. The time went so fast."

"Yes, it did."

"Do I give you the gift certificate?"

"No, just hand it to Lynn at the register by the entrance where you came in. I'll get you a glass of water." He touched the door handle and paused. Georgia finally became quiet. Kellie left and headed to the men's room to take a piss and wash his hands and face, then get Georgia a glass of water.

Once he had, he took a peek back at his room. The door was still closed so he gave Georgia a few more minutes. After ten, she emerged looking exhausted and ruffled. He handed her the glass, but all she did was sip it and hand it back.

That's what happens when you talk about things that stress you out for an hour. You don't relax.

43

"When you get home, drink plenty of water." Kellie left the glass on a table and walked her to the front entrance.

"Thank you, Kellie." She set her purse on the counter and dug into it for her gift certificate.

"You are very welcome." He waved and returned to his room to clean up the sheets and get it ready again for the next client. The craving for caffeine was strong, but Kellie didn't like to drink too much coffee during the weekday. He allowed himself one cup on Saturday and Sunday morning. That was it.

The sheets placed in the laundry, changed into his gym shorts, Kellie grabbed his mat to join the yoga group. When he entered the room he stopped short.

Monty was already there, stretching on a foam mat.

Kellie didn't think Monty would be a yoga kind of guy. Instantly Kellie reconsidered. Before he backed out, Monty met his gaze. The man didn't show emotion either way. The perfect poker face. But with Monty now aware he was in the class, Kellie felt obligated to participate.

Since he did not get a sweet smile or greeting, Kellie placed his mat down far enough away from Monty to not have to interact with him. *Why did he make another appointment with me? How awkward is this?*

Nearly a dozen people joined the class. It was a large room with mirrors on the front wall behind the instructor, Sharita. She called the group to begin, and they stretched silently with her guidance.

No matter where Kellie turned, Monty was either in his direct field of vision or reflected in the mirrors. It was up to Kellie to stop looking at him. *If I only could.*

Sharita had them stand tall, and breathe deep. Kellie knew the routine well. Soon they would be on all fours, legs spread, going into positions as if they were demonstrating the Kama Sutra.

44

Since he normally did the class topless, Kellie removed his t-shirt and tossed it near his mat. Most of the men did the same, including Monty. The women were in sports bras and tight pants, but Kellie barely noticed them. His cock began to react, so he had to force himself to not stare at Monty.

Reaching his arms out to the side, concentrating on his breathing, Kellie tuned into Sharita's voice, forcing himself to let go of the useless attraction he felt.

He was doing well until they lowered into the downward dog position. Kellie looked through his legs and could see Monty. Yes, he was breathing deeply, pushing his pelvis down, yadda, yadda, but all Kellie wanted to do was sit on the sidelines and watch Monty do his poses.

He needed Scott to call. For that moron to give a shit. To take him out for dinner. Anything to get over this crazy crush.

Look at his arms. Will you look at his fucking arms?

Kellie's cock went stiff and he wanted to leave the class. Again Kellie chided himself, beating himself up for losing control and again tenting his baggie gym shorts. It was insane.

Slowly they moved to another pose. It was picture perfect for viewing Monty's package as if he were exposing himself to Kellie.

His body was out of control. Kellie had to leave before he humiliated himself. Once they were seated on the mat, Kellie curled his fingers around his shirt, gripped the mat, and tried to exit without a scene. He caught Monty watching him in the mirror as he left the class.

Once he returned the mat to the rack outside the room, Kellie held his shirt in front of his crotch and made for his private massage room. He closed himself in and caught his breath.

His cock was throbbing and his nerves were shot. He dug through his personal belongings which he had locked in a cabinet and found his phone. He dialed. Voicemail picked up. "Scott, it's me. Look, I need to get laid. You available tonight? Call me." He disconnected and sat down on the chair, trying to think.

~

Scott never did call.

Kellie had one last appointment scheduled before he could go home and drop dead. He couldn't recall being this tired.

Juan Ramirez, a pastry chef for one of the elite eateries on Rodeo Drive, was a client of his for a year. Soft as the dough he kneaded, Juan was one of Kellie's favorites. He was a gentle man, always on time, and really seemed to enjoy the sessions.

The older man was married with five children ranging in ages from twenty to eight, and though they did discuss family, Juan didn't go on and on during his time on the table. He did, however, sport wood each visit. But he told Kellie it was because he imagined Angelina Jolie giving him the massage.

The hour passed quickly since Juan stayed quiet and allowed Kellie to get on with the task of making him feel more relaxed.

By eight p.m. Kellie had fresh sheets on his table and prepared the room for tomorrow. He did work Saturdays, but only four appointments, just like his week days.

Before he left the club he took a look at his schedule. Lynn had gone home at five and her evening replacement, Carmen, was busy on the phone. Three appointments scheduled for tomorrow. He could sleep in until ten.

Kellie turned a few pages to see how his week was shaping up. He noticed Monty's name had been penciled in on Tuesday. Kellie thought it was strange since he could have sworn Lynn had showed him an appointment on Thursday. He skimmed the pages quickly. There was one on Thursday too. "What the...?"

"You okay?" Carmen asked, stepping closer to him.

"I just think there may be an error. I had a new client yesterday and he couldn't have made two appointments for next week."

46

"Why not? You have several clients who see you twice. Look. Lenny Silverman, Mike Murphy…"

"Okay." Kellie shrugged. "If it's a mistake I'll find out Tuesday." He put the book back under the counter. "Have a good night, Carmen."

"You too, Kel."

He left the club, a shoulder bag slung over his arm with his personal items, and walked to where he parked his car. As he did, he checked his phone. No calls.

"Fine, Scott. I can't compete with three-way sex with two television stars…so fuck off." He began to grow angry about too many things in his life that had not gone right.

Losing his job as a real estate agent, the foreclosure on his home, no luck with men, and now getting a migraine as he thought about his past failures. "Whatever." Kellie imagined a meal alone and didn't feel like cooking. Life was frustrating at the moment and he wasn't sure how to fix it.

Chapter 6

Most people lived for the weekends to be set free from work. With Kellie it was the opposite. Weekends dragged for him. He was trying to save money, so even though Tyson and a few other friends tried to temp him out to dance and drink, Kellie didn't go. He hung out by himself, cleaned the house, did the laundry and food shopping, and took long hikes alone in Escondido Canyon.

Tuesday brought anxiety. Kellie tried not to stress but maybe once he knew Monty better, he'd feel less intimidated. This time he wore briefs, so as not to tent out his yoga pants. Lesson learned.

"Hi, sweetie!" Lynn blew him kisses as he walked through the front entrance.

"Hello, my dove." Kellie threw them back. When he met her smile he noticed her trying to be discreet while tilting her head to the lounge area.

Kellie looked over his shoulder and spotted Monty, sitting with his legs cross in a chair, an open magazine on his lap. Kellie checked his watch. He had ten minutes until the appointment so he wasn't late. Inhaling a deep breath to calm down, Kellie said, "Monty?"

He looked up over the magazine, his gaze smoldering and a little terrifying to Kellie.

"I'll need just a minute."

Monty nodded, looking back at his magazine.

Kellie pressed his lips to Lynn's ear to whisper, "Why does he hate me?"

"Shut up." She laughed and gave him a push towards the spa area.

The vibes between them were terrible. Kellie felt as if he had done something to offend Monty, but if he had, why did Monty come back? It didn't make sense.

Kellie locked his wallet and keys in the cabinet, turned on the music and made sure the stones were warming. He stepped out of his flip-flops and clipped his canvas belt around his hips.

The room ready, Kellie washed his hands, inspected his face and hair in the mirror and returned to call Monty back to his room. This time Monty was staring into space, his hands folded on his lap. The man seemed unhappy or preoccupied. Kellie didn't know if he'd ever see him smile.

"Monty?"

He perked up and approached Kellie.

On the tip of Kellie's tongue were so many things. But Monty's demeanor kept them behind his teeth. As Monty entered Kellie's private room, the soothing sounds of surf and sea brought with it some slight tension relief. Kellie said, "The same?"

"Yes. I'm in agony."

Pain. Chronic pain would make a serious difference in a person's life. Kellie crouched in front of Monty who was sitting on the chair, taking off his shoes. "Can you tell me about it?"

"My neck, my back..." Monty rolled his shoulders and shrugged as if to exaggerate where he meant.

"Was it an injury?"

Monty's expression appeared full of irony. "It's a combination of things." He took off his shirt, tossing it in a wicker basket beside the chair. The sight of his chest and abs instantly turned Kellie into mush.

Kellie stood, moving to the door to let Monty undress in private. "I'll be back."

Monty nodded, appearing grim.

Kellie closed the door behind him, slightly less tense and more concerned. He prepared oils for Monty, taking special care.

Chelsea entered the room, meeting Kellie's gaze. She had her canvas belt already on and appeared tired.

"Just finish a client?" Kellie asked.

"Yes. Are you just starting?"

"That guy I told you about. Monty Gresham. He's back."

"The guy you thought wanted a female massage therapist?"

"Yup."

"Magic hands."

"Maybe." Kellie slipped the pump bottle into the loop holder and checked his watch.

"It's going to be a long week." Chelsea used the back of her hand to wipe her hair away from her face.

"I don't know. I like the way it's starting out." Kellie winked and returned to the massage room. He pressed his ear against it and knocked. He heard nothing so he opened it.

Monty was in position, lying face down on the massage table.

Kellie closed the door behind him, straightening the sheet and making sure the cushion under Monty's ankles was in the right place. Before he greased up, Kellie stood at the head of the table, staring at Monty's entire body from top down. He cupped his hair gently, holding it for a moment, trying to get bad vibes to leave and good ones to enter. Monty took a deep slow inhale and exhale, as if releasing the strain of the world that was on his shoulders.

The fire ignited in Kellie. There was no way to stop it.

This time his cock was contained in a pair of cotton briefs and wouldn't humiliate him. The attraction began to burn into physical heat. Kellie quickly raised his shirt over his head and hung it on a hook by the sink. He resumed his light caresses down Monty's broad hot back, feeling he too was an inferno.

"Are you hot?"

"I'm okay."

Kellie folded back the sheet to Monty's hips and ran his hands along his satiny skin. *A lover. That's what it feels like touching you. You are like my lover.*

The sensuality was hitting Kellie hard. He pumped oil into his hand and the scent of lavender, citrus, and peppermint pervaded the small space. Wind chimes, humpback whale songs, and Native American chants carried in the calmness, blocking out the noise of the hall, people chatting, cell phones ringing...

Us. Us alone.

Kellie hadn't tied his hair back. He didn't know how he forgot. It wasn't long, just long enough to get a tiny ponytail. It hung around his face and now that his hands were greasy, Kellie tried to decide how much it bothered him.

Standing back at the head of the table, Kellie ran both his palms on either side of Monty's spine from his neck to his ass.

Monty inhaled and exhaled slowly, moaning with his exhale.

The sexy sound sent the goose pimples rising on Kellie's arms and his cock throbbing between his legs.

He used broad sweeping movements to get Monty to relax enough for a deep tissue massage. He loosened Monty's arm from the sheet, allowing it to dangle off the side of the table. Kellie added oil to his hands and began digging into the knots inside Monty's shoulder blade.

Monty took a few deep breaths to consciously let go of the tissue Kellie was working on.

As he felt the tension—which was not releasing—in Monty, Kellie wanted to know what the man did. Was he still with the Navy SEALs? Did he work in an office now? What did he do? Would his questions ever be answered, or was this a purely sensory relationship? Touch but don't talk.

Kellie was too intimidated to begin a conversation. This was the opposite of Georgia. She wouldn't shut up, Monty wouldn't utter a peep.

"You all right?" He couldn't resist. The silence sucked.

"Yeah."

Kellie checked on the massage stones and used oil on them. He ran the hot stone down Monty's tight muscle and Monty gave one of the most sensual moans Kellie had heard from him yet. Kellie continued exactly what he was doing, working the smooth stone in and around the worst of Monty's tension.

If this were Tyson or Lenny, Kellie could have joked about that wonderful groan. He would have asked, 'Do you sound like that when you're coming?' With those men he could joke. No way he would dare with Monty.

As the stones cooled, Kellie placed them back into the warmer, using his elbow and forearm to dig in deep.

"Too hard?"

"No."

Kellie rolled his elbow over Monty's knot, feeling it move like a lump of bundled wire. He let up, caressing Monty lightly, affectionately, because it's what he felt. Affection.

He picked up Monty's arm from where it hung, using his hip to hold it up until he rubbed more oil into his hands. Monty's fingers moved as he did.

Kellie nearly hyperventilated as Monty appeared to touch Kellie, returning his affection. Not knowing if he was imagining it, Kellie continued, rubbing Monty's fingers and palm, working down his forearm to his bulging biceps and deltoid.

Monty's hips shifted on the table, immediately drawing Kellie's eye. It usually meant a growing hard-on. But with Monty, Kellie figured it was just a stiff back, not a stiff cock.

Finishing his right arm, Kellie tucked it back under the sheet, and moved to the head of the table, again running his palms down Monty's back to his ass. He used the tips of his fingers to push into the hollows of Monty's gluts and felt Monty tense his bottom.

Kellie was so turned on by the subtle gestures he was dripping with perspiration. On his way to massage Monty's left side, Kellie peeked at the thermostat and quickly lowered it so the air conditioning kicked in.

He was only ten minutes into this massage. Half of him didn't want it to end, and the other half was craving getting away from Monty so he didn't embarrass himself. Kellie released Monty's right arm from the sheet, resting it on the table. He pumped oil into his hand and smoothed from Monty's wrist to his shoulder, squeezing his rock hard biceps and yearning to get to know him, understand him...make love to him.

A drop of perspiration rolled down Kellie's temple. He used his upper arm to wipe it off. *I am losing my mind!*

His cock felt cramped in the confinement of his briefs when it usually dangled free as he massaged clients. It was thick and pulsating, distracting Kellie from focusing on what he was doing. As he raised Monty's arm to work higher on it, he intended on placing it against his hip, as usual. Monty spread his fingers in anticipation of touching him and caught Kellie right in the groin. The temptation to allow the caress on his cock was nearly enough to make him scream in frustration. There was no mistake Monty had to know what he had touched. Kellie tried to be casual as he guided Monty's hand to his hip, working Monty's arm as rolling drops of sweat began running down Kellie's face and chest.

Monty's hips moved again. Kellie knew all the signs. This man had to be getting an erection. Now they were both shifting their postures and growing awkward. The question of Monty's sexuality began in Kellie's mind. But so many straight men had grown hard with him, it held no definitive answer.

The clock ticking sounded like a time bomb. Kellie never realized he could hear it over the music, but the sound on the CD was just ocean waves at the moment.

Kellie finished Monty's arm and tucked it away gently. He smoothed his hands up and down Monty's back and began adjusting the sheet to get at his legs.

Trying to feel cool as the air conditioning blew on him, Kellie raised one of Monty's legs to part them, tucking the sheet between to preserve Monty's modesty.

He exposed one side of Monty's ass cheek and as he wrapped the sheet under the opposite leg, he brushed his fingers over what felt like a cock. Kellie blinked and noticed Monty's dick was pointing down between his thighs, not stiff, but not soft either. The darker color, shape of Monty's head and the thickness of his shaft against his wrinkled ball sack was enough to make Kellie clench his jaw in longing.

Proceeding with the massage, forcing himself to not look at that fabulous dick, Kellie hid it from his sight and pumped oil into his palm, rubbing his hands together. He took one look at Monty's tight ass and went for it, squeezing it, digging into his hip flexor as his own briefs became damp with pre-cum and perspiration.

He needed a cold shower. Badly.

The sight of Monty's endowment brought back a recollection. Kellie at seventeen, getting his first massage with JC.

He too was face down, legs spread, but no sheet. JC had his hands between his thighs, massaging the root of Kellie's cock

54

right above his rim. Kellie reached under himself to straighten out his erection and JC said, "Push it down."

Kellie did, feeling it stretch underneath him. The minute he settled onto the table again, JC used his fingertips to stroke it, over and through his testicles. Kellie moaned at the pleasure and spread his legs wider. "Feels so good. Wow."

"Looks amazing too, Kelsey."

"Do you massage everyone like this?"

"No."

"It feels so nice. Why not?"

"I only do it to the clients I like best."

Kellie smiled into the soft bedding. "I'm glad you like me."

"You're a beautiful boy. And so sweet."

Kellie didn't feel sweet. He felt horny. "I never knew massages could make you want to come."

"Mine do. If you do it right, you'll accomplish more than just getting rid of aches and pains. You'll release tension."

"Wow." Kellie tried to do a split on the table as JC's focus was completely on his genitals.

"Just wait 'til you turn over."

Hearing the laughter in JC's voice, Kellie smiled. "Believe me. I can't."

Kellie was panting. He licked the saltiness off his lips and wiped his face with his upper arm again. Working his way down Monty's leg to his calf, then his foot, Kellie stared between the man's legs. Even with the sheet covering, Kellie envisioned what that cock looked like since his glimpse. And he liked it.

Never before had Kellie worked himself into this state. For three years plus during the training, he had detached himself from the sensual side to focus on the simple art of massage. This was wrong, unprofessional, and could get him to lose his license and job. Having already lost his career in real estate, Kellie couldn't face the humiliation of failure, yet again.

He finished Monty's left leg and had to reposition the sheet to do his right. Unwinding it from where he had tucked it, Kellie shook it out and covered the left side, exposing Monty's right butt cheek and entire right leg, including that vicious scar on his calf. As he tucked in the sheet, he tried not to look but did anyway. Monty's cock was nearly crimson and veins showed down its length. Kellie imagined Monty wanted to raise his hips and flip his dick upright but may be too humiliated.

Weighing up the idea of saying something to allow Monty the chance to get comfortable, admitting he had seen that big engorged dick, wasn't something Kellie imagined doing. With someone else, yes. Not with Monty.

Certainly the man was confident enough to do as he liked. Unless the realization that a man had exited him was too much for Monty to admit.

If that was the case, it wasn't Kellie's problem.

He gingerly tucked the sheet between Monty's thighs, resisting the urge to run his finger down that fabulous appendage and get accused of molestation.

Once the sheet had been arranged correctly, Kellie again oiled his hands and wiped at the perspiration on his face with his upper arms. Resuming the massage, Kellie grabbed that hunk of ass and gave it a good deep tissue rub. Monty whimpered. *Whimpered.*

"Too hard?" Kellie immediately let up.

"No."

With the one word answer came more deep breaths. Kellie continued where he left off, imagining chewing on Monty's ass and licking down the crack to his rim. Kellie ran his hands over the soft hair on Monty's thigh to his calf, being gentle along the scar. He bent his knee as he did with the first leg, coating it with oil and making sure he took care of every aching muscle this man may have. He paid attention to his toes and arch, finishing his legs and loosening the sheet to cover him up once more. Standing beside the table, Kellie said, "Okay." He used a towel to wipe his face, then lifted the sheet and said, "Scoot down and roll over."

It took a minute but soon the table creaked and shook as Monty turned face up. Kellie waited, staring at the sheet, trying to calm down now that Monty could see him. He draped the sheet back over him and noticed Monty's right hand holding onto his cock. He didn't say anything. Kellie removed the face rest, folding it down, adjusting the pillow under Monty's knees. Letting Monty deal with his body for a moment, Kellie checked on the massage stones and then rolled the stool to the head of the table, sitting down.

"It's normal, babe."

Monty slowly released his cock and rested his hand to his side.

It appeared Monty had gotten his body back under his control.

Kellie wished he had been that successful with himself. No chance. His crotch was damp and his dick needed release. He folded the sheet under Monty's nipples and again took the stones out of the heater. He rubbed them together with oil, and used them to roll under Monty's neck to his shoulders.

"Oh, Christ…"

"Good?"

"Fuck yeah."

Kellie glanced down and noticed the sheet beginning to move on Monty's cock.

Since Monty had broken the ice Kellie said, "Your job must be very hard."

57

Monty replied with an exhale that said it all. He kept his eyes closed and his face passive.

"Your back is one of the worst I've ever dealt with. I'm glad you're doing yoga. That will help."

"It's the stress."

"Are you a Navy SEAL?" Kellie tossed the stones back into the heater and used his hands to rub Monty.

"Was. Now I'm going to hold training camps for civilians."

"Wow." Kellie bit his lip on his excitement.

"No shit. It will be fucking hard work for the recruits and us."

Kellie allowed Monty to fall back into silence, not wanting to make Monty speak if he didn't want to. He rolled his palms down Monty's chest over his nipples seeing his cock respond, most likely against Monty's will. *I can relate, bud.*

Kellie continued, standing to work Monty's chest and abdomen, folding the sheet at Monty's pubic bush.

"Knew I'd get hard."

"Stop worrying. We all do." Kellie worked as low as he dared, giving Monty's belly a nice rub. He glanced at him, seeing Monty's light eyes sizzling into his. The charge of electricity that hit Kellie nearly knocked him down. He refocused on his work and watched the sheet rise, as if by magic, near where he massaged.

There it was. A full blown erection. But no happy ending in sight.

The temptation was painful. Kellie spent too much time near it, hovering under it, close to it—digging his fingers into Monty's hips, sides, staring at it, wanting it—and once again running with tickling drops of sweat as his body went into overload.

Kellie pretended it didn't interest him, being attentive with the rest of Monty's body, until he had gone round the world of his anatomy. He washed his hands, sat on the stool and cupped

Monty's head, holding it still. Monty blew out a long exhale and closed his eyes.

Kellie got lost on Monty's features, his dark eyebrows and long lashes. He ran the tips of his fingers through Monty's thick hair, into his scalp and all the pressure points of his head.

Monty opened his mouth to moan, his cock standing straight out from his body at one point, to laying against it the next.

Kellie didn't have an appointment right after this, so he took his time. He used his thumbs to draw circles around Monty's temples, his fingertips to trace the details of his face; his forehead, cheekbones, lips...

Kellie watched Monty's eyelashes flutter as if he had reached a higher plane. Kellie had been there before. After a good massage, you're lightheaded and euphoric.

Cupping Monty's head, Kellie raised it off the table and manipulated it side to side, tilting it, pulling traction to ease Monty's soreness. He reached down Monty's chest to the sheet, dragging it up to fold down at his neck. As he did he felt Monty's exhale brush under his chin.

Sitting still, in contact with this man, not wanting to let go, Kellie closed his eyes and tried to draw out Monty's negative energy. He rose up, making a pass with his hands about a foot above Monty's body, using circular movements.

"What the fuck?" Monty inhaled sharply. "I can feel that!"

"It's your aura, babe. It's huge."

"What? My aura? You're stroking my aura?"

"Yes." Kellie may have thought wicked things, but he didn't say them.

Monty lay perfectly still.

Kellie traced his aura with his hands above Monty's torso, closing his eyes to sense where it was. "You're so incredibly powerful."

"What color is it?"

"Light blue." The question surprised Kellie. Monty didn't seem like the kind of guy who would ask the color of his aura.

"Never have I felt that before."

Kellie shook out his arms, relaxing them to his sides and looked at Monty. "How do you feel?"

"Unbelievable." Monty actually smiled. "Thank you."

"Take your time getting up. I'll get you a glass of water."

"Thanks."

Because it was over, Kellie felt let down. He closed the door behind him, and actually sensed separation anxiety. Hundreds of clients had been under his care, and not once had Kellie been this attached and attracted. It was bound to happen.

He stopped at the men's room, tied back his hair, urinated, and washed his hands and face. He stared at his naked chest and finally began to cool down. His crotch was soaking wet and he needed a shower badly. Before he returned to Monty, Kellie filled a large glass with purified water. He knocked lightly.

"Come in." Monty was dressed, seated on the chair putting his shoes on. He took the water. "Thank you."

Kellie picked his shirt up from the hook and put it on. It seemed more professional and there was a dress code in the spa. He watched Monty guzzle the water.

"That's some scar you have on your leg." Kellie leaned against the table.

"My calf muscle was filleted off in training. Had it reattached."

"Fuck." Kellie cringed. "Is it numb?"

"No. They did a decent job." He looked for a place to set the empty glass.

Kellie took it, placing it near the sink.

"Am I keeping you?" Monty finished dressing and slumped in the chair.

"No."

"I can't believe you found my aura. I never believed it existed."

"It's a trip. I know."

"Son of a bitch." Monty laughed shyly. "I felt the sensation when you were nearly two feet above me. How is that possible?"

"Just is."

"Sorry about the wood earlier." Monty's cheeks grew rosy.

"Don't be. It's normal. Most guys get hard. I figured that's why you preferred a woman, so you didn't get one with a guy. Right?"

"I couldn't get an erection with a woman."

Kellie paused to see if he heard right. He didn't reply as he thought it out.

"I wanted a woman because it wouldn't feel sexual. I'm gay."

You're gay? Kellie choked and swallowed his surprise. "Oh. Me too." He shrugged trying to play it down. "You like the yoga class?"

"I do. Why did you leave last time? You did ten minutes and took off."

There was no way Kellie was going to admit the real reason. "I remembered I had a client."

Monty stood, appearing stiff and completely exhausted.

"Are you off today?"

"No. I have to get back there." Monty patted his pockets as if he were trying to get his bearings and find things. "I swear, I feel so disoriented."

"Sit."

"I'm okay. I'll go get a fruit smoothie."

"That's a good idea. Get your focus back before you're behind the wheel."

"Thanks. I'll see you Thursday."

Kellie had to think for a minute and wondered if he missed the conversation that had to do with making a date. Then he got it. "Right. Your next appointment."

Monty stepped out of the room, not looking back.

Kellie removed the sheets from the table and dumped them in the laundry room. He came back with fresh linens and refitted the table. Once it was done, Kellie turned off the CD player and checked the time to see when his yoga class began. He had around a half hour.

Hoping for Tyson's company to keep him busy for a few minutes, Kellie scanned the workout room for him. He noticed Monty talking with another man at the juice bar. He was actually smiling. Flirting?

Suddenly Kellie felt like the 'hired help'. In no way could he compete with the posh clientele. He avoided the area and kept searching for his friend.

~

Monty sipped his banana/pineapple protein shake, nodding his head. His longtime friend and another former SEAL, Brandon Kennedy, was beside him. "How's the networking? Did you speak to the management?"

"Yes, but I want you to close the deal." Brandon looked down at the drink in Monty's hand. "You fit right in here. Knew you'd love it in LA."

"So far." Monty noticed Kellie standing near the weight room, looking around.

Brandon turned to where Monty was staring. "Someone I should meet?"

"No. That's just my new massage therapist." Monty held back the straw and gulped down the thick liquid.

"Give me a fucking break, Monty. Now you have a male masseuse? How gay is that?" He shook his head then asked, "Which guy?"

62

"Ponytail, black yoga pants and shirt."

"Figures. He's gay right?"

Monty didn't answer that question. "You should book a massage. You're too uptight. And I know if my neck and back always ache, so do yours."

Brandon gave his attention back to Monty. "So? Do you still think this gym is too pretentious and snobby to get us clients?"

"It is, but these are the type of people who think they want our elite training." Monty used the straw to finish the rest of the drink, using it as a shovel with the cup to his mouth.

They were standing near swivel stools at the counter of the juice bar, which had all the resemblance of a chic downtown club but without the noise and booze.

There were two baristas behind the counter—one male, one female—whirring healthy concoctions for the thirsty gym junkies.

"Are you handing out business cards, Monty? Have you gotten us any referrals?"

"Some. I still think discussing promotion with management and getting posters on the wall is the way to go." Monty felt Brandon's stare on his profile. Without turning to look he asked, "What?" Monty was keeping track of Kellie in the room. Kellie had hooked up with a handsome, slim, black man who was in a club uniform.

"Have you spoken to anyone from your family since you moved here?"

"No." Monty thanked the young man behind the counter as he took Monty's empty glass.

"Can I get you guys anything else? There's granola and seed muffins. Just made this morning."

"Granola? Are you out of your mind?" Brandon expressed his distaste.

"Don't act like a Neanderthal around this place. We have to fit in to get referrals. Split one with me."

"You can't eat a whole muffin?" Brandon still appeared repulsed.

Monty shook his head at him.

"Fine. Gimme one." Brandon removed his wallet from his back pocket.

Monty heard Brandon mutter under his breath, "This LA mentality is rubbing off on you. Next thing you'll do is have a caviar facial."

"Shut the fuck up." Monty shoved him.

Brandon put a ten on the counter as the young man placed the enormous muffin on a plate before him.

"Jesus!" Brandon couldn't believe the size of it.

"I take it you've never ordered a muffin here." The young man behind the counter laughed.

Monty broke a piece off the top and ate it.

"Give me some of that." Brandon tore a chunk off.

The young man laughed as he brought Brandon change, saying, "I'll get you a knife."

"Anyway," Brandon said, "So you're all settled in? Got the remodel of your home finished?"

"Yeah. All done." He took the knife from the young man. "Thanks."

"No problem."

Monty cut the muffin in half, breaking more pieces off of it to eat. He glanced up and noticed Kellie laughing with the second man.

Brandon turned to look again. "You have a thing for your gay masseuse?"

"I don't know." Monty didn't want to have a thing for him. He needed to feel more settled in the new location and in this new business venture before he even thought about a

64

relationship. He assumed the young man of color and Kellie were a couple judging by their body language.

Brandon looked at Monty. "He's not your type. What's with the ponytail?"

"What do you know about my type?" Monty ate a big chunk of the muffin.

"Everything. After ten years of friendship in the service do you really think I don't know you?"

"I don't have a type." Monty brushed his hands off.

"Sure ya don't, Montgomery."

"You and my mother are the only ones that call me that."

"Since when are you attracted to barefoot men with ponytails?" Brandon took another look at Kellie who was laughing with the handsome black man. "Bet he's vegan and drives a Prius."

Monty caught Kellie's light eyes. The connection was powerful, as if they had already touched intimately. And maybe they had.

Brandon turned from one to the other, reading into it, as he was trained to do. Monty didn't care what Brandon thought.

Monty broke the stare first, trying to get his own read of Kellie's interest.

"What kind of a massage was it?" he asked. "Did he give you a happy ending? Suck your dick?"

"No. Shut up." Monty checked his watch. "I want to take that yoga class that's coming up."

"Next thing you'll tell me is you're eating tofu and avocado sprout sandwiches." Brandon backed away from the counter. "You and I have to get back to the center. Now."

"You go. I want to take this class. And besides, you're the one who told me I should live in LA. You're the one who suggested I recruit from this gym." Monty brushed crumbs from his shirt.

"You're turning into a yoga-loving tofu-eater and you're blaming me?"

"Blame you?" Monty noticed Kellie walk towards the yoga room. "I may thank you." Monty whacked Brandon's chest with the back of his hand. "See ya later."

"You better be at the center after that class."

"Sure. See you there." Monty grabbed a mat from outside the room and entered, scoping out a spot. He didn't hesitate to place his mat next to Kellie's, loosening up after he did.

~

Kellie sat on the mat, stretching out his legs as Monty placed his beside him. He smiled. Were they friends now? Or just massage therapist and client? "I thought you had to get back to work."

"I will. After this." Monty asked, "Was that your boyfriend?"

"What? Was who my boyfriend?" Kellie wished he had the nerve to ask Monty the same question about the man he was sharing a muffin with.

Instead of answering verbally, Monty tilted his head to the area outside the room.

"Tyson? No. He's a friend. He's a personal trainer here."

Monty nodded and his focus moved to the influx of people preparing for the class.

Kellie figured he'd ask the same thing, since Monty had. "Was that yours?"

A smile formed on Monty's lips. "No."

Okay. We established we're both available. Now what?

Sharita entered the class. She clapped her hands, stood in front of the group and asked, "Ready?"

Kellie and Monty both rose to their feet.

"I have a love hate relationship with this shit." Monty began mirroring the instructor's warm up moves.

Kellie laughed to himself.

"My fucking body is so stiff. I'm not very flexible."

"Takes time." Kellie reached out his arms and noticed when Monty did, they were just about touching fingertips. It felt nice.

"I'm an impatient man."

"Are you?" Kellie lowered his voice so they didn't disturb the other students.

"I can hear the sarcasm."

"Sorry. Uh. Maybe we shouldn't talk so much in class."

"Probably."

As the positions began to get challenging, Kellie watched Monty in the mirror's reflection. He had taken the class so often, he didn't need Sharita's guidance and was getting off on the way Monty looked when he moved. Much to Kellie's delight when they got to the downward dog, the class was facing the left wall, so he got a grand view of Monty's backside and spread legs in his gym shorts.

Though he was supposed to keep his head down, and look between his own legs for the proper form, Kellie kept staring at Monty's ass for as long as he desired...until Monty noticed.

Since Monty was in the correct pose, he was looking through his own legs at Kellie. Kellie was about to turn away in embarrassment when Monty's mouth curled into a wicked smile.

The sensual rush from that look went right between Kellie's legs, making his dick swell. Kellie did not look away as they held their pose and breathed. Instead, he imagined fucking Monty while he was in that position.

The downward dog morphed into the child pose, and Kellie was left huffing for breath as his excitement grew. It seemed he would have to wear briefs from now on. Three years of dangling free in his yoga pants, never thinking of sex to the extent where he could embarrass himself, had come and gone.

One man.

How could one man set Kellie's world on fire?

Though he wasn't religious, Kelly was spiritual. He was convinced the powers-that-be had plans for him. Fate brought people in and out of Kellie's world his entire life and each person he had met, he had learned a lesson from. Even with the ones who broke his heart, Kellie had found something good to grow from.

Through the tumultuous economy where he'd lost his career and house, his real estate friends fleeing the area to try and rebuild their lives, Kellie still found strength.

He was in a better place mentally. With the training for message therapy came an entirely new lifestyle. Eating well, exercise, growing his hair slightly longer than it had been, reducing his carbon footprint, being earth conscious…

He wasn't the same man he had been five years ago. He felt healthy and kept a positive view of his future.

Yes, there had been setbacks along the way—failed relationships, stinging hookups without a follow-up phone call—but Kellie lived and learned.

Hearing Monty's deep breathing beside him, Kellie wondered what fate had in store next. Was Monty the dream man he had been waiting for all his life? Probably not. One thing Kellie learned over his twenty-seven years, there were no knights in shining armor to rescue him. And he didn't think he needed one. Maybe he was the knight to rescue his man.

He didn't believe in romance. He wasn't a chick with a dick who mooned over lovers, begged them to call or felt insecure until they showed up with roses and knelt on one knee. That was pure bullshit and he knew it.

Still, some people crossed his path that were…interesting.

Monty Gresham was one of those men.

The tough ex-Navy SEAL. With the execution of the worst terrorist in this century had come a new hero—the special forces of the United States Navy. By far the most acclaimed men on the planet since their daring deed. Was he falling prey to that fantasy?

Kellie sat cross-legged and straightened his back, inhaling, as he thought about it. Monty, beside him, was focused on the class, the instructor, and his posture.

Kellie didn't think Monty's past job held any mystique. It was glamorous, but Kellie wasn't uniform mad. It didn't diminish his opinion of Monty either. On the contrary. In a spa where spoiled celebrities abound, living off their family fortunes and doing little to impact society in a positive way, Kellie admired Monty's work ethic and confidence. But if Monty had been a retail manager at a computer store, Kellie would have had the same opinion.

Right?

Kellie glanced at Monty's tattoo. Wrong. *I hate lying to myself.*

~

Monty didn't find yoga easy. But he never gave up on anything he did. His tendons didn't stretch like they had in his twenties. But as with everything else he did, practice would make perfect.

Seeing Kellie's perfection gave Monty something to aspire to. Monty was a fitness junkie and expected the men in his life to take care of themselves as well. It was too easy to sit in front of the TV or computer and do nothing. That's why after his stint with the Navy SEALs, Monty began his fitness business. In an area in the country where every new fad was in vogue, Monty figured LA would be a great place to recruit clients for his SEAL fitness training. He just had to get it up and running. He, Brandon, and several other former SEALs joined ranks to rebuild an old warehouse into a 'maximum'-high-tech training center.

The tough part about the job was getting the word out. The members of this spa would be ideal, at least the few who worked out. Many sat and socialized, sipping wheatgrass shots and getting pedicures.

He held his feet together as he stretched his legs, elbows on his knees. His tendons complained and ached but Monty bore it.

Beside him, Kellie was showing off his amazing flexibility. After seeing Kellie shirtless during their last massage session, Monty knew the man worked out hard with weights. Since his skin coloring and hair were relatively fair, Kellie had no hair on his chest. Monty figured Kellie was in his mid-twenties.

A few moments to breathe deeply and relax came and went, and then Sharita ended their class with a smile.

Kellie got to his feet, rolling up the mat while Monty unfolded his legs and relieved his aching knees before he stood.

He and Kellie exchanged glances. It appeared Kellie wanted to say something. Monty waited.

Kellie said, "Well, catch ya later."

"Bye." Monty watched him walk out of the room, not looking back. It didn't appear there was much chance of them becoming anything but massage therapist and client.

He stood, picking up the mat and thinking about everything he had to do. Without people signing up to take their exercise course, they wouldn't last six months.

Monty put his mat into a rack and checked the time. He headed to the manager's office, just to touch base with him about the things Brandon had already discussed.

He looked around for Kellie but didn't see him any longer.

Chapter 7

Wednesday morning, Kellie made sure his room was ready and headed to the lounge to find Lenny. Lenny was sitting with his hands interlaced on his lap and immediately stood when Kellie smiled at him.

Lenny approached him as Kellie led the way to his room. "How are you, Lenny?"

"I'm doing well. How about you?"

"I'm fine too." Kellie gestured for Lenny to enter his room. "The usual?"

"Yes. This time I'd like the full release package." Lenny gave Kellie a sly smile.

"I'm sure your wife will be happy to oblige when you get home. See you in a minute." Kellie closed the door behind him and went to mix Lenny's oils, smiling. When he returned and knocked he heard Lenny acknowledge him. Kellie poked his head in to see Lenny face down on the table, relaxed.

He adjusted the sheet as well as the pillow under Lenny's ankles then stood next to him running his hands up and down his back over the sheet before he started. "How was your weekend?"

"Good, Kellie. No complaints. My grandchildren were over and the house was full of noise and laughter."

"Sounds nice." Kellie folded the sheet down to Lenny's waist and pumped oil on his hands, rubbing them together. The music playing was of soft flute sounds of the Andes. Just what Lenny liked.

"Do you see your family?"

Kellie stood at the head of the table and ran both his hands down Lenny's back on either side of his spine. Lenny moaned and his legs shifted. "No. Not much anymore," Kellie said.

"Are you still dating Scott?"

"I'm not sure. I don't think so. He vanished on me." Kellie worked Lenny's shoulders and neck.

"So what do you do on your time off to have fun?"

Kellie laughed at the fact that he didn't know. "I guess I just enjoy my 'me' time."

Lenny grew quiet as Kellie worked his back and shoulders. After a while Lenny said, "You're too good a man to go to waste."

Kellie smiled, working Lenny's right arm. "Well, I have a fantasy man."

"Oh?"

"A new client."

"Is he gay?"

"Yes. Amazing, huh?"

"Why don't you ask him out?"

"I don't know. It just doesn't feel right. I think he likes our professional relationship."

It grew quiet again as Kellie continued working Lenny's sore muscles.

"So…" Lenny said softly through the face rest, "You won't ask him out because you think he may not be your client if you do?"

"Yes. It's not against the rules, it's just I'm not getting that vibe from him." Kellie thought about Monty as he folded the sheet to cover Lenny's back and exposed one leg to massage to his foot.

"Well, let me tell you something, Kellie."

"What, Lenny?"

"If he comes in for regular massage sessions with you, he'll fall madly in love with you."

Kellie smiled. "Is that right?"

"I know I have."

Hearing the smile behind Lenny's words, Kellie broke up with laughter. "Thank you, Mr. Silverman. From you that's a high compliment."

"My pleasure." Lenny sighed. "Literally."

~

By late afternoon Kellie had worked out, taken a spinning class and was ready for Natalie Cushman. He found her in the lounge using her black nail polished fingers to text on her phone, biting her lower lip as she did.

"Nat?"

She looked up, smiling brightly and approached him. "Hello, handsome!"

They exchanged a wonderful hug and air kisses for the comic effect. He held her around her waist as she tucked her phone into her purse. "How's the glamorous world of Adam Lewis?"

"Busy. He's really got a stable load of prima donnas."

Kellie gestured for Natalie to enter the room first, crossing his arms and leaning on the door frame as she sat down to take off her army boots.

"I'm just glad he handles the difficult ones. They get on my nerves."

"I hear ya. I see the celebs float around here a lot. They don't even work out. They just gossip and sip smoothies."

"Oh, honey!" She flapped her hand at him. "They have personal trainers who give them a workout at home. They come here for the pampering."

"True. I guess that would explain why Adam never shows up. Home gym?"

"Yup. He and Jack do their thing in their own home." Natalie took off her silver cuff bracelet.

"Okay. I'll let you get undressed. Face down, my pet."

"Okie-dokie."

He smiled as he closed the door, wondering what wonderful stories Natalie would have for him today.

Once he'd mixed his oil and returned to Natalie, he did his usual preparations and began a relaxation massage which he knew she loved.

"I have someone I want you to meet."

"Really?" Kellie admired Natalie's tattoos as he massaged her back. "Who?"

"His name is Tony Spagna. Adam just signed him after he appeared in *Being Screwed*."

"What's he like?" Kellie raised Natalie's hand out of the sheet and allowed it to dangle off the side.

"From New York, rough around the edges. But needs a good man to keep him in line."

"Keep him in line?" Kellie didn't like the sound of that.

"Did you catch *Got Men?* That reality show about the six gay guys they forced to come out?"

"Yes. It made me cringe."

"Well? Remember him?"

Kellie thought about the line up on that reality show. He groaned. "Oh no. No way."

"Why not? He's cute?"

"He's mental. I'll pass. Thanks anyway."

"Just think about it."

Kellie knew one reason he disliked being single—being matched up with losers.

With one more appointment to go to finish his Wednesday, Kellie shared a protein smoothie with Tyson as he took a break between clients as well.

"Penny for your thoughts, Kel?"

"Hm?" Kellie handed him the cold shake and slouched on the sofa. "I'm thinking about Monty again. I can't stop. I must be getting a crush on the guy."

"So? Get a crush. He's gay. He's available." Tyson shrugged.

"Yeah, but..."

"Yeah but what?" Tyson handed Kellie back the drink.

"You just know when someone likes you. They look at you a certain way. Monty doesn't."

"And nothing from Scott? At all?" Tyson leaned against Kellie's arm.

"Nothing. He dropped off the planet." Kellie finished the smoothie, holding the cup against his thigh. "I think being a chauffeur he gets a lot of opportunities for sex. You know?" Kellie felt Tyson rest his head on his shoulder so he put his free hand on Tyson's thigh. "Can you imagine how many drunk men come onto him?"

"Yes. Easily. He is cute."

"Yeah. He is."

"Well, I have a date for Friday night."

"Oh? Tell me about him."

Tyson took a deep inhale of air and sighed. "Let's see. He's one of my new clients, aspiring actor—aren't they all?—and only twenty-four."

"Sounds promising."

"The physical attraction is there, and we talk easily when we're working out together. What more can you ask for?"

Kellie sat up with a jolt. Monty was talking with the manager, shaking the man's hand as they headed towards the front desk area, near the exit.

Tyson said quietly, "There's your crush."

"What's he asking Phil?"

"Maybe he's trying to get a job here."

"No." Kellie admired Monty's outfit. Monty was in black slacks with a tight sleeveless crewneck shirt, showing off his tattooed shoulders. "He told me he has his own training camp."

"Ahh," Tyson said, "Joining forces with the owners then."

"Something like that. Maybe just being allowed to advertise here."

"True."

Kellie met Monty's eye. The split second they connected, Kellie smiled, his insides lighting with fire. Monty showed no emotion, shaking the hand of the manager and exchanging words.

"He's just going to leave?" Tyson asked. "He's not even going to come here and talk to you?"

"See what I mean?" Kellie's heart sank. "I'm not his type."

"His loss."

"Fuck it." Kellie stood, tossing out the paper cup into the trash. "I have to get ready for my last client."

"Okay, Kel. Catch ya later."

Kellie gave Monty one last glance before he lost sight of him. Monty wasn't looking back.

"Whatever..." Kellie exhaled in defeat and headed to his room.

~

Monty finished up his negotiation to get the spa to refer members to his elite form of exercise. He waited for Phil to leave and looked for Kellie. He was gone. He took out his phone and called Brandon as he left the building. "Hey. We got the go ahead on putting up posters and running ads linking to this spa."

"Good. That just may push us into the black."

"I'm hoping. We need to make enough money to hire a real advertising sales person."

"We're not there yet. You do pretty well with your Lieutenant Commander background."

Monty removed his keys from his pocket. "I do my best."

"It's our mantra. What are you doing now?"

"Heading home." Monty checked his watch, then glanced over his shoulder.

"Alone again?"

"Don't rub it in. See ya."

"Bye."

He flipped the phone closed and thought about Kellie. *What the hell.* He returned to the reception desk and stood waiting as the woman spoke on the phone. When she ended her call, he asked, "Can I speak to Kellie Hamilton?"

"Do you have an appointment?" She flipped pages of a planner.

"No." The moment he replied, Kellie appeared and signaled to a man who was in the lounge.

"Drake? I'm ready for you now."

The receptionist said, "There he is."

Monty watched Kellie greet Drake and walk behind the wall to where his massage room was. He said, "Thanks," to the woman behind the counter and left.

~

"So what's new with you, girl?" Drake sat down on the chair and took off his sandals.

"Not much, Drake. The usual." Kellie leaned against the doorframe watching him. "Any new plays you've written opening up?"

"Yes! I have one coming to the Coast Playhouse this November. It's a musical based on my friend's romantic comedy novel."

"So you wrote the screen play?"

"I did." Drake smiled sweetly, his long lashes looked as if he used mascara and his lips always appeared glossed. Drake was wispy and thin, a petit male with the drive of a lion to succeed. "I gave my boyfriend the lead. Is that nepotism?"

"Yes, but heck, this is Hollywood after all." Kellie moved away from the doorframe. "I'll let you finish undressing. Just the usual? Upper back and neck?"

"I want your hands all over me this time, Kelsey." Drake puckered his lips flirtatiously.

"You got it." Kellie smiled and closed the door behind him, heading to mix oils. His smile fell quickly as he thought about the cool treatment from Monty.

When he returned, Drake was laying face down, the sheets barely covering him. Kellie adjusted them, making Drake more comfortable with the pillow under his legs.

"You haven't even touched me and I'm fully erect."

Kellie shook his head. "You were born horny." He folded the sheet at Drake's waist and with both hands pressed down on his back gently.

"Fuck. Let me fix it."

Kellie stepped back as Drake adjusted himself and returned to his position, his head against the face rest. It took a minute before Drake settled down. Once he did, Kellie resumed what he was doing. "Breathe."

Drake inhaled and exhaled. "And I jacked off in the shower before I came here…what is it about you?"

"It's not me. It's just the comfortable touch." Kellie pumped oils into his hands.

"Comfortable? I got news for you, sweetie, it's friggin' erotic."

Kellie began smoothing his hands over Drake's shoulders and upper back.

JC came to mind again. Whenever Kellie was reminded about how sensual a massage could be, he thought of that man.

How could he not?

The first few massages JC gave him ended with hand jobs. It was typical for JC to spend nearly fifteen minutes massaging between Kellie's legs. While Kellie lay flat on his back on the table, JC teased him until he was writhing on the soft padding. How could Kellie not want to get another massage over and over again? JC gave him the sexual release without any of the baggage of a relationship.

The first time JC leaned down to envelop Kellie's cock into his mouth, Kellie nearly hyperventilated. At seventeen, he had never had sex with a man, nor a blowjob. Having a man as old as JC perform oral sex with him was beyond anything Kellie had ever imagined.

Using one hand to jack him off, JC sucked and orally fucked Kellie until he came in his mouth. Kellie remembered the first time—his eyes wide, staring at JC in awe and his body shivering with chills.

He heard Drake moan softly and felt a pout form on his lips. Kellie felt let down by men at the moment. He didn't like looking for love. He always believed love will find you.

Chapter 8

Thursday morning, Kellie stood behind Lynn looking over her shoulder. Mike, Tess, and then *Mr. Gresham…* that was his day so far. Monty was coming in at five-thirty. Kellie tried not to feel excited. He had no reason to.

He headed to his room to make sure it was ready for his first client, then hit the gym for his morning workout.

~

Monty skimmed the pages of a men's fitness magazine. He'd already had a full day of work. Clients were signing up for the first session at his training camp, booking spots and arranging housing.

He and Brandon devised a client daily schedule for both the military training and the gourmet meals in between. The resort was all-inclusive for two weeks. Monty liked to think of it as The Ritz meets Boot Camp.

With a headache he could not shake, and feeling stiffness in his low back, Monty was ready for this massage. It brought temporary relief to his pain and satisfied a craving he had for being touched by a man. Yes, he'd thought he wanted a woman to massage him at first, but now that he had experienced Kellie? He only wanted Kellie.

His mobile phone vibrated. Monty took it out of his pocket and read a message from Brandon. He called him, tossing the magazine on the low coffee table and moving towards the exit so he wouldn't disturb anyone.

"What?" Monty asked when Brandon picked up.

"You said the cook can start immediately, right?"

"Yes. He said he was unemployed."

"He's not answering his phone."

"Hang on." Monty scrolled through his list of numbers and then said, "Is this the number you called?" He rattled it off.

"No. I had the wrong one. Bye."

Monty disconnected the line and looked up. Kellie was standing by the receptionist desk waiting for him.

The sight of that young man in his baggie black yoga pants and sleeveless tank top and ponytail pleased Monty. He approached him, staring into Kellie's light blue eyes. "Are you a vegetarian?"

"Yes. Why?"

Monty smiled to himself as he passed by him, headed to the massage room. Thinking of Brandon's appraisal, which in fact was a form of profiling for Brandon, Monty asked, "Drive a Prius?"

"Are you spying on me?"

Monty entered the small room and spun around to see Kellie's expression of bewilderment. "No. Just a good guess."

Kellie didn't look amused. He said, "I'll be back in a minute," and shut the door.

Monty began undressing, tossing his clothing onto the chair. As he did, he read Kellie's certificates—his California license and the degree he received from a local college. The music was the same as last time—chimes, whales, ocean waves. Monty climbed naked on the table, tugging the sheet to cover his ass, and positioned his head on the face rest. Staring at the floor below him, anticipating Kellie's touch, Monty felt his cock thicken. He adjusted it so it lay upright, assuming he would get hard again. Just about ready to fall asleep from his exhaustion, Monty heard a knock and then the door open. He watched for Kellie's feet through the donut shaped cushion, then felt him straightening out the sheet and pillow.

"Same thing, Monty?" Kellie ran his hand lightly over Monty's back, making Monty's cock throb.

"Yes."

"Okay, babe."

Babe. Was it affection or what he said to all the clients? Monty began inhaling and exhaling deeply, letting go the stress he built up for decades. Massage was relatively new to him. It wasn't until recently that he had gone to a massage therapist. He wasn't too impressed with the technique of his previous masseuse and surely hadn't reached any type of meditative plane like he had with Kellie. Kellie was a master. Perhaps that was why he was in a club so elite. All the employees of this establishment were top in their field. It was what Monty aspired to for his own business.

He heard Kellie pump oil into his hands and rub them together. The scent of peppermint and lavender pervaded the air and instantly Monty felt better. Kellie's contact sent a shockwave of pure pleasure through Monty. *Oh, yes. I love your touch.*

Timing his breathing with Kellie's movements, Monty was able to exhale as Kellie pushed down on his back, making some of his vertebrae crack back into place. "I needed that."

Kellie chuckled.

Keeping his eyes open, Monty watched as Kellie's feet made passing steps around him. Kellie's long reach made Monty tingle from his toes to his scalp.

He moaned, low, long and deep as Kellie began working the knots between his shoulder blades. *Fuck!* Monty's cock was thick and throbbing under him. This was by no means a massage with the intent to seduce, and maybe that was why it did.

Images of slimy ads in the back of gay magazines for 'massages' read like whorehouse come-ons. Hinting the customer would be satisfied in every way... Happy endings...

The thought revolted Monty. Overseas he'd been to those types of businesses, his fellow officers pretending it was a gag to go, getting drunk and letting some foreigner jerk you off after getting a rubdown. It sucked. Back in those days, Monty would rather service himself than be forced into having a woman try to jack him off.

But he'd bowed to the pressure, especially when he was young and stupid.

Kellie's hands made long sweeps from his neck to his hips. The oil, the perfect skin to skin lube. Monty blew out several breaths, getting the urge to hump the table under him. Or hump the massage therapist.

Was it the temptation? Knowing he could not be sexual with Kellie here? Was that the turn on?

Everything about Kellie was a turn on, who was he kidding? A vegan and a Prius. Could Brandon have guessed it any more precisely? He and Kellie were opposite. Nothing was better in Monty's opinion than a good filet mignon or barbeque pork ribs. He drove a brand new, gas-guzzling, fire-engine red Camaro. What on earth would they discuss if they had a drink together?

Kellie folded the sheet to expose Monty's leg.

Monty blew a few deep breaths in and out in anticipation of getting his thighs touched. He was so excited he was wondering if the hour would be a loss. Nothing he was thinking or feeling was making him relax.

All right. Stop. Focus on letting go your tension or this is going to be for nothing.

Monty halted his internal dialog and tuned into the contact between him and Kellie. Kellie parted Monty's legs and wrapped the sheet between them, exposing one leg at a time.

Visualizing Kellie as he used more oil to work on his leg, Monty began to feel that floating sensation again. He lost himself on listening to Kellie's soft breaths, the shush of his bare feet on the parquet floor. And his amazingly strong hands.

Kellie was a big man, nearly six feet, with broad shoulders and a rounded chest. Monty began to imagine kissing him. Rustling noises and the pause in the message distracted Monty. He spotted Kellie's feet near the head of the table before he returned to massage Monty's second leg. Kellie paid special attention to Monty's toes and arch, rubbing against the scar Monty knew he had on his calf. It was an accident he'd sooner forget. Crawling under razor wire had its drawbacks.

Kellie finished Monty's legs and lowered the sheet down his backside. Though the pain Monty felt in his hips was excruciating, having Kellie touch his ass made up for it.

Another few breaths in and out and Monty tried not to flinch as Kellie dug into his hip flexor. He whimpered without meaning to. The pain and pleasure combination was akin to S&M. Kellie dug deep into his hips, but kept massaging around the tender area as well, over his low back and near his ass crack.

Monty telepathically told Kellie to get dirty with him. Of course it was nonsense. But it made for a better fantasy.

It worked with the whores overseas. 'Touch my ass.' 'Touch my balls.' 'Touch my cock.' Those sluts did anything you wanted.

Kelsey Hamilton was not a slut.

He was the perfect gentleman and professional to a fault. Monty figured if he did or said anything lewd, Kellie would kindly tell him not to call for another appointment. He had to admire the guy for his willpower. Lord knew what kind of celebrities walked through the door.

"Okay, babe." Kellie held up the sheet as a blind. "Scoot down and roll over."

Monty knew he was sporting serious wood. Since he did last time, and would most likely every time, he didn't flinch. He rolled over and scooted down, just like the man had asked. He opened his eyes and stared at Kellie as Kellie arranged the sheet properly. He knew now why Kellie had paused earlier. He had removed his shirt. Monty could see Kellie gleaming with sweat and it made his cock bounce when he did.

The shorter hair had loosened from Kellie's rubber band. It fell around his oval face in wispy light brown locks. Kellie adjusted the pillow so it propped up Monty's knees. Monty raised his legs up to assist him.

"How you doin', big guy?" Kellie rested his hand on Monty's chest.

"Too good." Monty glanced at the sheet where it tented.

A wry smile on Kellie's lips, he folded the sheet down on Monty's chest and pumped oil into his palms.

Monty watched. Last time he didn't, trying to let go of his tension. Not this time. He wanted to see this man in action.

Kellie ran his fingers and palms across Monty's pectoral muscles, along his shoulder, down his arm to his hand. He picked up Monty's arm and rested it on his hip as he pumped more oil. Monty moved his fingers, deliberately touching Kellie. Though he stared at Kellie's face for a reaction, Kellie didn't give him one. Instead, Kellie continued working Monty's forearm, hand and fingers. Movement under the sheet caught both their eye. Monty's cock had a mind of its own and was happy to let Kellie know everything he did made him excited.

The urge to grip it and jack off was strong. Kellie's touch made Monty so horny he was going insane.

Kellie's expression was calm, though he was running with perspiration. It wasn't hot in the room, but Kellie was the one working up a sweat. Monty lay passive, yet still his back was soaking the sheet under him. Passion. Passion that was bubbling under the surface had Monty drenched. That was his excuse.

Kellie rested Monty's right arm back onto the table, moving behind him to his left.

With the same care and deliberation, Kellie massaged Monty's left side. Once all his limbs were attended, Kellie sat on a stool behind Monty's head to work his neck and shoulders. Monty closed his eyes again, not wanting to miss the tension release in an area where he hurt the most.

Kellie used the hot stones on him, making Monty whimper at the pleasure. The stones ran over his knotted muscles, causing them to ache and feel good simultaneously. Ten minutes later, Kellie washed his hands at the sink and returned to sit on the stool. He began digging his fingertips into Monty's scalp through his hair. Monty's cock began shifting under the sheet in earnest. Monty was sick of being embarrassed by it. *Yes, you fucking turn me on. Okay? Sheesh.*

Monty parted his lips to exhale from the intense pleasure Kellie was generating, both through his head and down into his groin. "Kel, that is so fucking good."

"I'm glad."

It sounded very generic. Certainly not personal. Kellie must say that to all the men and women he massaged. What did Monty expect him to say? 'Wow! Wonderful, Monty! Let's date!'

Monty was so distracted this time, when Kellie reached over his body to find his aura, Monty felt nothing. No, he felt something. Disappointment.

"Okay, babe." Kellie touched Monty over the sheet on his solar plexus.

86

Monty moved like lightening to grab his hand, causing Kellie to jump and appear startled.

They met eyes.

Seeing Kellie's apprehension, Monty softened his hold on Kellie's hand and said, "Thanks."

"You're welcome." Kellie smiled and pressed his fingers wide on Monty's chest.

As Kellie drew back to leave, Monty allowed his hand to slip off Kellie's.

"Take your time getting up. I'll get you water."

Monty nodded, watching Kellie close the door behind him.

~

Kellie was shaking as he walked into the restroom. He stood at the sink and stuck his hand into his briefs, feeling how sticky he had become. Keeping the sessions professional was not easy. But Kellie couldn't read Monty. And even if he could, Kellie would not risk his professionalism for anyone. *Ask me out! Is it that hard for a Navy SEAL to ask a man for a date? You fuckers killed the country's enemy number one. Come on.*

Kellie washed his hands and face and stared at himself. "Am I a vegetarian? Do I drive a Prius? You think I'm a parody of a liberal Californian. What could we have in common other than a physical attraction?"

But what an attraction it was. Kellie was in lust with the man. Rubbing Monty felt intimate and sensual. Not like with his other clients. With Monty, Kellie was having sex. Sex with his hands, his elbows and his forearms, pressing against Monty's hot skin. No, they weren't fucking each other, but they were making love. Kellie had the same afterglow he would from loving a man. Monty's reactions to his touch, his soft whimpers, gave Kellie the intimate fantasy he craved.

He met his eyes in the mirror and said, "I could fall in love with that man."

87

~

Feeling oily but good, Monty sat on the padded metal chair in the corner of the small room. He put his shoes on and sat still, looking around at the small details. A shelf with crystals and stone carvings, CDs neatly placed on a rack, the sink with its towels and stone heater, music and lighting designed to soothe.

"Monty?"

"Come in."

Kellie held a glass of water for him.

Monty took it, gulping it down. "Thanks."

"How do you feel?"

"Good." He watched Kellie walk to a hook on the wall, remove his shirt and put it on.

"Do you normally massage topless?" Monty finished the water and set the glass beside him on the floor.

"Uh. Why? Does it offend you?"

"Offend me?" Monty sat up straight. "No. You can do it naked. I won't be offended."

Kellie appeared shy. "I just get really heated up sometimes."

"I get 'heated up' every time you touch me."

His cheeks going crimson, Kellie folded his arms over his chest defensively and said, "It happens often."

"I can imagine." On the tip of Monty's tongue was the question, *Do you ever date your clients?* Monty knew shrinks couldn't but didn't imagine there was a code like that for massage therapists. Even still, he didn't ask. He stood, taking the glass with him, and handing it to Kellie. "Thanks."

"Did you already book your next appointment?" Kellie took the glass from him.

"I've got every Tuesday and Thursday at five-thirty booked."

Kellie appeared surprised. "Booked? As in…from now on?"

"If I'm available."

Kellie nodded, going shy again.

Monty imagined closing the gap between them and caressing his cheek. Instead, he walked through the door. "See ya."

"See ya."

It felt as if Kellie was staring after him, maybe watching his ass. The temptation to turn around to see, to give him a last smile or wink was strong. But Monty's pride was stronger. He didn't turn back.

~

Kellie stripped the sheets, raising them up to get a sniff. The oil scent was so pungent, he barely caught scent of Monty. He touched his nose to the place on the linen that would have been under Monty's cock and inhaled it. A slight aroma of cologne or musky soap still lingered. Kellie sat on the massage table, hugging the sheets, staring down the empty corridor.

Chapter 9

Kellie's stress level was making him crazy. By Saturday he was already craving Monty and wishing the weekend was gone. He dialed Chelsea's cell phone number, drumming his fingers on his kitchen table as he sat with an empty mug of tea.

"Kellie?"

"Hey, babe."

"What's up?"

"I was wondering if you had a free hour or two where we could swap rubs."

"Oh, thank God! I'm dying and I thought you were too busy. Yes, please."

"You have your table home?"

"I do. Come over."

"Be there in five." Kellie pocketed his phone and pumped his fist. "Thank fuck!" He and Chelsea exchanged massages ever since they met at the spa. He loved her technique and not only did she give wonderful massages, she was a great sounding board and a good friend.

Kellie parked in the driveway of her modest three bedroom home in Inglewood. Though they were getting paid decently, none of them had yet acquired the financing to buy luxury condos or palatial mansions in the suburbs of Los Angeles. On the contrary, they all seemed to be scraping by but managing.

Chelsea was a single mom with a teenage son. Drew split the time with Chelsea and his grandmother, Chelsea's mother. But on weekends Drew was with Chelsea.

Kellie knocked, looking at her lawn, which was in need of new sod or at least a weed-whack. He certainly didn't hold that against her. But if he had a fifteen-year-old son, the young man would earn his room and board. It was good enough for Kellie to do for his dad, it would be good enough for his offspring.

He heard Chelsea shouting through the door for Drew to answer it. It opened and before Kellie could step inside, Drew had resumed his slouching in front of the television with his friend, gaming controls in their eager fists. Kellie closed the door behind him. "Hi, Drew."

"She's in the back."

Not taking offense, because this is how teenagers behaved everywhere, Kellie headed to where Chelsea had her home massage room set up. It was a small bedroom with one window covered by blinds. To Kellie it appeared to be an attempt at feeling like the salon but without the expense.

It didn't matter to Kellie. It was all they needed to exchange rubs. Seeing Chelsea fitting the sheet on the table, Kellie slipped off his flip-flops and assisted her. She appeared rushed and disheveled. "Wow. You want to go first?"

"No. I get last dibs."

"I hear ya."

She rolled her shoulder around like it was sore. "We need to do this weekly. You know?"

"I do. Let's make sure we do." Kellie took off his shirt and tossed it on a folding chair she had set in the corner.

"What music would you like?" she asked.

"You pick. As long as it's not too intrusive, I'm good."

She placed a CD in the portable player and turned it on. "Be back in a minute."

"Okay." Kellie stripped off his clothing and lay face down on the table, very happy Chelsea wanted to swap massages. Once he got himself comfortable, he could hear Chelsea telling her son to not bother her for an hour.

Kellie imagined the boy and his friend could spend all day playing games. He'd never liked video games and didn't see the attraction.

She knocked.

"I'm ready."

The door opened and Kellie felt Chelsea going through the preparations he did with each client—adjusting the foot pillow, the sheet, checking on the massage stones...

As if Chelsea needed to get herself into focus, she placed both hands on Kellie's back and took deep breaths. He did the same, preparing to let go of all his horrible stress.

Once they had both filled and released air from their lungs several times, Chelsea folded back the sheet to Kellie's hips and pumped oil into her hands. At the first healing touch, Kellie unwound and moaned. "Christ, why did we wait so long?"

"Because we're both swamped."

"I'm not that swamped on the weekends."

"Lucky you."

As Chelsea dug into Kellie's shoulders for the knots, he said, "Chelsea."

"What, sweetie?"

"I have a huge crush on a client."

"Which one?"

"Monty Gresham."

"Do I know him?"

"He's the one I almost referred to you because in the beginning he wanted a female therapist."

"Uh…"

"Navy SEAL tattoos on either shoulder."

"Oh! Him! He's really hot, Kellie. Is he gay?"

"Yes."

"Has he shown an interest?" She scooted around the table to his opposite side, letting his right arm dangle loose from the table.

"Yes and no. He gets hard."

"All the men get hard with you."

"Do all the men get hard with you too?"

"Maybe seventy percent. Some are gay and I just don't do it for them. I think some of the guys prefer it that way, like Monty thought he did."

"True. I think they don't want to be turned on. Some even feel like its cheating."

"I know. Silly, huh?"

"I thought it was silly, too, before I met Monty."

"What do you mean?" Chelsea rubbed his fingers and palm.

"Well, normally when I massage someone, that's all it is. A rub."

"Please tell me you're not sexually gratifying him."

"No, you kidding? Risk my job? Have him complain? Not going to happen."

"Then what do you mean?" She let his arm dangle from the table and dug inside his shoulder blade. She found a knot and worked it with her elbow.

Kellie blew a few breaths out trying to get it to let go without much success. "Have you ever massaged someone and it felt was very sensual, but it was just the usual technique, like you do with other clients?"

"Um."

"I mean, I'm not doing anything different to him than I do with everyone else. Nothing inappropriate. But still, I get so horny touching him, I feel as if we're fucking."

"Wow."

"So, I'm nuts and you never felt that way."

"No. I have one client I love massaging. He's straight and I think he's really sexy."

"Does he get hard?"

"Yes." She laughed.

"Would you ask him out?"

"He's married."

"Oh."

"So. No." She stood at the head of the table and ran her hands along Kellie's back to his hips. "But I feel very close to him. Like we have some kind of connection that's deeper than just a client. Though neither of us says it. It's all body language."

"If he was single would you ask him out?"

"Oh hell yes."

"I want to ask Monty to go out for a drink, but I sometimes I get the feeling it's servant to master between us, and not in an S&M way, in a class way."

"Oh, yeck. Not really, Kellie."

"Yes, really. I feel as if he's a celebrity high class businessman, and I'm a lowly masseuse."

"He's a celebrity?"

"No. I only compared him to one because of his status with the armed services. After all, the Navy SEALs are all the rage after the mission in Pakistan."

"Does he make you feel that way? Or are you projecting?"

"See. This is what I don't know."

"So, you're afraid if you say something about becoming social, he may get offended and not see you as a client any longer."

"Or worse. Complain to Phil. All I need is someone to say my gayness is offensive and I'm done."

"Shut up. Everyone knows the work ethic you have there. If someone said I did something inappropriate would you believe them?"

"No."

"There ya go."

"Mom?" Drew called through the door.

"I told you not to bother me, Drew."

"Can we order pizza?"

"Sure." She added, "My wallet is in my purse in the bedroom."

"'kay."

"Sorry, Kel."

"Don't be." He sighed and closed his eyes, enjoying the rest of his massage in silence.

~

Monty tugged at the equipment to make sure it was sturdy. He and a dozen other men were putting the finishing touches on the training facility. They finally had enough people sign up to fill a class. Their first. If this went well, the referrals would be worth the effort.

Monty leaped up to the first rung of the inverted ladder, reaching hand over hand to swing across the length, making sure it was stable. He got to the end and dropped off, rubbing his right shoulder as he did.

"Hey, old man!"

"Shut the fuck up, Brandon." Monty met him near the obstacle course.

"Shoulder giving you problems?"

"No. You are." Monty went into a boxing stance and pretended to spar with Brandon, who eagerly did the same. They took a couple swipes at each other until another SEAL buddy approached with paperwork.

"Right," Cliff held out a piece of printed paper. "Menu. Have a look."

Both Brandon and Monty stopped horsing around to read it.

"Fucking vegetarian selection?" Brandon made a face. "Is this because you're in love with your masseuse?"

"Shut up!" Monty pushed him hard until Brandon stumbled. "Have you sampled the food, Cliff?"

"Yes. The chef prepared all of it. Fucking amazing."

"Good."

Brandon snatched the menu from Monty to read thoroughly.

Monty left him to it and did a walkthrough of all the equipment, testing it, hanging his weight on it, swinging from it.

The steel and chrome appearance of their facility was perfection. They may not have all the talent for design but they sure as shit knew who to hire to do it. Monty stood still, doing a one-eighty of the entire facility. "Love it!" he shouted loudly, causing the rest of the men to turn to look. They began whooping it up like Tim Taylor's tool man grunts, sounding like a bunch of macho apes. Monty couldn't be happier.

Brandon rushed him like a linebacker. Monty stood his ground until he was about to be tackled, turning sideways to allow Brandon to miss.

"You fucker! We did it!" Brandon picked Monty up to spin around.

Monty rubbed Brandon's head with his knuckles as punishment, but gave in and hugged Brandon. "Now let me down before I fuck you."

Brandon allowed Monty to roll down his chest to his feet. "If I wasn't married, I'd let you."

Monty announced to the throng who were still celebrating, "Straight, married Brandon Field just offered to let me fuck him!"

Catcalls and whistles surrounded them.

"I'm so horny, I may take it." Monty went for a grab at Brandon's dick.

Brandon dodged him, laughing. "Ask out your masseuse. He'll fuck you."

"Shut up and get busy."

Brandon winked, walking away.

Monty wondered what 'his masseuse' was up to today. If he had his way, he would fuck Kellie. Every day.

Peeking over Lynn's shoulder to make sure 'his man'—yes,
did indeed see the name Monty Gresham at the five-thirty spot

Chapter 10

Somehow Kellie had killed the weekend.

His errands, his food shopping, reading, sleeping, had turned
Saturday into Tuesday morning.

He didn't ask why, he was just glad it did.

Lynn was behind the desk, the headset on her ear, talking
Kellie had no idea what he would do without her.

Peeking over Lynn's shoulder to make sure 'his man'—yes,
did indeed see the name Monty Gresham at the five-thirty spot

She spun around to slap his arm and giggle at his antics.

Kellie didn't care who knew. *Yes, I have a crush on the man.
So? What are ya gonna do about it?*

He danced behind her, around her, with her, and then dancing
on the way to his workout routine he slammed into someone.

Blinking and about to apologize, Kellie gulped loudly at

"Having a good day?" Monty asked.

"Yes. Sorry."

"Did you enjoy your weekend as much as you're enjoying

Kellie gave Monty a head to toe inspection. Not because he needed to, because he wanted to. Fabulous Monty was wearing dark slacks and a short-sleeved button down shirt, looking sharp and business-like, as he carried a briefcase.

"I'm happier here. Now. Here." Kellie pointed to the floor in front of him.

"I hope you're still this happy for our appointment."

Kellie had an urge to tell him he was happy *because* of the appointment, but again, deemed it inappropriate. "Count on it."

Monty cupped Kellie's jaw.

The touch of this man's hand nearly made Kellie's legs buckle. In a split second, Monty had retreated to do, whatever he had planned to do before their appointment, leaving Kellie chomping at the bit for more of him.

This time as Kellie stared, Monty did indeed look back, giving him a sensual glance.

"Great. Now I need to jack off." Kellie spun around and headed to his massage room to calm down.

~

On his way to show the manager, Phil, his advertising posters, and hopefully put them up inside the salon today, Monty looked around at the men and women trying hard to keep in shape. The world was filled with individuals, all a wonderful variety of sizes, shapes, and colors.

It fascinated Monty how one person could stick out from the rest. One man. Nature worked in bizarre ways. Though Monty had studied psychology and human behavior, he couldn't pinpoint to a T what made two people attracted to each other. Yes, he'd heard it all—pheromones, nature, nurture, your mother, your father…

But when someone crossed his path he grew hungry for, Monty took notice.

He stood at Phil's door about to knock. With the amount of hours he'd spent building his own facility, creating a regiment to kick the ass of any client, Monty had enough exercise. When he was given time away from the job, he was drawn here. Here to see Kellie. When it came to dealing with this particular salon now, Monty volunteered, and Brandon didn't deny him the treat.

He knocked. "Phil?"

"Come in."

Monty opened the door and noticed the man appeared busy. "Can I show you the posters?"

"Just drop them off. I'll make sure they get pinned up on the walls."

Monty removed the stack from his briefcase, placing them on a vacant chair. "Thanks."

"No problem. I wish you good luck on your grand opening."

"We'll need it. Make sure you give us plenty of your promo material to display. I think our clients will overlap."

"You got it."

Monty left, closing the door behind him. He walked through the palatial spa area, standing to watch swimmers in the lap pool, pausing to glance at the whirlpool and sauna, but feeling empty.

His life had been so complicated. For two decades of service Monty didn't have time to breathe. Suddenly he was given the opportunity to pause and inhale. The SEAL training retreat was nearly complete. Their first session was booked, and all that he could do, he had done, at least until something new came up, which did constantly.

Monty had no idea how he could feel lonely and isolated in a building filled with people.

Over the years he'd built up a lot of rage and resentment towards life and politics. Maybe now was the time to start letting go.

He sighed loudly and decided to spend some time here unwinding before he headed back to the training center. He dropped his briefcase in his car, and took a canvas bag with shorts and a t-shirt back into the salon.

~

Kellie fussed with the details of his room. He wiped down the shelves, rearranged his crystals, folded sheets, straightened the pictures and wall mirror… Why was he a nervous wreck?

He had two appointments and his yoga class to go before he had Monty naked and lying on the table. Not only that, Kellie needed to do his morning workout. Mike Murphy would be coming for his appointment in an hour and a half. Kellie had hid in his massage room since bumping—literally—into Monty.

"This is stupid." Kellie pulled the rubber band out of his hair and wrapped it up tighter. He looked into the mirror as he did and blew out a breath of air in frustration. "Go work out! So what if Monty is out there?"

Straightening up his appearance, Kellie left his massage room and tried to think only of what he had to do before Mike showed up for his appointment.

He didn't see Monty in the weight room. Tyson spotted him while helping someone workout, and waved. Kellie waved back.

Fine. He's gone. Good. Kellie stretched in front of the mirrors and went into exercise mode.

A half hour later, sweat running down his chest and temples, Kellie checked the time—he needed to rinse in the shower before Mike's appointment. He walked past the yoga room on his way to the locker room and backtracked as he did. Monty was lying, face up, alone in the room. He was holding one knee, looking like he was stretching the muscles of his low back.

Kellie watched him for a moment.

101

Below Monty's gym shorts, Kellie could see all the sinewy muscles in Monty's thigh flex. Kellie didn't want to disturb him. It appeared the man liked solitude.

He tried to envision what Monty's life in the Navy SEALs could have been like. Other than the media version, he really had no idea. Just before Kellie continued on to the shower, Monty must have felt Kellie's presence. He turned his head towards the door and released his leg, allowing it to rest on the floor.

Kellie's breath caught in his throat. They didn't wave, smile, or do anything two friends would do under these circumstances.

The odd vibe was too much for Kellie. He walked away, needing to get back on his schedule. He was spending too much time thinking about this man.

~

Monty watched Kellie leave. Once he did, he stared at the ceiling, contemplating. The relationship between him and Kellie had become a strange game. Monty found it peculiar that two men who touched intimately, could still be tiptoeing around each other.

Monty felt slightly out of his element. Spending time in a high end Hollywood health resort was the opposite of what he had been accustomed to. He was more at home lying in a trench staring at the stars.

Brandon was the ringmaster of the new training camp. How many nights did they talk about what they would do when they finished their service? Brandon dreamt big. Brandon spoke of a reality TV series which featured their new facility, and of course, bringing the biggest stars in LA to their retreat. Their new intensive training spa aspired to become a bizarre cross between country club cuisine and punishing boot camp. With his charisma and intelligence, Brandon had convinced twelve of their colleagues to invest their money and time into this venture.

102

It looked great on paper. Time would tell how they did as the first session drew near.

Monty stood, feeling the sense of dizziness from lying prone and moving to vertical too quickly. Once it passed, he made his way to the locker room and, consciously or unconsciously, hunted down Kellie.

When he spotted him with a towel around his hips, walking out of the shower, Monty ducked behind a row of lockers. Standing hidden, he watched as Kellie finished drying his hair with the same towel, naked in front of his open locker door.

Monty inhaled deeply as he got his first look at this man's cock and ass. Soft, Kellie's dick appeared slightly larger than average, but not huge, and cut, which Monty preferred. The lack of tan lines gave Monty the impression Kellie either sunbathed nude, or didn't tan at all and his natural skin color was bronze.

That handsome black personal trainer appeared beside Kellie, joking with him and smiling. Monty backed away and changed out of his workout clothing. He had a few errands to do before his five-thirty appointment with Kellie.

~

Kellie pulled his briefs up his thighs.

Tyson touched his arm to get his attention.

When Kellie looked at Tyson he saw Tyson's focus was somewhere behind Kellie. "What?"

"That man you like was just checking out your attributes."

Kellie jerked his head in the direction, seeing no one there. "You sure?"

"Am I sure?"

"How long was he there?" Kellie put his yoga pants on over his briefs.

"I don't know but the minute I showed he split." Tyson leaned against the lockers opposite Kellie.

Kellie ran his hands back through his hair tiredly. He sat down on the bench between rows of lockers and felt drained.

Tyson stood behind him, combing his fingers back through his hair, drawing it into a ponytail. "What's going on with him?"

"Nothing. Just a lot of tension." Kellie handed Tyson the rubber band he had around his wrist. Tyson took it and fastened back Kellie's hair affectionately.

Once he did, Tyson sat next to Kellie and leaned on him. "Ask him out. What's stopping you?"

"He intimidates the shit out of me."

"Why?"

"A million reasons. But mostly because I just don't think he likes me."

"Why would he be checking out the goods?"

"Hell, I see his? He wanted to see mine?"

"You saw his cock? Did you peek?"

"Unintentionally. When I went to wrap the sheet around his leg, it was pointing down." Kellie shivered to express to Tyson his desire. "What a fucking cock."

"Did he know you spotted it?"

"He must. I had no idea it was there and I just about grabbed onto it when I wrapped the sheet between his legs."

"Love when you do that to me. I am so hard now. Gah! I have to meet a new client." Tyson sat up and checked his watch.

"Shit!" Kellie jumped to his feet. "I have Mike Murphy waiting for me. I have to go." He dove into his shirt and closed the locker. Tyson walked to the exit with him. Kellie tossed his wet towel into the laundry bin on his way.

"Catch you later for a smoothie." Tyson squeezed Kellie's arm.

"Okay." Kellie hurried to the waiting area and spotted Mike reading a magazine. "Mike?"

He looked up.

"Come on back."

Mike's expression brightened and he tossed the magazine aside. He gave Kellie a touch on his back as they made their way. "You always look so good." Mike ran his hand to Kellie's bottom.

Kellie didn't mind that from Mike. He was a dear friend. "Any casting calls?" He gestured for Mike to enter the room first.

"Yes. A few irons in the fire." Mike sat on the chair and removed his shoes and socks.

"The usual?"

"Unless you're including happy endings."

"Nope. But your stress will be gone even without it."

"Says you." Mike winked.

"I'll be back."

"Can't wait."

Kellie closed the door behind him and tried to get back on target with his work.

~

Monty returned to the club slightly later than he would have liked. Since it was five-thirty the city was bumper to bumper exhaust-spewing-beasts for miles. Finally parked, jogging to the entrance, Monty headed to the reception desk and said, "I've got an appointment with Kellie. Should I go right back? I'm late."

Before the woman could answer, Monty did what he said he would do. He strode down the corridor, avoiding people chatting about their pedicures and facials, past employees texting and chewing gum like it was taffy, and finally to the door with the name '*Kellie, Massage Therapy*' on it. It was ajar so he opened it. Kellie was sitting on the chair in the corner, head in hands. When Kellie looked up, he seemed surprised. Like perhaps he'd thought Monty would not show up.

"I'm sorry." Monty closed the door behind him.

"It's okay." Kellie stood, appearing tired or upset.

"You can cut it short if you have an appointment after me."

"No. You're my last one for the day. It's fine. Let me let you get ready. I have to mix your oils."

Monty stopped him with a hand on Kellie's muscular upper arm. Kellie didn't react or look Monty's way.

"The traffic was a nightmare. I'm not used to this."

Slowly Kellie met Monty's stare. The look was smoldering with sexuality. It made Monty's throat tighten and chills cover his skin. "Please don't worry. I'm just glad you made it."

The urge to take Kellie into his arms was killing Monty. The closeness of their posture, the sense of attachment he felt, all worked into torture. Loosening his hold on Kellie's arm, Monty let his hand drop to his side. The staring match was explosive, as if something would happen between them.

Monty toed off his shoes and tugged his shirt over his head.

Kellie appeared conflicted and reached for the doorknob.

Monty drew closer, his breathing feeling labored as the craving to kiss and touch Kellie grew.

"I'll let you get ready." Kellie's Adam's apple moved with his swallow, showing his nerves. He opened the door and passed through it, closing it behind him.

Monty looked down at his crotch. As he opened his pants, his cock emerged from it, thick and hard.

~

Kellie couldn't breathe. He rushed to the room where he kept his oils and braced his hands on the counter near a sink.

"Kellie?"

Hearing Chelsea's voice, Kellie looked up.

"What's wrong?" She hurried towards him.

"I can't do this."

"Can't do what?"

Kellie tilted his head in the direction of his massage room. "Monty. He's there."

"And?"

Kellie didn't even know how to express his feelings about Monty to Chelsea.

"Did he cross the line?"

"No." Kellie shook his head to reinforce his words. "But if I go in there right now, I may."

"You won't. You'll click into professional mode, Kel. And if you want to touch him that way, just ask him out!" She lowered her voice and leaned against him so they couldn't be overheard. "So, he says no. You think you'd be the first to get rejected?"

"I would lose him. If he doesn't like me 'that way'," Kellie used his fingers like quotation marks for the last two words, "then I'll create a bad vibe and he'll vanish."

"You like him that much?" She rubbed his back.

Kellie met her eyes. "I think I do."

~

Monty lay perfectly still, listening. Was it taking longer than usual for Kellie to get ready? Did he cross a line and upset him?

He was about to get up and look for Kellie when he heard him knock. Monty didn't answer, but he did lean up on his arms and watch the door. It opened and Kellie peeked in, wearing his canvas belt with his oil bottle hanging from it. That was a good sign. Monty relaxed again, his head against the face rest and his arms at his sides. He felt and heard Kellie walking around, straightening up the sheet, adjusting the cushion all as if there was an elephant in the room.

After a few moments of preparation, Kellie stroked Monty's back gently. The amount Monty had been craving Kellie's touch, both for his healing technique and for his affection, created a pain in Monty's chest. Longing. Having been independent for as long as he could remember, the only thing Monty could relate his feeling for Kellie to was his trust in his fellow SEALs. They were so close-knit, none of them had ever let the other down. And that behavior continued in their civilian life.

Maybe that was why Monty didn't have a lover. How could an ordinary man compete with the bond Monty had created with his team?

Kellie folded back the sheet. His touch was feather light. "Are we doing the same today?"

"Yes."

Kellie added oil to his hands and ran them down Monty's back to his hips.

Seeing Kellie's bare feet through the hole in the face cushion, Monty moaned softly at the first healing caress. This time, he shut down his thoughts and focused on breathing and letting go his stress. He wanted that light headiness. He wanted to feel Kellie stroke his aura.

~

Other than the music and some sounds of conversation from outside the room, it was silent. Kellie needed to pretend this was just like any other massage and he wasn't falling for a client. It wasn't against the rules, it wasn't unheard of, but unless Monty made the first move, Kellie would not cross that line.

He intended, however, to give Monty the best full body rub Monty had ever experienced. There were no rules against that. Hearing Monty's measured breathing, knowing Monty was working on pure relaxation, Kellie grew warm and excited. He removed his shirt quickly, tossing it on the protruding hook, and resumed his massage. On Monty's left side, admiring his eagle tattoo, Kellie got lost on it, imagining running his tongue over it.

He loosened Monty's arm from the sheet, allowing it to hang off the table, then worked Monty's neck and upper back, deep, like he wanted it.

108

Twenty minutes of silence, pure indulgence, Kellie used the stones on Monty's back, making him whimper and moan in pleasure. Kellie had no doubt Monty was as hard as he was at the moment, seeing Monty's hips shifting to find a comfortable spot for an erection. No matter how cool Kellie tried to make the room, he was running in perspiration and his crotch was damp and pulsating.

After Monty's back was rubbed, Kellie raised the sheet to cover it, and moved to the foot of the table. He exposed Monty's right leg and wrapped the sheet between Monty's legs to preserve his modesty. Yes, Kellie could have gotten a sweet glance at his balls but he didn't.

Taking extra time on Monty's horrendous scar, Kellie had mixed a special bottle to help fade it. He pumped it into his palm and began working over that calf muscle, feeling sorrow for the injury which must have been a nightmare. The urge to run kisses over it to show his compassion was strong, but Kellie moved on to Monty's foot, bending his knee, holding it upright, attentive to his every toe and pressure points on his sole. He exposed Monty's perfect ass, one cheek at a time, and again had the pleasure of kneading it, feeling where Monty's pain reflex occurred inside his hip flexor area. That ass. That perfect tight ass tormented Kellie.

Monty's left leg and hip done as well, Kellie walked beside Monty, raised the sheet and said, "Okay, my love, scoot down and roll over."

A low groan preceded movement. Kellie waited before lowering the sheet. No erection this time. Kellie didn't regard it either way.

He lowered the face rest and adjusted the pillow under Monty's knees.

Sitting behind him, Kellie folded the sheet just under Monty's nipples and began working his neck and shoulders from underneath.

Monty's lips parted to a sigh and his eyes stayed closed.

Kellie was able to stare at him freely. It's all he wanted to do. Images of the two of them, sharing a bottle of wine, gazing into each other's eyes, haunted him.

Monty was so pliable, Kellie was able to tilt his head to the side easily, massaging Monty's neck and upper shoulders. Kellie oiled his hands and stood, pushing the sheet down with his fingertips. He caressed Monty's chest over his nipples, working his pectoral muscles and sternum. When he reached all the way down Monty's torso to his abdomen, the sheet finally tented. Kellie made a few long swooping palm rubs from Monty's shoulders to his hips, then stood beside him to explore the external oblique muscles and abdominal.

A breathy moan made the hair stand on Kellie's neck. Monty's cock could no longer ignore the sensual touch. Kellie had been hard for the whole hour, able to look at every sinewy muscle he was caressing.

He tugged the sheet up to Monty's neck, washed his hands and sat on the stool at the head of the table. With all the affection of a lover, Kellie cupped Monty's head in his hands and held it, gently pulling traction to release the strain in his neck. He dug his fingertips into Monty's scalp, through his thick brown hair, rubbing in a circular motion until Monty's cock was like a pole under the sheet.

"*Oh, God...*" Monty whimpered, his eyes still closed.

The charge of electricity sent to Kellie's groin from the sensual words was strong.

Kellie closed his eyes and kept his hands still for a moment. His heart was beating so hard under his ribs he was nearly in pain. Tears stung his eyes and the amount he wanted this man was growing unreasonable.

He shook himself out of it, sat up and traced Monty's features with his index fingers, up and down his nose, around his eyes, forehead and cheeks, to his lips. Monty's hips shifted and his cock moved, pressing against the cotton sheet.

"Okay, my love," Kellie whispered close to Monty.

Monty unfurled his hands from the sheet and reached over his head, touching Kellie's face.

Kellie closed his eyes and let go a stressful sigh.

Monty tickled his fingertips over Kellie's cheeks and jaw.

With both hands, Kellie held Monty's hands against his face. He kissed each of his palms and bit back a whimper.

One of Monty's knees bent, moving the sheet as he did.

Kellie didn't want this to go where it was headed. He couldn't let it. With a squeeze on each of Monty's hands, he placed them down on Monty's own chest, standing.

"Kellie." Monty held his cock over the material.

Kellie shook his head no, and left the room. He felt drunk, high, and dizzy from the intense contact. He entered the restroom and propped his hands on the sink trying to recuperate.

~

Monty couldn't move.

The session had been mind blowing.

His thoughts were disoriented and his limbs felt like lead. He bent both knees and tried to wake out of the strange stupor. After rubbing his face, he reached between his legs and squeezed his cock. It was rock hard and he was going out of his mind.

He jerked it a couple times and knew he could come. It was just out of the question. No way. Reluctantly he let go of his dick and moaned. With everything feeling like a huge effort, Monty sat up, the sheet on his lap, his legs dangling off the table. He stared at his clothing, imagining standing and getting dressed. He simply couldn't at the moment.

A knock at the door made him blink his eyes.

It opened and Kellie looked at the chair then saw him on the table. Kellie held a glass of water.

Monty reached for it.

Kellie stepped in, closing the door after he gave Monty the glass. Monty sucked it down, thirsty for a drink. Kellie sat on the chair, hands folded on his lap.

Once Monty drank the entire contents, he felt slightly more alert. "Holy crap. That took everything out of me."

"I'm sorry." Kellie appeared sheepish.

"Don't be. It was unbelievable."

Kellie stood, took the glass from him and set it by the sink. He reached for his shirt and before he put it on, Monty stopped him. He touched Kellie's arm and turned Kellie to face him.

"I can't do anything here, Monty."

"I'm not asking you to."

"Do you want to…?"

"To?" Monty held Kellie's hand.

Kellie glanced down at the clasp. "Go out to dinner with me?"

"Yes."

The relief on Kellie's face was adorable. Monty asked, "What took you so long?"

"Are you kidding?" Kellie laughed nervously. "You intimidate the shit out of me."

Monty reached around Kellie's back and held him, resting his head against him.

~

Kellie caressed him gently, kissing his hair. He held Monty's head, not wanting to let go. He backed up and gave him a smile that felt mushy and affectionate. "Are you free tonight?"

112

"What day is it?" Monty appeared seriously disoriented from the power of the massage.

"Thursday. Or would you like a sexier day of the week?" Kellie pushed Monty's hair back from his forehead.

"Thursday." Monty's brow furrowed. "Um…"

Kellie expected enthusiasm and didn't get it. "Let me step out again and you can get dressed. I think this session really fucked with your head."

"Shit. No kidding. I can't think straight. All the blood went to my cock."

"I'll give you a few more minutes." Kellie put his shirt on, took the glass and left. He tried not to take offense. Monty was just feeling groggy.

Once he got rid of the glass, Kellie stepped out of the spa area to look at the men and women working out. Tyson was still busy, training new clients. The man was always booked. Personal trainers were all the rage.

Ten minutes of staring off into space, and Kellie felt a light touch on his back. He woke up and found Monty standing behind him.

"I can't tonight." Monty frowned. "While you rubbed me to near unconsciousness, my business partner has been going out of his mind."

"Okay." Kellie was disappointed but understood.

"What's your weekend like?"

"Let me check." Kellie walked to Lynn's desk, taking her appointment book out to see what she had booked for him. Monty stood on the opposite side of the reception counter.

"Looks like I'm busy both Friday and Saturday evenings. How about Sunday?"

"Okay. So far I'm free. How do you want to work this?" Monty held his mobile phone.

"Let me give you my cell phone number."

"Ready." Monty smiled, as if prepared to take it. He pushed numbers into this keypad while Kellie spoke them. "Okay. I'll call you Sunday afternoon, meanwhile, think of a place I can wine and dine you."

"Sounds perfect."

"Bye." Monty waved and left, his strut always confident and masculine.

"Sigh," Kellie said to Lynn, who had eavesdropped.

"At least you have a date."

"True. Just hate waiting." Kellie made a silly face at her and returned to his room to strip the linens and replace them with fresh ones.

Chapter 11

Sunday afternoon came.

And went.

No phone call, no contact from the former-Navy SEAL.

Kellie was trying not to be furious. He hadn't taken Monty's cell phone information home. The plan was for Monty to call him. He didn't. Get over it.

A glass of wine in Kellie's hand as he sat in his den watching television, Kellie knew trying to date this man would be a painful disaster. Monty had 'unattainable' written all over him. Kellie understood that from the start. Why he knew it, he couldn't explain. But some men who were sought after never let you claim the prize.

The worst end of this deal, which Kellie knew would happen, was either Monty would cancel his appointments, or he would show and the awkwardness would be palpable.

When his phone rang, Kellie's heart pumped. He reached for it and checked the caller ID. "Hi, Tyson."

"Don't sound so disappointed. Oh. Wait. It's Sunday night and you're supposed to be with Prince Charming."

"Yup. I knew it."

"Do you want me to take you out to dinner?"

Kellie checked the time. It was nearing nine. "No. How about tomorrow?"

"Deal. You pick the spot, my treat."

"How's it going with your new man?"

"Good. He just thinks dates are for the end of the week. Of course no one wants to go out while we're off."

"I know." Kellie sighed loudly. "Well, you got me. Thanks for calling and for the offer for dinner tomorrow."

"My pleasure. You want to vent?"

"No. I'm too worn out. I'll just veg."

"Okay, sweetheart. I'm here if you need a shoulder."

"Thanks, Ty." Kellie hung up and stared into space.

~

"Try it now!" Monty was boiling hot and standing in front of an electrical panel with a man holding a flashlight at it.

"Nothing!" Brandon called back.

"Fuck!" Monty stormed out of the basement of their developing facility and approached the lineman outside their premises.

"Anything?" The man in the bucket truck shouted down to Monty.

"No! Come on, man! We have work to do before the grand opening!"

"Don't worry. I'll get you juice."

Monty threw up his hands in frustration.

Brandon grabbed Monty on his shoulder. "Look, he'll get it done. Do you want me to order pizza for the guys?"

"What the hell time is it?" Monty looked at his watch. "Ten? Fuck!" He patted his pockets for his phone, then took off into the building again when he couldn't find it.

In the dark, using a flashlight, Monty located a pile of his things and removed his phone. He cursed himself at having forgotten his date. A date that meant the world to him.

The lights flickered and went out. He left the building and used the streetlights to see his cell phone, dialing.

"Hello."

"Kel…"

"Hi." His voice sounded flat and tired.

"I'm so fucking sorry."

"It's okay."

Monty knew it was not okay. "We had a power surge overload the circuits at the new place and it completely burned out the wiring. We open tomorrow for media-review tours and…" Monty sighed and leaned against a car that was parked in the lot out front. "I'm sorry."

"I said it's okay."

"Let me make it up to you. I feel like crap." He checked his watch. "Did you already eat?"

"Yes."

"Wow, that was a stupid question. I haven't." Monty didn't know what to say. "When are you free?"

"I don't know. I have to check my schedule again."

"Fuck. Kel…"

"Look, I'm kind of tired. I'm going to bed."

Monty felt a pain jab him at the guilt. "Okay. I'm sorry."

"You don't have to keep apologizing."

"I feel like I do."

"See you Tuesday for your appointment."

"Yes. I'll be there." Monty heard Kellie disconnect the line. He looked up at Brandon who was walking closer.

"I ordered ten pizzas. You think that will be enough?"

The lights came on and the sound of men cheering echoed in the area.

"Yes." Monty ran his hand through his hair. "I was supposed to go out to dinner with Kellie tonight."

"Yeah, so? My wife had dinner for me too. Life of a new business owner, suck it up." He walked away.

After Brandon left, Monty said under his breath, "Yeah, but yours wasn't a first date." He kicked himself for remembering so late. But there was nothing he could do about it now.

~

Kellie kept busy Monday. Another day off to murder, kill, waste, or whatever one does with time not well spent. He had dinner with Tyson so that made for a nice evening and the day wasn't a total loss.

Though he needed a hobby, he didn't have disposable income. The bankruptcy and foreclosure left his credit rating in the pits, so Kellie curbed his desire to shop, eat out, and do frivolous things he used to do as a real estate agent.

Keeping a tight hold on purse strings made for a dull life. Since he did his exercise routine at the salon all week, he didn't have to spend time exercising outside of it. So he strolled around the beach, hiked the canyon, or sipped coffee in a park—people watching, but not interacting too often. When he got together with friends it was normally for in home get-togethers, or a drink at happy hour.

But he lived for his work. He always had.

Tuesday morning, Kellie was glad to be back in his grove. If he didn't try to date and just went on with his life, he was fine. Happier. His past attempts at meeting someone who was more than just a sex partner had failed. Scott being the most recent, and if he admitted it, Monty was a failure as well.

Kellie wasn't sure what he did to put men off, but no one seemed to call back or see him after a few dates.

As he placed linen on his table, Kellie wondered if the fact that he touched naked men may put off a potential partner from giving him a chance at finding real love. If he dated a man who did what he did, he certainly wouldn't hold that against him. But then again, he was biased.

His day was going well, as planned. Kellie was most calm when things went smoothly. His morning workout was finished, two clients done, and his yoga class was behind him.

One thing lingered before he could go home and forget everything at the salon. Monty Gresham.

The man now had a standing appointment for every Tuesday and Thursday at five-thirty. One last check with Lynn and Kellie knew Monty had not canceled. Why should he? He wasn't the one who was humiliated. Kellie hadn't stood him up.

But Monty had called him to apologize. He called and was starting a new business.

Guilt surfaced as Kellie thought about Monty trying to begin a venture as big as the one he was planning. Maybe he was being too hard on the guy.

Fresh linens on the table, a new CD playing sounds of waterfalls and birds chirping, and Kellie was ready for anything.

He poked his head around the corner first. Yes. Monty was there. He wasn't reading a magazine. Monty appeared to be looking for him. The minute Monty spotted him, Monty hopped to his feet with a worried expression on his face.

Kellie pretended this was just a client here for massage therapy. He smiled and said, "I'm ready for you."

Monty walked beside him down the hall to the massage room. "Kellie, I'm sorry. Forgive me."

"Don't worry." Kellie laughed, brushing it off as trivial. "Just get ready and I'll be back soon."

Monty did not look happy. He stood still, staring at Kellie as Kellie shut the door and went to mix his oil. Though he tried to make light of it, Monty hadn't called him all day Monday. So? Nothing ventured, nothing gained.

~

He removed his clothing, feeling like he had really let Kellie down. And he had. Why didn't he call him? Because he was so incredibly busy he couldn't sit down for a second and do anything rational.

The last minute details of the upcoming session turned out to be major issues—plumbing, lighting, passing state inspections, last minute permits and fees...all leading to so much pressure and headache, Monty ended up dropping dead at near midnight each day. And more so the last two days because of orientation and tours, media and interviews.

The new training session was set to begin this coming weekend, and he felt as if his life would be gone for two weeks until he and the rest of the guys had succeeded in getting the maiden voyage under their belts.

This first enrollment would make or break them. Brandon had arranged news coverage, reviewers, the works.

Monty lay down on the table, tugging the sheet over his legs but grew frustrated trying to cover up and ignored it. He stared through the face rest thinking, but soon shut his eyes and began breathing deeply. Timing at the moment wasn't conducive to love. Though he would have liked to begin a relationship with Kellie, maybe this wasn't a good week to do it.

A knock on the door and then the sound of it opening alerted Monty Kellie was back. The door closed and the familiar routine of Kellie straightening the sheet and cushion commenced.

Seeing Kellie's bare feet as he moved around the table, Monty sank both in his heart and from his physical exhaustion. Without a comment, Kellie oiled his hands and rolled his palms down Monty's back to his hips. Monty moaned in pleasure. His life had become as hectic as it had been while he was in the service.

It didn't matter he would love to have an easy life now. Things dropped in your lap and you either went for them or you didn't. If it was hard? So what? He was trained to deal with hard. In comparison to what he'd been through in the past? The ordeal of starting up a business was nothing.

But Monty was tired. Very tired.

As Kellie changed up his routine, never rubbing him the same way twice, which Monty liked, he closed his eyes and immediately fell into the floating sensation he'd come to expect from Kellie's fabulous sessions.

Kellie removed Monty's arm from the sheet, making Monty's fingers curl involuntarily as he rubbed his forearm. When Kellie raised Monty's arm up to let it dangle from the table, Monty spread wide his fingers and touched Kellie's leg. The minute he made contact, Monty reached for him. Kellie stopped what he was doing.

His eyes still shut, Monty felt Kellie's hip and held it, giving it a loving squeeze. Gently, Kellie raised his arm up and allowed it to hang over the table as he intended, then he went back to working the knots in Monty's shoulder.

Monty wanted to touch him. He'd had his chance Sunday night when he was supposed to go out on their date, but he screwed it up. There was no way to prevent the attraction Monty felt the moment he and Kellie were in the room together. And that didn't begin to describe the intense desire he had when Kellie caressed him.

The touch of Kellie's hands went straight to his groin. Monty shifted on the table, forgetting to set his dick upright. It was growing hard while pointing down, between his legs.

Monty inhaled and exhaled in a sigh, letting it thicken where it was. He was too tired to raise up and shift it, and he didn't care where it was. As Kellie's probing into his knots between his shoulder blades grew deeper, Monty floated with the pain/pleasure combo. He began to think his love of pain was going to bring him into a masochistic relationship. Being a SEAL, if you couldn't tolerate pain, you were useless.

Monty not only tolerated it, he learned to get off on it.

Mind over torture. It was all in the head. Once you got control of yourself, no matter the situation, you could manage anything.

He caught himself from drifting off, thinking about his work in Iraq and Afghanistan. The secret missions in Pakistan and Libya...the list of what his special-forces team did was endless...and necessary. But it didn't define him any longer. Or at least he hoped it didn't. The former-Navy SEAL wanted to be redefined as a businessman and loyal partner.

Kellie folded the sheet to cover Monty's back and exposed his left leg. Monty knew his thick cock was pressed downwards. The yearning Monty had for Kellie to brush his hand against it was strong. He curled his fingers into a fist and spread his legs, just a little.

The sheet was tucked under his right leg, and Kellie brushed his hand over Monty's cock but it felt unintentional at best.

Monty moaned and then bit his lip to shut up.

Kellie pumped oil, bending Monty's leg to hold his foot upright. Monty shifted his hips on the table, then thought, 'fuck it.' He reached between his legs and set his dick upright.

Kellie paused as he did, obviously aware of what Monty was doing. There wasn't a need to be modest any longer. It seemed getting an erection with Kellie was common for most men.

Once Monty settled down, Kellie continued rubbing his leg. His toes were attended, his arch and ankle. Monty didn't know how much he ached until the areas of his body that caused him pain were tended.

His right leg was exposed as his left was covered. Kellie allowed Monty's foot to rest against him as he rubbed oil between his hands. Monty breathed deeply again and then realized Kellie was spending time on the scar on his calf. The curved line of the slice was being catered to, specially.

Monty didn't know what to think. No one, not even himself, had given that injury much thought. He was sliced, sent to the medic unit, stitched up, and was back on duty. He'd even pulled the stitches out himself in order to prevent having to leave his team.

Monty wanted to imagine Kellie cared a great deal for him to be so nurturing, but Kellie most likely gave all his clients the same TLC.

His legs tended, covered, and Kellie standing beside him on the table, Monty knew it was time to roll over. Indeed, Kellie raised the sheet and said, "Okay, babe. Scoot down and roll over."

Monty opened his eyes and obeyed, watching Kellie hold the sheet between them, preserving Monty's modesty. Kellie replaced the sheet again and they caught gazes. Kellie didn't smile. He fixed the cushion to lay under Monty's knees, and folded the face rest down. Business as usual.

"Kellie."

"Hm?" Kellie appeared distracted, as if deep in his thoughts.

"Have you forgiven me?"

"Huh? Oh. Yes." He folded the sheet down to Monty's chest.

At the moment Monty was not hard, but he knew watching Kellie massage him would change that.

Kellie checked on the stones in the heater and sat down on a stool behind Monty to work his neck and shoulders. "I probably shouldn't socialize with my clients anyway."

Monty didn't believe a word of it. Kellie was hurt. He shook off the sheet from his arms and reached backwards, over his head to touch Kellie.

At first Kellie moved back, but soon stayed still.

Kellie stopped massaging Monty's neck and lowered his gaze somewhere below Monty's head, maybe staring at the floor or his own bare feet. Monty caressed Kellie's hair, tugging some of it out of the rubber band so it fell around his handsome face.

Kellie parted his lips as if he was going to speak, but he said nothing. Monty began drawing Kellie lower for an upside down kiss. He arched his back and reached as far as he could, using his power to pull Kellie down. They brushed lips.

Kellie whimpered and the sheet tented between Monty's legs.

With his tongue, Monty traced Kellie's lips. The fire the act sent to Monty's groin was intense.

~

All Kellie wanted to do was get this session done without feeling like a jilted boyfriend. At first it seemed possible, it was business as usual. Until…

Until Monty reached for him.

The touch of Monty's lips on his was electric. Kellie didn't know if this was an apology or a proposition. Either way, Kellie wasn't sure he wanted it to go any farther than the light lip tickling.

This was work. Monty had an opportunity to see him socially where they could be free to fuck. What Kellie had to decide was whether he was going to hold a pathetic grudge against this man, or get the fuck over it.

Monty held Kellie's head by his hair and dipped his tongue into Kellie's mouth.

Okay. I'm over it!

Kellie kept their mouths together but walked around the table so they could kiss the right way, not upside down. He leaned against the table, lowering down to his elbows and cupped Monty's face. As the kissing grew more frantic, Kellie felt Monty shift his legs on the table, bending his knees.

124

Without limits between them, this sensual dancing of tongues could become humping dicks. Kellie had to decide what the hell he intended on doing.

When Monty yanked the sheet off himself, exposing his fantastic body, Kellie blinked and caught his breath as he looked. The peeks and glimpses of Monty naked did nothing to prepare Kellie for how attracted he was to him.

The temptation to go with his impulses was strong in Kellie. But with that impulse came a sense of right and wrong, not to mention the sting of last man he dated, Scott, not calling him after they had sex.

Kellie slowed them down. He backed up and smiled at Monty.

Monty was panting, his chest heaving as if he were going a little crazy.

"I'm not sure this is a good idea." Kellie tugged at the sheet, trying to cover Monty's nakedness.

"Then why am I so sure it is?" Monty pulled on his own cock a few times.

"When are you free?" Kellie's attention kept being drawn to Monty playing with himself. How easy would it be to grab that beautiful cock and stick it into his mouth? Too easy.

"Now."

Kellie smiled at the compliment. "You know what I mean."

"Kel, I'm not asking for some slimy happy ending."

"Aren't you?" Kellie teased, but did he know for sure?

"No." Monty released his cock and rested his arms beside him on the table.

"Do you want me to finish your massage?" Kellie tugged the sheet up, covering Monty's cock.

Monty lowered his legs to the table, looking weary. Once Kellie had him covered properly he rested his right hand on Monty's chest. "What are you doing after this?"

Monty appeared to think. "I don't know until I check my messages."

Kellie got his answer. He stood back from Monty, returned to his stool and resumed where he had left off.

"I'm not trying to be evasive."

"It's okay. Just relax." Kellie felt Monty's neck muscles tense.

"It's just this new business. Though there are a dozen of us, it seems it's falling on mine and Brandon's shoulders."

"That happens sometimes." Kellie didn't blame Monty. Not any longer. He remembered when his life was turned upside down three years ago. No work, no home, living at a friend's house until he got through massage training…life wasn't easy. And at that time, even the thought of trying a new relationship was out of the question.

"But it doesn't mean I don't want to be with you." Monty's gaze connected with Kellie's.

Kellie ran his hands down Monty's chest and kissed his forehead, sitting up again and smiling at him.

"Fuck it. Am I your last appointment?"

"Yes."

"Let me take you out to dinner."

"You sure you don't want to check your voicemails first?"

"I'm not even going to turn my phone on until after we conclude our first 'date'."

Kellie reached for the warm stones and coated them in oil. He used them to slide under Monty's shoulders and rub his neck. Monty closed his eyes and moaned, relaxing against the table under him.

As Kellie finished up, he couldn't stop thinking about that kiss. He washed his hands, sat behind Monty again, and held his head. Closing his eyes, Kellie felt so close to Monty at that moment, he lowered down to press his lips against Monty's forehead. "Okay, baby. You take your time and I'll get you a glass of water." Kellie pecked his lips against Monty's forehead again and released him, scooting back on the stool.

He stood, tucking his hair back behind his ear, and began heading to the door. In a flash, Monty was on his feet, pinning Kellie against the closed door.

Kellie's breath caught in his throat and he blinked as he gazed into Monty's blue eyes. With both his hands, Monty cupped Kellie's face and kissed him, opening his mouth and urging Kellie to do the same.

This time Kellie gave in. He threw up his hands to fate, who would either send him an incredible boyfriend or crucify him with another ego-smashing disaster. It wasn't his to decide.

Having an oily naked man seduce you was either incredibly sexy or insane.

Sexy!

Kellie reached his arms around Monty, one hand behind Monty's head, and the other on his perfect ass. As if waiting for a sign that this was okay, Monty growled as he became aggressive, opening Kellie's mouth wider with his tongue. Kellie's cock pulsated in his pants. Without looking, he reached for the doorknob and turned the lock. Once they were secure in their tiny room, Kellie returned his hand to caressing Monty's tight ass, running his palms over each globe of his cheeks.

Monty parted from their kiss, dragging Kellie's shirt over his head. Kellie let it drop to the floor. Next Monty untied the drawstring of his yoga pants and jerked them down Kellie's thighs with his briefs.

Kellie's cock sprang out of the material, connecting to Monty's erection.

After Monty helped Kellie remove all his clothing, they stood facing each other, staring into each other's eyes. Monty ran his fingertips down Kellie's side, making Kellie tingle.

The chills continued until Monty was holding Kellie's cock between his fingers.

"Wow." Kellie began panting. "Some first date."

"Should I stop?"

"No."

Monty leaned forward for more kissing, pressing Kellie's back against the door harder. He held the very tip of Kellie's cock, pinching it and twisting it gently between his index finger and thumb. Kellie sucked on Monty's tongue in his mouth, spreading his stance and holding onto Monty's ass.

Voices from outside the doorway, laughter, people coming and going to their appointments or using the cell phone were just muffled noise. All Kellie could hear distinctly was his and Monty's breathing and the sounds of a waterfall and birds from the CD.

Monty coaxed Kellie away from the door and spun them around so Kellie's back was to the table. Monty hoisted Kellie up by his waist, sitting him on it.

Kellie tried not to be too impressed with Monty's strength. Monty was slightly bigger than he was, in height and in bulk.

When Monty spread Kellie's knees apart and knelt down on the floor, Kellie nearly swooned. Monty took a moment to admire Kellie's anatomy, stroking the length of Kellie's cock softly and handling his balls, which were soft and pliable in the heat of the room.

Just as Kellie was able to calm down and breathe normally, Monty gripped the base of his cock and drew it deeply into his mouth, nearly to his fingers.

Kellie whimpered and gripped the bedding on top of the massage table. He watched, unable to look away and not wanting to. Monty framed Kellie's cock in both hands, allowing it to protrude between them. Little sucking noises accompanied Monty's head bobbing up and down between Kellie's thighs.

Though Kellie may have fantasized a 'happy ending' of some kind occurring in this room, he never imagined it would be his cock getting serviced.

Seeing Monty relax his arms across Kellie's thighs, Kellie admired those well-earned Navy SEAL tattoos. There was nothing Kellie wanted to do more than sit across a table with Monty and hear about his life…that was…until he had his cock in Monty's mouth.

Now there was nothing he wanted to do more than come.

As the urge to climax grew stronger, Kellie felt strange. He was violating club rules. Didn't the manager, Lindsey, get fired for having sex in the sauna?

Fuck it…

"Ahhh…Monty! I'm there." Kellie closed his eyes and rode the waves of pleasure. Monty made a sound of delight and milked Kellie's cock as it stayed inside his mouth. Kellie huffed loud breaths and leaned on his arms while he recuperated.

Monty released Kellie's cock and glanced up at him, smiling. "I take it you liked it."

"Shit." Kellie nodded, pushing his hair back from his face.

Monty dragged Kellie's ass to the edge of the table. Then he dug into the pile of clothing that lay on the chair. When Monty produced a rubber, he asked Kellie, "May I?"

Fear and doubt invaded Kellie's good mood. Not only was this wrong, he wondered if after they made love, he would never hear from Monty again.

"Babe?"

"Huh?" Kellie returned his focus to Monty's expression.

"No?"

"Um." Kellie bit his lower lip as he thought about it.

Monty got the hint. He tossed the condom package with his clothes and stared down at his cock, which had gone soft during the short debate.

129

Kellie reached for him, drawing him closer, between his knees. He rested his hand on Monty's neck and reached to kiss his lips. While he had Monty's mouth occupied, Kellie ran Monty's soft cock through his fingers. Monty deepened the kiss, holding Kellie around his back.

Kellie began jerking Monty off. Monty parted from the kiss to watch, resting his forehead on Kellie's. "Harder."

Kellie fisted Monty's cock strongly, quickening the pace. He listened for a clue as to how close Monty was. This behavior in his closed massage room was not sitting well with Kellie. The longer it went on, the more inappropriate it felt.

Monty made some guttural sounds, as if he may be getting closer. Now was not the time for Monty to be riding the edge.

Almost as if Monty were growing impatient with himself as well, he wrapped both his hands around Kellie's to help him jack off.

Kellie was slightly uneasy with the roughness Monty was using to get off. When the grip of Monty's fingers began to make Kellie's knuckles sore, he felt Monty's cock pulsate strongly and white cream shot out from Monty's slit, coating Kellie's cock and pubic hair. Kellie stopped moving his hand, but Monty kept fisting himself hard, sending more white blobs of cum out of his cock.

Kellie was overwhelmed in too many ways. He had to wait for Monty to unclench his hands to be able to let go. When Monty did, Kellie's fingers felt as if they had the circulation cut off. He opened and closed his fingers to get back the sensation, blinking at Monty. "You like it that hard?"

Monty's cheeks grew red and he stepped back from contact with Kellie.

"I have to clean myself up. I don't feel right doing this here." Kellie didn't know why he felt angry, but he did. He hopped off the table and stood at the sink to wash himself off. Behind him he heard Monty getting dressed.

Shaking his head to admonish himself, Kellie knew this was going to be bad all the way around and he never should have done it.

~

Monty felt slightly humiliated. He put his clothing on, his back towards Kellie, feeling greasy from the oil and now, like a sexual deviant. *"You like it that hard?"*

This was his fault. He shouldn't have seduced Kellie this way. The right way would have been to go to dinner and get to know each other. Not have sex in a spa. Once he was completely dressed he checked his phone. The number of missed voicemails and texts were annoying. Before he put the phone to his ear to listen to them, he spun around. Kellie was tucking in his shirt, looking let down.

Monty pocketed his phone and approached him. "This is my fault. I never should have got us going in here."

"We're both to blame."

"I don't know if I can do dinner tonight. I just checked my phone messages and there's a load. Can you wait while I listen to them?"

"Sure. Uh, let me just go to the men's room." Kellie pointed outside the door.

Monty nodded, stepping back to give him space to open it. After Kellie left the room, Monty stuck the phone to his ear.

~

Kellie entered the men's room and relieved himself. He was so angry at what he did, he wasn't sure he even wanted to have dinner with Monty any longer.

He leaned on the sink and stared at his reflection. His hair was long when it wasn't tied back. It gave him the appearance of a liberal surfer dude. At first it was what he thought he needed for the image here. Now he wanted a drastic change.

Leaving the men's room, Kellie noticed Tyson looking for him. When they spotted each other, they closed the gap between them.

"Did the appointment run overtime?" Tyson asked, tucking a strand of hair behind Kellie's ear.

"He's still in my room. I have to talk to you about what just happened." Kellie took a peek down that hall.

"Oh?"

"Not good. I mean, not really."

"Happy ending?"

"I can't talk here." Kellie glanced up and found Monty on his way down the hall, giving him and Tyson an inspection, as if he assumed they were talking about him.

"Hi." Monty nodded his head to Tyson.

Kellie said, "Monty, this is Tyson, Tyson, Monty."

"Hey." Tyson shook his hand. "Okay, Kel. Catch ya later."

"Right. Bye." Kellie waited for Tyson to go, then turned his attention back towards Monty.

"I can make it to dinner tonight. I'd like to shower and change. Can I pick you up?"

Though the contact in the massage room had unsettled Kellie, he said, "Yes."

Monty held Kellie's chin gently, with his thumb and index finger. "I won't let you down this time."

Kellie felt his cheeks blush from both his attraction to Monty and the thought someone might see them in such an intimate pose. "Okay." Kellie lowered his eyelashes and backed away.

"Do you want me to pick you up here?"

"No. I need to go home and get ready too."

Monty pressed his lips to Kellie's ear and said, "You don't need to change a thing. You're fantastic."

Chills covered Kellie's skin and yes, he melted at the incredible passion coming from Monty. Seeing Chelsea spy their flirting, Kellie stepped back and brushed his hair away from his face which he knew was a nervous gesture. "Did I give you my address?" His cheeks were on fire.

"No." Monty smiled wickedly.

"Let me write it down for you." Kellie tried to appear professional since they were now in the middle of a busy area of the club. He walked behind the front desk where Lynn was making appointments and removed a pad and pen. After jotting it down, Kellie scooted around the counter to meet Monty by the exit door. He folded the paper and pressed it into Monty's palm, all the while staring into Monty's sky blue eyes. "Seven?"

"Perfect." Monty appeared as if he may lean in for a quick peck on the lips, but soon backed up and gave Kellie a wink instead.

Kellie stared after him as he walked outside into the parking lot, getting that 'crush' butterfly sensation in his belly. He took a deep breath and made his way back to his room to clean it up and head home. Chelsea intercepted him.

With her hand on Kellie's chest to stop him, she smiled. "You made a date with Mr. Wonderful."

"I did."

"When?"

"Tonight."

"Look how flushed you are!" She giggled and touched his cheek. "Did you guys make love?"

"No." Kellie's smile dropped and he grabbed Chelsea to pull her aside to chide her. "I wouldn't do that here."

"Wow. Then your massages with that guy must be fucking awesome."

"Let me clean up the room and head home." The magnitude of what Kellie had done hit him hard.

"Okay. Let me know when you want our next massage swap. I'm already dying."

"Okay." Kellie returned to his massage room and began stripping the sheets. He looked around in paranoia, as if a camera or spy would have seen what he and Monty did, and he would be fired. Losing another career when the economy is at its lowest was not something Kellie needed to go through...again.

He brought the sheets to the laundry area, dumped them off, picked up clean ones and returned to make the bed for his morning appointment. He had Lenny coming in at ten-thirty, so he made sure everything was perfect for him.

One last look around the room and he gathered his personal items and locked the door.

Chapter 12

Monty shaved his face at the bathroom sink, swishing the razor in the basin full of water. He let the sink drain and turned on the shower, climbing in and scrubbing the residue of oil off his skin. He soaped up his cock and ran it through his palm thinking of sucking Kellie. He had to be mindful of Kellie's wishes and respect them. Doing risky things was something that had become second nature to Monty. So exchanging sex acts with a man he was growing fond of in a locked private room did not qualify as risky in his book. But then, he didn't work there—Kellie did. Monty had to respect Kellie's high moral standards and the fact that he knew mixing sex with massage was wrong. Kellie didn't work in a whorehouse nor was he a slut.

Monty finished up in the shower and as he dried off, his home phone rang. He groaned and allowed the towel to drape over his shoulders as he walked to the kitchen to pick up the extension.

"What?" He read the caller ID was Brandon.

"You up for a radio interview?"

"Sure. When?"

"Twenty minutes?"

"What? No." Monty shook his head and checked the wall clock. "Brandon, I have a date with Kellie and I'm not fucking it up this time. Ask Zak to do it."

"You and I are the management behind this operation."

"No. I'm going out to dinner. If you can't handle an interview one on one, then don't get involved in the promo." Monty used the end of the towel to wipe his dripping hair.

"You going to get like this? Three days before our first session?"

"Are you and Kathy getting a divorce?"

"What?"

Monty leaned against the kitchen counter and folded his arm over his chest. "You heard me."

It was silent on the other end.

"When you got through with your last tour you told me you were going to devote your time to Kathy."

"With this new set up, I'm too busy."

"She waited for you, ya dick." When the other end of the line grew silent again, Monty walked to his bedroom and threw the towel on the bed. "Don't fuck it up." He took clean briefs and socks out of his dresser drawer.

"I don't wanna talk about it."

"You should. You should go talk to someone. Are you going to let fifteen years of marriage go to waste?"

Brandon didn't reply again.

"Man, I have to get ready. I told Kel I'd be there to get him at seven."

"Fine. I'll do the fucking interview on my own."

The line disconnected so Monty tossed the phone on the bed and finished getting dressed.

~

Kellie raced around his apartment getting ready. He blew his hair dry after his shower, and now wished he had cut it short. He intended on it, soon. After debating on letting it hang loose or tying it up, Kellie threw up his hands and left it loose.

He dabbed on cologne, put on his best black slacks and favorite crew neck shirt, checked for cash, his mobile phone, his keys, and then paced the small apartment straightening it up for when Monty showed.

His apartment security buzzer sounded. Kellie raced to it, pushing the button to unlock the door. He dashed to the bathroom mirror and checked on his appearance, tucked in his shirt, looked at his ass in the refection and then composed himself to answer the door. After a light knock he opened it.

"Scott?" Kellie choked.

"Hey, babe." Scott reached for a hug and kiss.

Kellie pushed him back in panic. "What are you doing here?"

"I was free. I thought we'd go out for a drink." Scott stalked Kellie. "Or better yet, stay in for one."

"I'm going out to dinner with a friend. He's going to be here any minute." Kellie dodged Scott's greedy fingers as they went for a grab of both his ass and cock.

"So? I've had three-ways before. With Keith O'Leary and Carl Bronson."

"I know. You've told me a hundred times." Kellie swatted Scott's hand away from his groin. "I'm serious, Scott. You have to leave before he gets here."

"Who is he?" Scott appeared to get defensive.

"He's a man I met at the club."

"Do I know him? What's his name?"

"You don't know him. Go home." Kellie walked to his front door to show Scott out.

"Why are you being so cold?" Scott looked like he had no intention of leaving.

"You never call me. I have no idea why you're even here."

"We can see other guys. I don't care if you date. I do."

Kellie rolled his eyes at the folly. "I don't want a boyfriend who 'dates'."

"So you're serious with this guy already? I just saw you last week. We fucked."

Kellie opened his door to gesture for Scott to leave and found Monty about to knock.

Kellie's stomach pinched. "Hi. Did someone let you in?"

"Yes." Monty instantly found Scott in the room. He said nothing but looked miffed.

"Uh, Scott Baldwin, this is Monty Gresham." Kellie gave Scott an obvious tilt of his head to scram.

"Nice to meet you, man." Scott extended his hand to Monty.

Monty took it.

Seeing Scott morph into his predatory cat mode, Kellie rubbed his forehead tiredly.

Scott said, "Invite him in, Kel. Let's all have a drink together." Scott tried to keep hold of Monty's hand but Monty drew it back with a jerk.

"I'm leaving." Kellie stood in the hall with Monty. "Don't be here when I get back."

Scott asked, "Where are you going for dinner? Mind if I join in?"

"I do mind." With Scott outside his apartment, Kellie double locked the door and stormed down the hall. When he glanced back, Monty and Scott were walking side by side behind him.

"What do you do, Monty?"

"I'm beginning a new business at the moment."

"Yeah? Doing what? You need a driver?"

Kellie rolled his eyes and continued making his way to the front exit of the apartment house.

"Not at the moment. Why? Are you a truck driver?"

"No. A chauffeur." Scott chuckled. "I wear the whole get up—cap, black suit...look the part if you need a special transport."

Kellie opened the door to outside.

"Here's my card." Scott handed Monty his business card. "Can I have yours?"

"I haven't made them yet. So, no." Monty reached for Kellie's hand.

Kellie clasped it. He studied Scott's reaction to the gesture.

Nothing fazed Scott. He was such a player, Kellie knew all the man was thinking was how to get into another three-way.

"So, Monty, how old are you?"

"We have to go, Scott," Kellie said, not wanting to deal with Scott at the moment.

"Nice meeting you." Monty gave Scott a sort-of smile and took his car keys out of his pocket.

"Yeah. Uh, call me…if you need a chauffeur, or anything…" Scott watched Kellie and Monty walk to Monty's car.

Kellie was led to a new cherry red Chevy Camaro and Monty used his remote to open the doors. They both climbed inside the sleek sports car and Kellie put his seatbelt on, glancing back to see Scott still watching.

"Boyfriend?" Monty asked, not smiling.

"No. Bad decision. We had two dates."

"He fuck you?"

"Unfortunately." Kellie ran his fingers through his hair.

Monty left the parking lot, chirping the tires on the tarmac but not being reckless, possibly just annoyed.

"I don't like him, Monty."

"Do you often fuck guys you don't like?"

"Yeah," Kellie replied with sarcasm, "And I give hand-jobs to all my clients, too."

Monty stayed quiet until they stopped at an intersection. "Where am I taking you for dinner?"

"Before Scott showed up, I was looking forward to my favorite Mexican place on Santa Monica Boulevard."

"And since he showed up?"

"Take a right here. I'm sorry. His timing sucks." Kellie rubbed Monty's knee affectionately. When Monty made no reaction, Kellie took it back and slouched in the bucket seat. This date suddenly had 'disaster' written all over it.

"Which way?"

"Keep going for a few blocks." Kellie stared at Monty's profile. "Are we kidding ourselves, Monty?"

"Kidding ourselves?" Monty glanced over at Kellie as he shifted gears. "What do you mean?"

"Nothing." Kellie could not read Monty, no matter how he tried. *How do I get information out of a former Navy SEAL when torture can't even make those guys talk?*

"Are we still headed to this Mexican place?"

"Yes. Is that okay?"

"Yes."

"Monty?"

"Hm?" Monty slowed for a traffic signal, put his hand inside Kellie's thigh and blinked his long lashes at him.

Suddenly Kellie forgot what he was going to ask. It was something silly about maybe Scott ruining their evening. Kellie glanced down at Monty's hand as it massaged his inseam. "Nothing. I'm good."

Monty cracked a smile.

By the time they pulled into the restaurant lot, Kellie was in heat. The caress, though subtle and not over his crotch, was delicious. One thing being a massage therapist taught Kellie, was that touch was everything—healing, compassionate—and most certainly showed attraction.

Monty parked, set the parking brake and shut off the ignition. Before he climbed out of the car, Kellie unfastened his seatbelt and turned towards Monty in the seat.

Monty waited, watching him.

Kellie reached up and cupped Monty's cheek, feeling his close shave. He drew nearer, parting his lips.

A low whimper escaped Monty's throat before they kissed. Monty opened his mouth, allowing Kellie to explore it with his tongue. Kellie felt Monty's passion spark, and Monty's legs straddled wider.

Kellie smiled at his expression after his kiss. "Are you hungry?"

"Yes." Monty licked his lip, but it wasn't to seduce, it was more of a taste after the kiss.

Their sessions together already made Kellie feel as if he was free to stroke Monty's chest and arms, his cheek, his neck...but this time it wasn't on a professional level. This time it was because they wanted to.

Kellie touched Monty's skin at his neck, where the top shirt button had been left open. The man was an inferno. Heat radiated off of him.

"You're going to get me so hot I'm not going to want to get out of this car."

"We have all night. That is...if you want—"

"I want." Monty took Kellie's hand from his throat and ran it down his body to his hard cock.

When Monty pressed Kellie's fingers around his bulge, Kellie felt his cock pulsate. He chuckled, "I started this."

"You did."

Seeing Monty's warm smile, Kellie went for another kiss. While their lips were connected, Kellie rubbed hot friction against Monty's cock where it had thickened under the zipper. When he heard Monty's stomach grumble, he began laughing and sat back in his seat. "I hear you. Okay—food then love."

Monty chuckled as he climbed out of the car. He armed and locked the doors, pocketing the key, then held out his hand for Kellie to hold.

"Wow. I'm impressed, Monty." Kellie brushed shoulders with him.

"It takes a lot to scare me, Kel."

"I can't imagine." Kellie felt like a million bucks with this hunk at his side. "Can you talk about it or is it all hush-hush?"

"I can talk about some things, but I don't necessarily want to." Monty opened the entrance door, holding it for Kellie.

Kellie released his hand and walked in, seeing a line. He gave his name to the hostess and stood beside Monty. "You wouldn't think a Tuesday evening would bring so many people out."

"The food must be good."

"It is. Some celebs pop in now and again." Kellie glanced around.

"Do you follow that stuff?"

"No." Kellie smiled shyly.

Monty cupped the back of Kellie's head through his hair. "You are so fucking cute."

Kellie's cheeks burned with his blush.

"How old did you say you were?"

"I didn't say. You never asked."

Monty made an expression of, 'well?'

"Twenty-seven."

Monty whistled. "Man, you're old."

Kellie laughed, since he knew Monty was thirty-eight from the form he had filled out when he first made an appointment for his massage. "Do you care about our age difference?"

"No. Do you?"

"No. I mean, it's not like it means anything, right?"

"Not to me." Monty perked up. "The hostess just said your name."

Kellie spun around and spotted the woman smiling at him, holding two menus. As Kellie followed her, Monty pinched and fondled his ass. Kellie loved his playfulness and kept a smile on his lips, wriggling his butt for more attention.

They were shown to a table in the main room, against a wall with a colorful mural of dancers and flowers painted on it.

The table was for four, but the two of them sat together, sitting side by side instead of across from each other. From there, they could see the entire room and a glimpse of the outdoor deck. No one was outside now that the evenings had turned cool.

Monty began perusing the menu as Kellie 'perused' him. A waiter brought water, a basket of tortilla chips, and salsa for them and asked, "Would you like to order a drink?"

Monty gestured for Kellie to order, and he stopped short as if just noticing Kellie was lost on him. Kellie shook himself out of his hypnotic trance on Monty. "Just the ice water, thanks."

"You sure?" Monty asked.

"Yes."

Monty said, "I'll take a Corona."

"Be right back." The waiter left.

With a wry smile on his lips, Monty asked, "AA?"

"No. I drink. Just not tonight. I want all my senses perfectly sober."

"Should I cancel my beer order?"

"No. You do what you like." Kellie rested his chin on his palm and gave Monty a silly smile.

~

Monty tried not to laugh. "I haven't been looked at like that for a very long time."

"I don't imagine you would…doing, you know. SEAL stuff."

Monty held back a loud laugh and covered his mouth. "No. Definitely not doing, 'SEAL stuff'."

"So how homophobic are the Navy's finest?"

"Don't Ask Don't Tell was still in full effect while I was there. We didn't discuss it, but those close to me knew."

"Did you ever do anything sexy with another…er…SEAL?"

"I won't kiss and tell either." Monty's light eyes shined.

143

"Darn."

"Would you tell me about Scott if I asked?"

"Yes. Of course." Kellie waited.

Monty drank from his glass of water, then said, "I don't give a shit," and laughed. "I'm not one of those guys who has to have details about your past, Kel. You and I are what count."

"Wow." Kellie was very pleased with that comment. "What are you looking for in a guy? Are you into a relationship? Or just sex?"

"A relationship with the right guy. I would love to have a 'partner'." Monty used his fingers as quotes when he said it. "But I know how tough my schedule is right now. So it would have to be a man who got it. You know?"

"I do. My work schedule sucks for a relationship as well."

The waiter brought Monty's beer with a quarter lime wedged in the neck, and placed a pitcher of water on the table for Kellie to refill his glass. "Do you need more time?"

"Oh." Kellie looked over the menu. "I usually get the vegetarian platter."

Monty scanned the selection. "I'll take the steak fajitas."

"Very good." The waiter took the menus and left.

Kellie smiled wryly. "Steak."

"Yeah, oh well. We can't agree on everything." Monty loaded up a chip with salsa and ate it.

"You're a real macho guy."

"So are you, surfer-dude." Monty tugged at Kellie's hair.

"I'm going to cut it. I grew it long for the interview."

"Shut the fuck up." Monty squeezed the lime into the beer neck and swigged it.

"I did. I figured I had to look the part. It worked. I got the job."

"How short are you going to cut it?" Monty caressed the hair back from Kellie's face.

"If you keep petting me, I won't."

"I kind of like it. You look very Southern Cal."

"Where are you from?"

"West Virginia." Monty pressed their knees together under the table. "Dye it blond for me."

Kellie broke up with laughter. "Oh, handsome, I'd dye my fucking pubes for a man like you."

"Yeah?"

"Yeah." Kellie's crotch tingled with his lustful thoughts.

"Shave 'em?" Monty said it as if he were a little boy swearing.

"Shave my balls?" Kellie squirmed in his chair.

Monty sipped his beer and shrugged innocently.

"What are you into? Hm?" Kellie propped his chin in his palm and gave Monty his dreamy gaze. *Yeah, I am infatuated with this guy. So what?*

"I don't know. It's been a long time since I've had the pleasure of a civilian man who I can play with."

"Play with me." Kellie licked his top lip.

"Get over here." Monty grabbed Kellie's hair and kissed him.

With Monty's tongue in his mouth, Kellie grunted and blinked in surprise. The kiss was brief but hotter than hell.

"Okay." Kellie crossed his legs and fussed with his hair. "Complete wood."

Monty gave him a sensual smile and finished his beer.

~

The food was as good as Kellie said it would be. Monty enjoyed it thoroughly and finished every bite.

Kellie pushed his empty plate away. "I can't eat dessert."

"I can." Monty reached under the table to Kellie's crotch. When Monty squeezed it, he made a face of ecstasy. It was so easy to be silly and have fun with Kellie. Monty missed behaving like a juvenile. He'd been the joker in high school and had to be the opposite in the military.

"Mm. Check, please!" Kellie raised his hand to an imaginary waiter.

It got Monty looking around for their server. He caught their waiter's eye and mouthed, 'the bill?'

The waiter acknowledged him.

Kellie leaned against Monty's shoulder to whisper in his ear. "Spotted a celeb. Wanna know who?"

"Sure." Monty didn't care much for Hollywood's elite, but he wouldn't mind a few famous stars sponsoring his new business.

"Mark Richfield, ten o'clock."

Monty looked left.

"No, that way!"

"That's two." Monty cracked up.

"Sorry. There."

Monty turned to look. "Who is Mark Richfield?"

"You know the guy who models for *Dangereux* cologne?"

"No. Which guy is he?"

Kellie mumbled out of the side of his mouth, "Pretty boy, long hair."

Monty scanned around. "Boy?"

"No. He's not a boy. Never mind."

"That's the best you can do for a celebrity in LA?" Monty laughed and spotted the waiter bringing the check. He took it and said, "Hang on," removing his wallet and tossing his credit card on the tray.

"I'll be right back."

"Thanks." Monty noticed Kellie looking at the model. "Which one is he?"

"Jesus, Monty. I can't point to the guy." Kellie bit his lip. "Okay. The table right before the window, four guys sitting together, he's the one with the brown hair, longer than mine. Way longer."

Monty took another peek. This time two of the men noticed him looking. The long-haired man and a handsome clean cut man sitting beside him. Monty turned back to Kellie. He shrugged.

Kellie mimicked Monty's shrug.

"Here you go, sir." The waiter handed Monty his credit card slip and card.

Monty added a tip and signed it. "Thanks."

"You're welcome. Have a nice night."

Monty put his card back into his wallet.

"So? You're not impressed with the famous model?"

"No. Should I be?"

"Guess not." Kellie laughed and stood from the table.

Monty held his hand as they made their way out of the dining room. He took another look at the model and said to Kellie, "I like the guy sitting next to him better."

"That's it. I'm cutting my hair tomorrow."

Monty got a handful of Kellie's ass and squeezed it, making him jump.

On the drive home they didn't speak much. Kellie held Monty's hand until he had to shift gears, then he'd shift with him.

Monty wasn't big on trivial conversation and was glad Kellie didn't jabber his ear off.

"Is the guest parking okay?" Monty asked as he slowed down.

"Yes. That's fine."

Monty shut the engine and said, "You seem tired."

"I may be tired, but I still want you to come up."

"Good." Monty exited the car and walked with Kellie to the entrance, aiming his key fob over his shoulder to arm and lock his car.

It made Kellie laugh, like Monty hoped it would.

Once they were inside, Monty chased Kellie down the hall, grabbing his ass and smacking it. Kellie scooted as fast as he could, fumbling for the key.

When Monty caught him at the door, he spooned him and picked him up off the ground, pushing his cock against Kellie's ass.

Kellie moaned and poked at the lock frantically.

As the door opened and Kellie nudged it backwards, Monty set him on his feet, entering and looking around. The first time he stuck his head in, all Monty noticed was Scott. Now he could get a better look at Kellie's home.

It was small, but clean. No clutter.

Kellie took off his shoes, so Monty did as well.

"I want to apologize for my apartment."

"Why?"

"I used to own a house. I got hit with a foreclosure."

"Sorry, Kel. A lot of people did. Are."

"Do you own a home?" Kellie headed down a short hall to a bedroom, tossing his keys, mobile phone, and wallet on the dresser.

Monty tackled him to the bed. He pinned Kellie's arms over his head and stared at him. Kellie panted, his eyes wide. Monty tugged Kellie's shirt out of his slacks and smoothed his hand over his skin. A small noise of delight erupted from Kellie.

"You...um...top?" Kellie chewed on his lower lip.

"I prefer bottom."

"What?"

Monty pushed Kellie's shirt up his chest and pinched his nipples.

148

"You? Bottom?"

Monty opened Kellie's pants. "You have a problem with that?"

"Problem?" Kellie laughed like he was giddy.

"Yeah. I asked if you have a problem..." Monty teased, yanking Kellie's pants down his legs.

Kellie raised his head off the bed to watch as he was quickly being stripped. "When we were together at the salon, after you gave me head, you just seemed..."

"Seemed?" Monty tugged Kellie's slacks off his legs with his briefs, next his socks. He spread Kellie's legs wide and sucked on his balls.

"Seemed like..." Kellie moaned and dug his fingers through Monty's hair.

Monty knew what he 'seemed' like. But what he had always wanted was to be ravished by someone else. He was hoping his vegan massage therapist who drove a Prius and didn't drink a beer with dinner was 'up' for it.

The taste and scent of Kellie's crotch was making Monty wild. He bent Kellie in two and got a look at his rim. "Fuck, that's nice." He poked his tongue into it.

"Holy shit! Monty, I swear, I didn't..."

"Didn't?" Monty massaged his saliva around the tiny rim, licking it again.

"I'm shutting up now."

Monty knelt on the bed and took off his shirt, tossing it on the floor. He held Kellie's thighs and ran long laps from his ass to his balls. He could see Kellie's hands gripping the bedspread on either side of him.

Monty enveloped Kellie's balls, closing his eyes and devouring him.

~

You're a bottom? Are you fucking kidding me?

Kellie wasn't sure if he was excited or disappointed. He'd envisioned Monty fucking his brains out. Not vice-versa.

Kellie stared at the ceiling as his groin was given a tongue bath and his cock throbbed and danced up and down it was so hard.

As Monty caught his breath and sat on his heels, Kellie tried to get over the preconceived notion he had. He stretched out his legs on the bed to relax.

"You look disappointed. Kel, I can fuck you." Monty stood off the bed and removed his slacks and briefs.

"Huh? No, I'm not disappointed." *Am I?*

Monty sat on the bed next to Kellie, his hand on Kellie's chest. "Whatever you want."

Kellie was intrigued. He rolled to his side, encouraging Monty to do the same so they mirrored each other. "If you could have your fantasy man make love to you, how would it be?"

Monty smiled shyly. "I'd be the ultimate sub."

"Have you ever fulfilled that fantasy before?"

"Once, before I enlisted. I was only eighteen."

Kellie opened his mouth to reply then shut up. After a second to think about it, he said, "Spread out on the bed, Gresham."

Monty's expression brightened up. He shifted to the center and lay flat on his back as Kellie climbed off. Kellie wasn't prepared with leather and toys, but he did want to give Monty what he craved. Domination.

"Don't move." Kellie pointed at Monty in warning.

Monty nodded, smiling excitedly.

After Kellie left the room and rooted around for the items he needed in the kitchen drawers, he returned, seeing Monty playing with himself, tugging on his hard cock. Kellie showed him silver duct tape and a pair of scissors.

Monty's face lit up and he immediately spread out his arms and legs to all four corners of the bed. Kellie unraveled a piece of tape, biting it to tear it, and secured Monty's wrist to his bed frame.

"Kel. Wow."

"You okay?" Kellie walked to the end of the bed and touched Monty's foot affectionately.

"I thought a lot about doing this." Monty swallowed nervously, making his Adam's apple move.

"And?"

"Keep going." Monty spread his legs farther apart.

Kellie taped both of Monty's ankles to the bed, walking around the far side to secure his hand. Before he did, he raised it off the bed and kissed it tenderly.

The binding done, Kellie stood back to look at Monty, helpless on his bed. Even though Monty was tied up, the powerful aura of this former Navy SEAL was like a glowing fire coming from Monty's hot sweaty skin.

Kellie placed the tape with the scissors he had brought, for an easy way to cut Monty free. "How about you give me a safe word?"

"Pride."

"Love it." Kellie winked. He removed lubrication and condoms from his nightstand, then dimmed the overhead ceiling light in favor of just his table lamp. They were both soft at the moment, but Kellie knew he would change that quickly. Sitting beside Monty, Kellie ran his fingers down his throat to his chest. Monty's ribcage rose and fell rapidly with anticipation.

Kellie was by no means a master of domination, but he had seen it on porn films and certainly knew the concept. And the fact that Monty had not been dominated since he was eighteen, gave Kellie the notion he should delve gently during their first foray. But if he and Monty stayed together for any length of time, he would learn.

151

Kellie crawled over Monty, a knee on either side of his hips. He lowered down and sucked at one of Monty's nipples. This wasn't any different from Monty being passive as Kellie gave him a body massage. Not yet, anyway.

As he nibbled Monty's nib, he noticed Monty's cock respond. All of Monty's muscles tensed and the bed made a creaking sound.

Kellie rolled to lie beside Monty, blowing into his ear and biting his earlobe. "Tell me what to do to you."

Monty closed his eyes and his fists clenched.

"Don't be shy. I'm here to please you. Tell me." Kellie kissed his way down Monty's neck.

A tiny whimper escaped Monty's lips. He thrust his hips off the bed, arching his back.

Kellie glanced downwards and Monty's cock was fully erect. He blinked in delight and spun around, climbing over Monty and engulfing his cock into his mouth.

"Scoot back."

Kellie inched backwards.

"More."

Pausing as he thought about it, Kellie felt a warm puff of breath against his bottom. The bed shook as Monty tried to reach him.

"More!"

Kellie jolted at the order and backed up until his knees were straddling Monty's chest. Who was he kidding? Even helpless and tied up, Monty gave the commands.

Under Kellie, Monty's body tensed and tugged at the tape. He was about to suggest cutting Monty free when Monty began sucking Kellie's balls into his mouth. Kellie inched backwards until Monty had access to anything he wanted to lick, suck or bite.

"Who's master here?" Kellie laughed, playing with Monty's stiff cock.

Monty just moaned in response, pressing his face against Kellie's testicles and the root of his cock.

Kellie reached between his own legs and pointed his dick towards Monty. Monty went wild trying to get to it. Kellie spread his legs over Monty's head and pushed his cock into Monty's eager mouth.

"I have never had my dick sucked like this." Kellie bobbed up and down, orally fucking Monty. "I like it!"

The bed began to creak and shake. Kellie glanced behind him and found Monty's fists clenched, the muscles in his arms bulging. He looked down Monty's body at his cock, which was blushing reddish purple and straight as an upright pole. Kellie dove on it, his cock pulling out of Monty's mouth as he did. He sucked it as deeply as he could, holding the base with both hands.

"Fuck..." Monty moaned like he was in pain. "Kel...oh, fucking, Kel."

Screw this. Kellie stumbled off the bed, his hands trembling with excitement as he tore a condom from the strip. He rolled it on Monty as Monty raised his head to watch.

Kellie slathered Monty's sheathed cock with lube and squatted down on it, pushing it into his ass.

Monty threw his head back and opened his mouth to gasp. The veins showed in both his neck and forearms as he flexed his body tightly.

Kellie worked Monty's cock in and out of his bottom until he was opened up and feeling fine. He braced himself on Monty's hips and humped him. His own cock was thick and bobbing with his motion. "How's that, bottom boy?" Kellie showed his teeth in his sexual grimace. "Huh? How's that?"

"Fuck!" Monty shouted like it was an answer.

"Yeah. Fuck you!" Kellie began to run with sweat.

"Fuck me...oh, motherfucker, fuck me." Monty bucked underneath Kellie, meeting Kellie's squats.

"You like it? Huh, soldier boy? You like what I'm dishing out?"

"Yes. Oh, *motherfucker*! Yes."

Kellie bounced like a pogo stick on Monty's long cock, using him like a dildo to give himself a good prostate rub. "Oh, Christ, this is nice."

Monty tensed his arms and legs, making the bed complain at the tugging. Monty huffed as he grew excited. "I want to fuck you!"

"You are fucking me. But not for long." Kellie felt Monty rising closer to a climax. He climbed off the bed, pulling the rubber off Monty's cock. Monty gasped and raised his head off the pillows to see what Kellie was doing.

Kellie sheathed his own dick, used the lube generously, and then cut Monty's ankles free. Monty appeared stunned and waited.

Kelly bent Monty in two, pressing his legs apart and backwards. He pushed his dick down between Monty's legs and inside his ass.

Waiting to see if Monty was okay, Kellie read his expression.

"Kel?"

"Yeah?"

"Fuck me!" Monty shouted, panting.

"Jeez!" Kellie slipped inside Monty easily, as if perhaps Monty either made love regularly or...played with toys.

Kellie closed his eyes and moaned as he deepened their connection. "You are a god."

Monty chuckled, but sounded like he was ready to combust.

Once Kellie was ready to really make love to his man, he grabbed Monty's cock with both his hands and said, "Ready for takeoff?"

"Jack me hard."

"I intend to." Kellie recalled the wild hand-job in the massage room. He thrust his hips in and out of Monty's ass, and began fisting as if he meant to make Monty come so hard it would spatter his ceiling.

"*Ohhh* god…" Monty closed his eyes and pressed his head into the pillows.

"Yeah?" Kellie began running in sweat from the effort. "Oh god? Is that all you got to say about it?" He edged the climax, biting his lip, wanting his man to come.

"Fuck…*oh fuck*!" Monty began bucking, as if the fisting wasn't fast or rough enough.

Kellie was glad he was in top form, because this was hard work. He shifted his knees apart and hammered into Monty, squeezing his cock and fisting him in a blur of movement.

A deep masculine grunt preceded Monty's open-mouthed gasp. Monty choked on his breath and arched his back, his arms bulging with veins and his roping muscles.

His cock erupted like a fountain of cream, coating Kellie's knuckles and spattering Monty's skin.

"Yeah. Oh, hell yeah!" Kellie closed his eyes and came, grinding his hips against Monty's body, chills washing over his soaked skin.

As he came he kept milking Monty's cock, coaxing more creamy drops to emerge, rolling down his hands.

"Holy shit…" Kellie blinked and caught his breath. Under him Monty was limp, eyes closed, looking like a fucking centerfold model.

With an effort, Kellie backed up, pulling out and climbing off Monty's body. He used the scissor to cut his arms free, then pulled the tape off like adhesive strips. Monty never flinched.

Once Kellie had removed the spent condom, he dropped on top of Monty's sweaty, sticky body and held him. Monty embraced him, breathing quickly and slowly calming down.

Kellie closed his eyes and listened to Monty's heartbeat.

Chapter 13

Monty held Kellie in his arms, thinking of sleep. Yes, he should check his phone for missed calls. Yes, he should get dressed and head home to be up early for work in the morning. But he didn't want to move.

This act of submission with Kellie was the closest Monty had come to what he really wanted in bed. And it was their first time. How fabulous was that? It could only get better from here.

Hearing deep breathing from his lover, Monty smiled. "Are you asleep?"

"Mm?"

Monty kissed his hair, running the length through his fingers. "Baby. Thank you."

"Mm." Kellie sighed, snuggling closer, using his legs to hold onto Monty as well as his arms.

"I don't want to move either."

"Mm." Kellie seemed to agree.

"If you set the alarm, I can stay."

With a supreme effort, Kellie moved. He looked exhausted as he leaned up on his arms. "Yes. Let me wash up."

"Me too." Monty smiled at his woozy expression.

Stumbling, reaching for the wall as he went, Kellie made it upright. Monty was behind him, making sure he didn't crash into anything. "I thought *I* was worn out."

"What the heck time is it?"

Monty checked his watch. "Eleven. I'm old. What's your excuse?"

"You wore me out!" Kellie laughed tiredly, splashing his face at the sink.

Monty stood beside him, opening the lid to the toilet. "I feel like I've been holding those two beers in me for hours."

Kellie chuckled again. He leaned on the sink and watched.

Monty smiled, giving it a good shake to finish. He was about to flush when Kellie said, "I'm next."

"Conserving water? Just how granola are you?" They swapped places.

"I'm eco-friendly. Not granola. I don't wear Birkenstocks and socks."

Monty washed up, using a cloth to wipe his sticky skin. "You are so California. Do you eat avocados?"

"I ate guacamole with dinner." Kellie flushed the toilet and rinsed his hands, using the running water Monty was washing up with. He handed Monty a packaged toothbrush and then scrubbed his teeth.

Monty felt Kellie leaning against his side, both sharing the water and the mirror. It made Monty laugh at Kellie. "I feel like I'm back at training camp and there are more men than sinks."

"If you did this with the guys in training, I'm fucking jealous." He spat out the toothpaste.

"Yeah, well. We got close, but not like how you're thinking."

"Too bad. It was a hell of a fantasy."

"Yeah. I had that dream too until I figured out reality." Monty rinsed his mouth and dried his face and crotch with a towel.

"How the hell did you get that cut on your calf?"

"Didn't I tell you? I thought you asked about it while I was getting a massage once." Monty left the bathroom, Kellie close behind, shutting the light.

158

"Was it while you were in combat?"

"No. In training."

"Do you want something to drink?" Kellie pointed over his shoulder.

"Sure." They both headed to the kitchen.

Monty leaned back against the counter as Kellie opened the refrigerator.

"Water?"

"Yes. Thanks."

Kellie removed a pitcher with a filter in it, pouring two glasses full, handing one to Monty.

"No plastic bottles." Monty cracked up.

"Small carbon footprint. What can I say?" Kellie set the pitcher on the counter near Monty.

"I guess we all should think of that shit. I never have. The military is so uh…"

"Consuming?"

"Yes. That'll work." Monty drank the water thirstily.

"If you need to check your voicemails, it's okay."

Monty moaned and knew he should. "My partner, Brandon, did a radio interview today. He wanted me to do it with him."

"Why didn't you?" Kellie leaned against the counter beside Monty.

"Because I wasn't going to break another date with you."

Kellie appeared surprised. "Don't put your business decisions off because of me. I'll feel like crap."

"Look." Monty set his empty glass on the counter. "I haven't had a fucking real social life in twenty fucking years. No way."

"Want more water?"

"I'm good."

Kellie put the pitcher back into the fridge and the glasses in the sink. "I'm awake now. Want to watch a little TV before we snuggle?"

"Sure."

Kellie headed back to the bedroom. He slipped on his briefs and tossed Monty his.

Monty caught it, putting them on. He stopped Kellie from walking out of the bedroom and held onto him. "How will this affect our massage sessions?"

Kellie smiled shyly. "It shouldn't affect them at all."

"Mm hm." Monty embraced Kellie, holding him close and resting his head against his. "Sure, Kelsey."

"Is Monty short for anything?"

"Montgomery."

"Like in Alabama?"

"Yes. Or if you ask my mom, like in Montgomery Clift."

"Montgomery from West Virginia." Kellie chuckled. "Could we be more opposite?"

"We're not opposite. We're the same in many ways."

Kellie leaned back and stared into Monty's eyes. "What was your rank in the Navy?"

"Lieutenant Commander."

"That sounds serious."

"It was. It's not who I am now." Monty brushed back Kellie's hair from his face.

"You're too young to have retired."

"Didn't reenlist."

"Why not?"

"Had enough." Monty held Kellie's hand and walked to the living room with him, where the television was located.

He sat down on the sofa as Kellie picked up the remote and snuggled against him. Monty loved the casual feel they had. It was already comfortable, but after all, Kellie had been touching him intimately during his sessions for two weeks.

He kissed Kellie's head and put his arm around his shoulder. Kellie unfolded a comforter and spread it out over their laps, nestling against Monty. He aimed the remote at the television, yawning as he did.

Monty combed his fingers through Kellie's hair, enjoying him—his calmness, his eco-friendly ways, and his amazing loving.

Under the warm white quilt, Kellie tucked his hand between Monty's legs, his fingers around his thigh. The channels were surfed for something suitable. When Comedy Central was chosen for their late night pundits, Monty smiled.

"Okay?"

"Sure." Monty wasn't going to watch anyway, and didn't mind the shows that were on. He would have expected nothing less from a man like Kellie. He stared at his profile, using two fingers to toy with Kellie's silky locks, wondering if he would miss them if Kellie cut them off. He didn't care either way. Monty wasn't fussy like that.

Kellie placed the remote on the coffee table and sank down to Monty's lap. Monty continued to caress him affectionately.

"Man. You feel so good." Kellie yawned again. "With you petting me, I'll go right out."

"Go out. I'll get you to bed."

"I can get used to this." Kellie kissed Monty's leg.

"So can I."

Kellie rolled over to face up, smiling at Monty. Using his index finger, Monty traced Kellie's features, similar to the way Kellie sometimes ended their massages. "If we date, do I get your services for free?" Monty teased.

"Oh, hell yeah."

"Oh? I didn't expect you to say that."

"I wouldn't charge my boyfriend."

Monty thought about that word. *Boyfriend.* "Do you want to be my boyfriend?"

"I get terrified when questions like that are asked." Kellie picked up the remote and muted the irritating commercial that was airing.

"Why?" Monty traced Kellie's lips lightly.

"Because it's putting my heart out there. I've done this before—i.e. Scott Baldwin?"

"Did you ask Scott to be your boyfriend?"

"No. I just figured it was possible. I'm glad I'm not with him now."

Monty leaned down for a kiss. Kellie met him halfway and relaxed again on Monty's lap.

"I liked you even before you asked me out."

"I liked you too." Monty continued to outline Kellie's features, loving his looks.

"I don't sense connections like we had, very often. Massaging you was pure adrenalin."

Monty smiled. "You stroked my aura."

"I did." Kellie's eyes gleamed.

"I don't let just anyone get away with that."

Kellie smiled contentedly. "Funny how fate works."

"Fate?" Monty made a silly face. "If you say we're soul mates I may dry heave."

"Okay. Promise." Kellie looked back at the TV, turning on the volume when the show returned.

While Kellie watched Steven Colbert, Monty stared at him, pulling his soft hair through his fingers. He caressed Kellie's arm, then neck and chest, pushing the puffy quilt lower so he could see Kellie's body.

"I may be asking *you* for a massage." Kellie glanced at him.

"I'd do it. Anytime."

Kellie faced Monty. They stared at each other for a few moments. "We connect."

"We do."

162

"Why?"

Monty shrugged.

Kellie rolled his body towards Monty, using his index finger in the waistband to peek into his briefs.

It made Monty chuckle. "Yes? You already know what it looks like."

"Can't get enough of it. I hate to tell you I loved it up my ass."

"Why do you hate to tell me that?" Monty kept caressing Kellie's upper arm and neck.

"Because you like to bottom."

"I can go either way. It's just that most men want me to top them."

"I can see why." Kellie ran his hand up Monty's chest.

"So can I. I do understand it." Kellie's touch never failed to stir Monty's cock. It began to show through his dark cotton boxer briefs.

Kellie held back the waistband again and nudged his dick upright. "Even your cock is just how I love it."

"Is it?"

"Yes. Straight, long and cut. What more can a man ask for?"

When Kellie wrapped his fingers around it, Monty tensed his stomach involuntarily.

"Nice abs."

"Thank you."

Kellie moved closer and took the head of Monty's cock gently into his mouth.

Monty leaned back on the couch and closed his eyes as the television show became just noise in the background.

Kellie lowered Monty's briefs and repositioned himself for a better angle. To help him, Monty widened his straddle and cupped the back of Kellie's hair to encourage him.

The attention Kellie was paying to his dick at the moment was not to get it to come. It was to enjoy it. And both Monty and Kellie were enjoying the light licking and sucking.

Closing his eyes again, resting his head on the cushions behind him, Monty drifted off to the sensation of Kellie's tongue doing a mini massage on his cock.

At one point, Kellie picked up the remote and shut off the TV. In the quiet of the room, he continued to suck the head of Monty's dick, slowly, circling his tongue around the tip, and drawing hard suction.

The relaxing sensation began to morph into an urge to orgasm. Monty used both his hands to caress Kellie, trying to let him know how much he was enjoying the blowjob.

A flash of being taped to the bed and fucked washed through Monty's mind. It made his groin tingle and his cock thicken even harder in Kellie's hot mouth.

"Kel...nice."

Kellie increased his depth and speed. The delicate licking soon became a heated act of lust.

The sexual acts between them still felt as if they were exploring. Monty knew this kind of contact would bring them closer and seal the bond between them. He had no doubt Kellie could sustain him for a long while. They'd had an unbelievable first date, if you didn't count the insanity in the massage room as one. Would their friendship withstand the chaos of two relationship-unfriendly careers?

As Kellie shifted his posture to kneel on the floor in front of Monty, Monty felt him dig into his briefs to his balls.

Monty watched, now that the view wasn't obscured. When Kellie opened his bright blue eyes and they connected, Monty felt his crotch surge with pleasure. He had no doubt he leaked pre-cum he was so excited.

164

Kellie used his talented fingers and hands to touch all the right stimulating places on Monty's genitals.

The urge to climax began in Monty in earnest. He sighed and cupped Kellie's cheek as Kellie bobbed up and down on his cock, using one hand to jerk the base and the other to rub hot friction under his nuts.

"Kel...I'm there." Monty clenched his jaw and was sent plummeting over the edge. The pleasure that raced from his ass to the tip of his cock was delicious and lasted nicely as Kellie continued working him top and bottom.

Kellie milked him strongly, just as hard as Monty liked it. He was glad he didn't have to keep reminding Kellie to squeeze tight. Kellie obviously got it.

Monty encouraged him to keep pulling on his dick for a little longer, loving the tiny aftershocks just as much as the climax.

When Kellie finally sat up, wiping his mouth, Monty slid low on the sofa, took off his briefs, and raised his heels to the cushions. "Fuck me."

Kellie appeared surprised but didn't hesitate. He leapt up and hurried to get what they needed.

Monty cupped his cock in his palm as it softened, feeling it move under his fingers. He was so satisfied he could weep.

Kellie returned, already rolling a condom on his cock and kneeling in front of Monty, pushing the coffee table out of the way. Monty held his knees and exposed his ass for Kellie to take.

Kellie put lubrication on three fingers and didn't hesitate as he entered Monty's ass. The penetration made Monty tingle from his nipples to his hole.

Kellie was much more aggressive this time, nearly fisting Monty before he fucked him. Monty was in heaven.

When it appeared Kellie was about to pop from the act of finger-fucking Monty, he removed his hand and scooted close, pushing his cock inside Monty, deep and quick.

Monty gripped Kellie by the nape of his neck and drew him to his mouth to kiss. As Monty devoured Kellie's tongue and lips, Kellie trust in to his heart's content, his respirations and moans escalating with his hip action.

At one point Kellie parted from Monty's kiss to gasp for breath. Monty stared at him as he rose to a climax. Though Kellie wasn't muscle-bound, he was ripped and fabulously fit. Every sinewy fiber showed under his smooth skin as he made love. He threw his head back and showed his teeth in a sensual snarl.

"That's it, babe." Monty's cock grew hard again from watching Kellie come. He looked down at their contact and grabbed his dick and balls, pulling them aside so he could see Kellie's cock inside him.

Kellie instantly watched as well, and choked as he came. "Fuck! Oh, fuck!" Kellie moaned and drove harder between Monty's legs.

"Baby, baby..." Monty held Kellie's jaw and kissed him again, tightening his embrace so he was squeezing him as close as he could without hurting Kellie. Inside Monty's body, Kellie's cock continued to throb as he recuperated.

Kellie gasped for air and huffed. "I love fucking you. *Oh-my-friggin-god.*"

Monty kept sweeping his gaze from their union to Kellie's handsome face and sated expression. "I love fucking you too."

Kellie blinked and dove onto Monty, embracing him just as tightly as Monty had hugged him.

Monty didn't know why if felt so good between them. It just did.

Chapter 14

Wednesday morning Kellie spotted Tyson as they arrived at the same time at the spa. He gave his friend a big smile and wave.

"Ooh, girl! Look at you!" Tyson bumped Kellie's hip with his own. "You finally get to play with that hunk you've been mooning over?"

"Yes." Kellie felt his cheeks grow warm. "You have a second?"

"I was just going to get a muffin for breakfast. You know how huge they are. Split it?"

"Sure. Let me dump my things off in my room and I'll meet you at the lounge."

Tyson threw Kellie a kiss and walked off.

A smile on his lips, Kellie headed to his massage room and tucked his belongings away, took off his light jacket and folded it in with his wallet and keys. He closed the cabinet he had secured them in and made sure his room was ready for Lenny and his ten-thirty appointment.

The morning spent with Monty had been brief. Kellie had slept so heavily he didn't remember anything until the alarm went off at seven so Monty could get out and do his new business owner thing. They didn't even get a chance to sip coffee. Monty showered, dressed and left.

Kellie was still riding the waves of last night and their coupling. He finished fussing with the room and left it to find Tyson.

Tyson had claimed a loveseat sofa, had a plate with a crumbly fruit muffin in front of him and sipped an iced coffee drink. Kellie dropped beside him heavily and leaned on Tyson's shoulder. "I want to say I'm in love, but that's so cliché."

Tyson handed Kellie the drink to share and broke off a chunk of the muffin for himself. "I knew you'd get it bad for him. He's so your type."

"Yeah. He is." Kellie sucked the iced coffee through a straw.

"So? Dish. Did he give you a good humping? I'm surprised you can sit."

"Uh. Funny thing about that."

"Yes?" Tyson took back the drink.

"He's a bottom."

Tyson choked on his swallow and blinked. "That macho-man is a bottom?"

Kellie shrugged. "Surprised me too."

"Can you top?"

"Can I?" Kellie laughed and pulled a chunk off the muffin to eat. "Do you think I can't?"

"I can't. I don't want to."

As he chewed the banana-blueberry muffin, Kellie's eyes unfocused into the busy salon. Techno music was playing in the aerobic room where a class was being held with a mix of dance and exercise. In the weight room, ten televisions were suspended in front of the bikes and treadmills. Clients were chatting and giggling as they walked to and from their treatments.

Tyson waved his hand in front of Kellie's face. "Earth to Kellie?"

"Huh?" Kellie perked up. "Sorry. What were we talking about?"

"Your top tootsie is really a bottom bum."

Kellie spotted Lenny entering the spa, signing in at the reception counter. He checked his watch. He still had ten minutes.

"Kel?"

"Hm?" Kellie spun around to Tyson.

"Where are you? Are you happy or upset with your new macho man?"

"I don't know." Kellie's hair was falling out of the rubber band. He unraveled it and wrapped it back up. "I'm going to cut it."

"Okay."

"Which stylist should I use? I went to Fergie last time."

"He really is the best one." Tyson pointed to a client. "There's my ten-fifteen." Tyson handed Kellie the rest of the coffee and jumped to his feet, greeting his first appointment of the day.

Kellie finished the drink and tossed out the remnants of the muffin with the cup. He brushed his hands of crumbs and straightened his appearance. With a smile, Kellie approached Lenny, who was reading a magazine. "I'm ready for you, Lenny."

Lenny's expression brightened and he stood, following Kellie to the massage room.

"How are you, handsome?" Lenny touched Kellie's shoulder as they walked together.

"Good, Lenny, how about you?"

"I can't complain, but sometimes I still do." Lenny laughed. He sat on the chair in the corner of the small room and removed his shoes.

"I'll be right back with your oils." Kellie smiled at him and shut the door behind him. As he prepared for Lenny's massage, Kellie didn't know why he had a nagging sensation in his gut.

169

But something told him he wouldn't hear from Monty again for a while.

~

"I may as well be back in uniform." Monty sat at a desk sifting paperwork while four of his colleagues stood around him impatiently. "Why am I running this show?"

Aaron crossed his arms and shifted his weight. "Because Brandon is useless."

"Come on, Monty, you know you're the one we always counted on." Dennis leaned both hands on the desk in front of Monty.

"I'm not a businessman, or an accountant, or a fucking secretary!" He inhaled and tried to calm down.

Thomas crouched beside him. "It should be an invoice with the logo from the construction company on top."

"You take this pile." Monty handed him a stack. "Here, Aaron, take this pile."

Aaron split his paperwork with Zak and pulled up a folding chair.

In silence they flipped papers and grumbled.

The door opened. Brandon stepped in. "Well? We're ready for our grand opening media blitz. What's the hold up?"

Monty glared at him. "The holdup is the fucking building inspector trying to give us a fucking permit so we can actually open!"

"I got it." Dennis waved an invoice and left the room.

Monty began gathering up the papers into a pile. "The rest of you, get the fuck out there and double check everything. Safety is our number one concern. You got it?"

"Got it." They filed out leaving Brandon standing in the doorway.

"You have to calm the fuck down, Monty." Brandon closed the door to give them privacy. "Bad enough I had to do everything last night while you fucked your masseuse."

Monty rose to his feet menacingly, leaning on his desk. "Do not…I repeat, do *not* take your family problems out on me. You got that?"

"You agreed to this venture. You and the rest of those guys." Brandon thumbed over his shoulder.

"I agreed to share the weight of this bullshit. Not take on the bulk of it."

"It's natural for the men to go to you. You were their commander."

"I didn't sign on for that." Monty sat back down, rubbing his forehead.

"I'm afraid you fucking did. We all did."

"How did the interview go?" Monty continued to stack the paperwork, knowing arguing with Brandon would not make things better.

"I have no idea. Personally? I think I sounded like an idiot. I would have preferred you had been there with me."

"You don't need me to hold your hand."

Brandon slammed both his palms on the desk in anger. "I need you to be my partner! Goddamn it, Monty!"

Monty scooted back his chair and folded his hands on his lap. He didn't need this aggravation.

Brandon slumped down on a chair and covered his face.

"What's going on with Kathy?"

"She left me." Brandon rubbed his eyes and appeared more exhausted than he had since boot camp.

Monty stood and walked around the desk to touch Brandon's shoulder. Brandon leaned his elbows on his legs and looked up at him. "I did this for her."

"You did this for you." Monty sat on the corner of the desk.

Brandon slouched low in the chair and kept rubbing his face and hair.

"Get into counseling."

"Fuck that."

A knock was heard at the office door. Dennis shouted through it, "Gentlemen, we're on. Get your asses out here."

"Come on, Brandon. We have to see this through. We all invested everything in this place—our money, our time, and now our families."

Brandon stood, tucking in his shirt to try and appear presentable.

Monty opened the door and stepped out. A team of reporters and cameramen were ready to film their grand opening. He extended his hand to each. "Montgomery Gresham, nice to meet you."

"Were you the senior officer for your team?" one asked.

Brandon replied, "Yes. If it weren't for Lieutenant Commander Gresham, none of us would be here today."

~

"Oh, Kellie," Lenny moaned as he said his name. "Your hands are magical."

Kellie chuckled to himself. He was just wrapping up Lenny's hour and a half massage, sitting on the stool behind him and rubbing his scalp. Holding still for a moment cupping Lenny's head, Kellie whispered, "There ya go."

"I can't believe I'm expected to get up."

"Take your time. I'll bring you water." Kellie stood and washed his hands. He smiled at Lenny and left, heading to the men's room to check his appearance. Once he finished, he filled a glass with water, took out his mobile phone and checked it for messages. One text message—from Scott. *'c me 2nite'*. Kellie deleted it. "Sure. Now that I have a hot man you want me." He scoffed. "You want a three-way, I mean."

172

He considered texting Monty, but Monty just didn't seem the texting kind. He was older, mature, and busy. After a few minutes, Kellie returned to his room to check on Lenny. Pressing his ear to the door, Kellie said, "Len?"

"Come in."

Kellie opened the door and handed Lenny the water as Lenny sat on the chair putting on his shoes and socks. "How you feel?"

"Fantastic." Lenny sipped the water.

"You look great. Retired life agrees with you." Kellie leaned against the massage table.

"I keep busier now than when I was working." He looked for a spot for the glass after taking a sip and Kellie took it from him, setting it by the sink.

"How are you?" Lenny's forehead furrowed deeply as if he were genuinely concerned.

"I'm okay, Lenny. Thanks for asking."

Lenny reached out to hold Kellie's hand and studied his expression. "You need a man in your life."

"I think I found one. But we just started dating."

"One of your clients?"

"Yes."

"I'm very happy for you." Lenny finished getting dressed and stood, holding the back of the chair for balance.

Kellie reached for him to make sure he was steady.

"Your massages never fail to make me feel very lightheaded." Lenny smiled. "You're my legal high."

Laughing, Kellie said, "Yes. I seem to have that effect on some people."

"I should already have a Friday appointment."

"You do. Every Wednesday and Friday at ten-thirty. No need to worry." Kellie held Lenny's arm as they stepped out of the room.

173

"I don't know what I would do without you. Your new man is a very lucky boy."

"Thanks, Len. You always make me feel good about myself." Kellie walked him out to the lounge area where he spotted his next client waiting, Neal. He gave Neal a wave in acknowledgement.

"You just don't worry about anything," Lenny said.

Kellie felt confused by the comment but smiled and nodded. "Thanks, Lenny. Drive carefully." Kellie approached Neal. "Let me just straighten up the room. I'll be right out."

"I'm early. You're good." Neal smiled.

Kellie headed back to his room, replacing the linens with fresh ones. He and Monty hadn't made any arrangements to see each other again socially. But, if things were normal, Kellie would see Monty for his scheduled massage tomorrow.

As he made the table ready for his next client, Kellie pouted. Was it good or bad he would see Monty for an appointment before he would get a second date?

"Good," Kellie tried to convince himself.

~

Thomas handed Monty the coffee he had requested. Without it, Monty couldn't keep up the frantic pace. "Thanks."

"No problem. Brandon wanted to know if you wanted to get food delivered?"

"What the hell time is it?" Monty checked his watch as he stood near his desk. "Jesus."

"Yeah. I know." Thomas shrugged.

Monty sipped the coffee and said, "I'll order something."

"Thanks. I'll let the guys know."

After Thomas left, Monty sat down at his desk, put his coffee aside, and picked up the phone. He flipped through a yellow pages directory and dialed. When the restaurant answered he asked, "You deliver?"

"No."

Aaron walked into his office, seeing he was on the phone and kept quiet.

Monty cupped the phone. "Can Zak go out and pick up some food? I'm sick of pizza and this sandwich shop doesn't deliver."

"We'll send someone out."

Monty went back to his call. "Okay, we'll pick it up. Can you put together a large deli platter with a ton of the meats and cheeses on it, some rolls or bagels, and any kind of side salad you have?" Monty checked his watch again. He cupped the phone and said to Aaron, "Eight? How the hell did it get to be eight o'clock?"

All Aaron did was shrug.

The man on the phone answered Monty's question, "Sure. For how many people?"

Monty cupped the phone again. "How many guys are still here?"

"Fifteen?" Aaron answered.

"Fifteen." Monty said into the phone.

"Be ready in twenty minutes."

"Thanks." Monty gave the man his name and phone number and hung up. He turned the phone book around and pointed to the address. "Here. Write it down." He tore a piece of paper off a pad and handed Aaron the pen as well.

"Fucking starving. I have the worst headache."

"Join the club." Monty rubbed his neck and thought of Kellie. He picked up the phone to call him when Aaron said, "Need you out on the obstacle course. Dennis has the posters for the instructions, but he says they're wrong."

Monty hung up the phone and followed Aaron out of his office. "Just like boot camp...he should know, he's done it enough."

Aaron laughed and continued leading Monty to one of the areas of the training facility.

~

Kellie entered his apartment, tired and frustrated. Was this all some game now? Call? Don't call?

He removed his shoes and headed to the bedroom to change out of his work clothing. The bed was disheveled from Monty's sleepover. Kellie didn't want to make it or strip the sheets. If he could catch a scent of Monty's cologne tonight, he'd be happy.

"Am I supposed to call him?" Kellie tried to think of how they left off. He changed into a pair of gym shorts and t-shirt, heading to the kitchen for a bite to eat and water. It was nearing nine. He had a late appointment book last minute so that meant he had to eat late.

He leaned over his answering machine and found it had one message. He hit play. His mother's voice said, "Hi, Kelsey, just seeing how you are. Hope work is good. Love you."

Kellie picked up the cordless and hit speed dial for her number.

"Hello, dear."

"Hi, Mom." Kellie poured water from the pitcher into a glass. "How are you?"

"I'm okay. Tired."

"Are you still enjoying your job at the salon?"

"Pretty much. I just wish I could make more money." Kellie checked on the various leftovers, sniffing the containers.

"The economy is still terrible. You remember my friend Mary? Her son lost his job now as well. He was a mortgage broker. Oh. It's horrible."

"I know. It hasn't come back in three years to where it was." Kellie sat at his kitchen table with a fork sticking out of a plastic bowl, ready to consume his leftover tofu and quinoa salad.

"Can you ask for a raise?"

176

"Not really. I can raise my prices or work more clients into each day. Or…I can work seven days a week." Kellie took a bite.

"Oh no. Don't do that."

"My back and shoulders can't take it anyway." Kellie rotated his arm to feel a sharp pain in the areas he'd just mentioned. "I met a guy, but I don't even want to tell you about him yet."

"Why not?"

"I just had one real date with him last night." Kellie ate more food and chewed, staring at bills that had been left on his kitchen table.

"Is he nice?"

"I think so. He's an ex-Navy SEAL."

"Does he know the men who killed Bin Laden?"

Kellie laughed. "I have no idea and I doubt he'd tell me. You know, everything is a secret squirrel mission with those guys."

"What's his name?"

"Montgomery Gresham." Kellie felt butterflies in his belly at saying his name.

"That sounds very official."

Kellie laughed. "Yeah. That pretty much is how he is."

"I hope this works out for you. You haven't dated anyone steadily in ages."

"With the chaos I've been through when I lost the house and my job?" Kellie sipped his water quickly between sentences. "I haven't really wanted to get into anything serious."

"But you must be lonely."

Kellie looked around his small abode. "I am. At least, I hope I'm not going to be from now on."

"Okay, Kelsey. Let me go. I just wanted to say hi."

"Thanks, Mom."

"Love you, sweetheart."

"You too. Say hi to Dad."

"I will. Bye."

"Bye." Kellie hung up and placed the phone on the table beside him. He continued eating, wondering if this connection with Monty was going to fizzle quickly. It always did with him and men.

~

At one a.m. Monty came through the door of his home. He stripped, brushed his teeth and went to bed. He had six hours until he had to be back at the training camp again. He thought he had left this frenetic pace behind. How wrong could he be?

Chapter 15

Kellie didn't know what to think.

Wednesday—nothing. Thursday—nothing.

Was this what relationships were like now? Hot sex, great passion, awesome vibes, and then ignore?

Kellie had just finished his session with Mike Murphy and placed fresh linens on the table for…Mr. Montgomery Gresham.

Why Kellie was annoyed with Monty for ignoring him since they had made love Tuesday night, he couldn't explain. Or maybe he could. Scott Baldwin.

Scott had done the same thing to him and Kellie was growing sick of it.

How many times had Kellie looked at his phone and wanted to call or text Monty? Dozens. Why didn't he?

Because Monty was opening a new business. Kellie couldn't imagine calling him and interrupting him. But—that was his excuse. Why hadn't Monty called him?

"Stop self-destructing." Kellie bundled up the dirty linens to take with him to the laundry area. He tossed them into a hamper and carried freshly cleaned ones back to his room. He did a check of his watch and seeing he had a half hour before Monty was supposed to show up, Kellie looked for Tyson.

He found him busy training someone on the weight machines, so Kellie sat in the lounge to daze off at nothing and stew. It was what he did best—beat himself up for every failed opportunity in his life. It didn't matter that hundreds of thousands of people had lost their jobs and homes since the economy tanked. He blamed himself for his timing and being in the wrong business. *Real estate? That was supposed to be the dream job. Buy property. Wasn't that the catch phrase for decades? I get my license and poof. Dead wrong.*

And the fact he hadn't had a steady boyfriend since...ever?

What am I doing wrong? I'm not clingy, I don't scare men off, do I? What could I be doing to chase them away? We've become a disposable society. People are thrown away just like plastic junk.

When he went to pull his hair back he felt nothing. It was chopped off in a conservative style. Fergie had just cut it this morning and Kellie knew it would take a while to get used to it.

He ran his fingers through it a few times. It was more like what he was used to. As a real estate agent, he had kept it cropped short, worn a business suit...did the dance.

His mood was sinking like it had when Scott fucked him over. In a small piece of his mind he hoped Monty didn't show for his massage, cancelled all his appointments and he never saw him again. It was just easier than being put through the mill each time he began a new relationship.

Before Kellie realized it, Tyson was standing next to his chair. Tyson nudged Kellie's knee with his own. "I can barely recognize you without the ponytail."

"It was barely a ponytail."

Tyson gestured for Kellie to move. "Scootch over."

He shared the loveseat with Tyson and they connected along one side.

"Talk to me."

"I don't know what to talk about. My life sucks."

"Then I won't tell you about my new beau. It would seem cruel." Tyson leaned his head on Kellie's shoulder.

"Does he text you?"

"Constantly. Little love notes. But I won't even show you."

"Sigh." Kellie laid his head on Tyson's and felt even more depressed. "It's me, right? I have some weird veggie-Prius vibe most guys think sucks. Right?"

"They don't know what they're missing."

"Yeah. That's the problem. They do. They have sex with me. Then they vanish. They know exactly what they're missing."

"Uh oh."

"What?"

"Isn't that your man? What'd he do to himself?"

Kellie sat upright and searched for Monty. He spotted him walking slowly, obviously in pain.

"Go. What are you waiting for?" Tyson pushed Kellie.

Kellie scrambled to his feet and hurried towards Monty. He met Monty at the desk where Monty signed in and Lynn was checking on his appointment in her books.

"I'm here, Lynn." Kellie nodded to her.

"Okay, Kel."

Kellie hooked Monty's elbow and walked with him back to his massage room. "What did you do?"

"Wrenched my back. I'm okay."

Kellie knew he wasn't 'okay'. He escorted him to his massage room and sat Monty on the chair, crouching to remove his shoes for him. "How did you do it?"

"You'll laugh."

"Believe me, I won't."

Monty unbuttoned his shirt and cringed when he shifted to take it off. "All I fucking did was lift up the dumpster lid to dump a bag of trash. A felt a zap and a tear and now I'm a cripple."

181

"Christ, I've done that. I reached over to take the laundry out of the dryer at home and the same thing happened to me." Kellie helped Monty undress. "I'll fix you up."

"God-fucking-damn it! I didn't even hurt myself this bad in the service."

"You filleted your calf." Kellie helped Monty stand so he could remove his lower half of clothing.

"That didn't hurt near as badly as this does. I'm getting fucking old."

"I was twenty when I tore my back up. So it's not age, it's posture." He glanced down at Monty's soft cock and balls as they were exposed. How was he supposed to be mad at the guy now?

Monty crawled over the table, face down, groaning in pain.

"All right, babe." Kellie raised the sheet over him, adjusting the cushion under his ankles. "Have you taken anything for it?"

"I don't do painkillers."

"How about over-the-counter stuff?"

"I have to buy some." Monty stiffened, then seemed to force himself to let go of his back soreness as he lay flat on his front.

"I have ibuprofen with me. Let me mix up some oil that will help your back."

"Please. I have to return to the training center tonight and I'm in fucking agony."

That ruled out a date. "Okay. I'll be right back." Kellie tried not to be selfish about this new relationship. The poor man.

~

It didn't matter if he was in pain. He had to be fine.

How fucking humiliating.

Monty had been lifting boxes, railroad ties, and eighteen wheeler truck tires for weeks. He flips the lid open on the dumpster and...wrenches his back?

The men who had seen it happen got a good laugh. Aaron, Dennis, Thomas...real funny to see the nearly forty-year-old moron get hurt. Monty knew if it had been a serious injury they wouldn't have laughed. He'd have killed them.

Now he had to let Kellie see him vulnerable too. Had his pride ever taken this kind of beating before?

"No." He closed his eyes as he looked through the face rest at the parquet floor. All through BUD training, being seen as weak was impossible. SEAL Basic Underwater Demolition training made grown men cry. Not him.

Never.

The door opened and closed. Monty listened as Kellie prepared things around him—the warm stones, something at the sink, Monty couldn't tell.

But the first moment Kellie laid his hands on his back, Monty moaned and knew he'd feel better for it. He had swallowed his pride to come and get Kellie's help. That had to mean something. He must really like the guy.

"You let me know if anything I do hurts you."

"It won't."

"How's the opening going?"

"I'm trying to pretend it's not a disaster."

Kellie made a sound of sympathy and began working on the spot Monty had torn, low back, near his left side. "You got it." He flinched and blew out a few breaths.

"Same area I did. I know how much it hurts."

"It can't hurt. I have to run a goddamn training session in two days."

"Let me treat you for it. Do you have time tomorrow to come in?"

"No." Monty clenched his fists as Kellie put more pressure on the painful spot.

"Not even a half hour?"

183

"By the time I drive here and back, it'll be two."

"I can come to you."

Monty thought about it. "You'd do that?"

"Of course. I have a portable table."

As Kellie worked on relieving Monty's pain, Monty thought about when he would have even a half hour of free time. With his thoughts vanishing under Kellie's skilled hands, Monty drifted off. Kellie began moving his palms in circular motions as if pushing the soreness away from its epicenter. He felt Kellie stop at one point, then noticed his bare feet near the front of the table. When Kellie resumed the massage, he used his elbows and forearms to dig deeply into the damaged muscle. It made Monty flinch and clench his jaw.

"I'll lighten up."

"You do what you have to do to get me one hundred percent."

"Promise."

Again Kellie paused and Monty heard him rubbing the stones together. Monty took a few deep breaths and wanted to feel the heat on him. Kellie massaged deeply into Monty's sore back with the warm smooth stones, making Monty moan from the pleasure and pain relief.

Monty nearly fell asleep at one point, he was so exhausted. Though he tried to sleep six hours last night, he tossed and turned and was lucky to get three.

Kellie had placed a heating pad on Monty's low back as he worked his limbs, neck, and shoulders.

"You are so knotted up."

Monty grunted in reply. He wasn't surprised. "I should have gotten a job as dog-walker. I must be out of my mind."

"Opening up a new business is always murder."

"No. This one in particular. I can kick myself."

"I'm sorry, Monty."

"Why? You're not the moron, I am."

Another few moments passed and Kellie removed the heating pad. He held up the sheet and said, "Scoot down and roll over."

"I have to move?" Monty forced himself to get to his elbows. He focused on his low back as he shifted downward on the table and rolled over. "Hey. It feels a little better."

"Good. After you take ibuprofen, it'll be even more tolerable." Kellie covered Monty with the sheet.

Monty looked at him. Something was different. He tilted his head and stared at Kellie as Kellie continued to fix the cushion under his knees and fuss with the sheet.

"You cut your hair."

Kellie smiled. "I didn't think you'd ever notice."

"I'm a selfish cunt. You'll learn that about me."

"I highly doubt that." Kellie loosened Monty's arm from the sheet and coated his own hands in oil. "But I have no doubt that's the rumor you perpetuate."

"True. Rule by attitude and terror. Just ask my dad." He spread his fingers out so he was touching Kellie's hip as Kellie massaged his forearm and biceps.

"If you talk about family you'll tense up."

"How did you get to know me so well so quickly?" Monty tucked his fingers into Kellie's yoga pants. "Do you always massage shirtless?"

"Only with you. You get me very hot." Kellie's blue eyes sparkled as he rubbed the oil into Monty's forearm.

Monty admired him with his short hair. "I like it better. I suppose I'm used to everyone around me having a buzz cut."

"Yeah. Even vegan-Prius drivers have to go butch every once in a while."

"You seriously never eat meat?"

"Yes, really. I mean, I won't scream if I ingest some accidentally."

"How does one accidentally eat meat?"

185

"Sometimes it's in food you don't think it will be in. Never mind." Kellie blushed, placed Monty's left arm down on the table and walked to the foot, exposing Monty's left leg. He bent Monty's knee and began pushing it backwards, doing Monty's low back exercises for him.

"They teach you a lot of moves in that massage school, don't they?"

"They do. And I spotted you doing these in the yoga room."

"Reconnaissance? I'm impressed."

"Does it hurt?" Kellie held Monty's foot and rolled his hip off the table as he bent Monty's knee tightly to his body.

"Not as badly as I expected it would. I thought I'd be screaming."

"Scream for me, baby." Kellie winked.

"Look what you did."

"What?"

Monty pointed at the tented sheet. "Now my dick is hard."

"Happens to the best of them." Kellie straightened out Monty's leg and rubbed oil on his hands to massage it.

Monty looked at the wall clock. "You shitting me? You've been rubbing me for nearly two hours?"

"Time flies when you're having fun."

"Am I your last appointment?"

"That I know of. Lynn doesn't usually book someone late unless she asks first."

"You don't have to do this." Monty felt guilty. Was this taking advantage?

"I want to." Kellie finished rubbing Monty's toes and moved to his right leg, bending it back as well, loosening up the low back muscles.

Monty closed his eyes. "That pulls on the tear. Fuck. Why did I do that?" He was so angry at himself he could kill someone.

"What do you have to do this weekend?"

186

"Not much. Just demonstrate the obstacle course, the water course, the calisthenics routine…"

"I get it." Kellie used his weight to push back Monty's leg until Monty cringed. "You need to heat it tonight. To be honest, I'd cold compress it and then heat it. Along with that, take ibuprofen and acetaminophen mixed. Two of each, every four hours."

"You do realize I'll never do that when I leave here."

"Why not?" Kellie lowered Monty's leg, oiled up and began rubbing it.

"Because I suck at taking care of myself."

"If you want to be able to move Saturday, you better get good at it."

"Come home with me."

Kellie perked up. "Huh?"

"Are you doing anything tonight?"

"You want me to play nursemaid?" Kellie laughed, straightening out the sheet as he moved back to Monty's upper body.

Monty gripped Kellie's arm. "I want you to play sex partner and boyfriend."

"Typical man. Still craving sex though he's in agony." Kellie rubbed Monty's right arm, the only limb left to attend.

Monty stuffed his fingers down Kellie's yoga pants like he had with his left hand. "The first time you gave me a massage you didn't wear anything under these. Why do you wear briefs all the time now?"

"Christ." Kellie's cheeks went crimson. "You knew that?"

"I make it my business to know everything." He ran his fingers up Kellie's crotch, feeling his hard-on. "The first time you and I had an appointment, you tented the fabric of the pants you were wearing. I was looking forward to seeing that again. But you started wearing briefs."

"I embarrassed myself." Kellie was adorable when he blushed. Monty was about to get dirty with him.

Kellie placed Monty's arm back on the table and washed his hands. He rolled the stool closer to the head of the table and dug his fingers into Monty's scalp.

"I tingle everywhere you touch me. I can't tell you how much I enjoy these sessions."

"I love it too. And you should pamper yourself."

Monty made a noise of disbelief. "Pamper myself. Babe, this is to keep the pain and headaches at a tolerable level. It's not pampering."

"Poor thing." Kellie bent down and kissed Monty's forehead.

Monty reached backwards and gripped his face. "Get the fuck over here."

Kellie lowered down and kissed him.

Monty ate at his mouth, bending his knees as the intensity made his cock throb.

Kellie gently ended the kiss and continued to massage Monty's scalp.

"You have any idea how much I want you to crawl between my legs and fuck me right now?" Monty reached under the sheet and tugged on his erect dick.

"How's your low back feel?"

"That's evasive."

"I can't fuck you in here. I shouldn't even kiss you."

"I do admire your integrity. But I'm fucking horny."

Kellie traced Monty's eyebrows, nose, lips, sensually, tenderly…

"You're going to make me want to jack off." Monty spread his knees and fisted his cock under the sheet.

"What a waste of spunk that would be." Kellie stood, walking around the table.

Monty tried to sit up quickly and felt his back pull. He slowed down and was furious with himself for not being able to leap off the table and pin Kellie to the wall like had done previously.

"I'll get you some ibuprofens and water. Take your time getting up."

Once Kellie left, Monty swore under his breath and sat up gingerly, wishing he could punch a hole in the wall he was so frustrated. "Real attractive, Monty. I'm sure moving like an eighty-year-old man is making Kellie excited." He shook his head and tried to psych himself up to get off the table.

~

Kellie shook two pills into his palm and then filled a glass of water. He returned, smiling to himself about being able to enjoy Monty for the evening. He looked forward to helping him get his back healed and ready for his big weekend.

Leaning his ear on the door, Kellie said, "You decent?"

Monty opened the door. He was fully dressed and looking annoyed.

"Here." Kellie held out the water.

Monty took it, gulping some down.

"Take these." Kellie opened his palm.

Monty picked up the two pills and swallowed them, finishing the water.

"Let me just check with Lynn before I go."

Monty nodded but his expression had changed.

Kellie took the empty glass from him. "You still in agony?"

"Look, maybe I should just head home and call it a night."

Kellie winced at the sting of the rejection. "Sure, Monty."

"I don't want to be a fucking burden on you. This sucks." He showed his teeth in his grimace.

"Burden on me?" Kellie put the glass down by the sink. "Monty, nothing gives me more satisfaction than taking care of people. I do it for a living."

189

"And you shouldn't be expected to do it for your friends off work."

Friends? Kellie was feeling sicker to his stomach by the moment. *A second ago I was his boyfriend and sex partner.*

"I'll call you." Monty pecked his cheek and left the room.

"Are you kidding me?" Kellie felt his eyes burn. He grew so angry he stormed after Monty. "If you don't want to date me, tell me."

"What?" Monty spun around, his car keys in his hand.

"I'm not playing this game again."

Monty looked around at a few people who could overhear their spat and brought Kellie to the side of the lounge area near a wall. "What are you talking about?"

"Just tell me you're not interested, okay? Spare me the nights of waiting for you to call." Kellie was about to explode he was so tired of the rejection.

"I am interested in you." Monty took another paranoid look around. "You want to talk about this in your room? Or air our crap where you work?"

"Forget it." Kellie threw up his hands and stormed back to his massage room, ripping the sheets from the table in fury.

The door closed behind him. He turned around to see Monty standing there.

"Sit." Monty pointed to the chair.

Kellie sat, the sheets balled up on his lap.

Monty tried to prop himself up on the side of the table, hoisting himself to sit on it. He cringed from pain and Kellie jolted as if to help him, but stayed put.

After a second to think, Monty said, "I am not the type of guy to look for help from anyone. Okay? It's out of my comfort zone."

"Fine."

"Stop looking so hurt."

"Can I be honest?"

"I expect nothing less."

"I get mixed vibes from you."

"I'm not doing that intentionally. I'm going through a lot of bullshit at the moment."

"So my timing sucks once more. Story of my life." Kellie fussed with the linens on his lap. "Fine. Call me whenever."

"Babe." Monty reached out to stop him from leaving the room. "If you feel compelled to come and play doctor for me, okay. But I will not be a model patient."

"I can take a hint, Monty." Kellie reached for the doorknob.

"I'm not hinting!" Monty cursed and tried to get off the table. "Fuck!" He grabbed his low back and looked at the ceiling as if for strength. "You think your timing sucks?"

Kellie put the linens on the chair and embraced Monty slowly. "Come here, old man."

"That kind of comment will get you spanked."

"You want me to spank you, sub-man." Kellie held Monty close, resting his chin on his shoulder.

"That's not the point."

"You are not a robot, and you are not indestructible. Sorry to have to inform you."

"Don't tell the crew at the fitness center that. After what we've all been through, they think I walk on water."

"That must be a very hard reputation to keep intact."

"You have no idea." Monty leaned against Kellie heavily.

"Let me baby you. Do it for me."

"You're out of your mind."

"I know." Kellie leaned back to smile at Monty.

"Fine. You want to play nurse to an invalid, that's your problem."

"Yes, it is. And I intend to take advantage of you."

"Yeah?" Monty brightened up.

"Yeah." Kellie kissed him.

Chapter 16

Kellie drove behind Monty's Camaro. As he did, he noticed Monty put on a Bluetooth or a headset. With the big grand opening of his Navy SEALs fitness center, Kellie began to feel as if he was intruding on Monty. Was he acting demanding? Or was this what Monty wanted as well?

As usual, Kellie second guessed himself. Bad past relationships tended to overshadow new ones.

He pulled up behind the Camaro in a driveway of a single family home in Culver City. Kellie knew the real estate in this area. He figured Monty must have paid in the mid-three-hundred thousand range for a tiny two bedroom cottage. It had a little bit of property to it, but not much.

He parked and shut off the ignition, seeing Monty struggle to get out of the low-slung sports car with his aching back. Kellie made a move to give him a hand but hesitated when Monty managed to do it himself.

"I used to sell homes in this county." Kellie met Monty at the front door.

"I bought it at auction. The place was a piece of shit."

"I hope you got a good deal."

"I did. I gutted it and remodeled it." Monty opened the door and Kellie took a look at the fresh off-white paint and wood floors. It was a small 1970's home, but now completely updated.

Kellie felt as if he and Monty were in the same boat. How nice would it be to own a huge house with ten thousand square feet instead of living in either an apartment or a seven hundred square foot cottage.

Kellie thought leaving the military after at least a decade of service should give a man some cash, but he said nothing. He didn't think it was his business to ask. And Monty may have put the bulk of his assets into his new business.

"Are the ibuprofens working?"

"I have no idea." Monty opened the refrigerator and removed two bottles of water, handing Kellie one.

Kellie looked around the rooms. No pictures were yet hung on the walls, and the smell of new paint and flooring still lingered.

"How long have you lived in California?"

"Eight months." He checked his mobile phone quickly. "Are you hungry?"

"Are you? I can eat I guess."

"I'd say we can throw steaks on the grill," Monty smiled as he spoke, "But…"

"Sorry."

"Shit, I can't even order a pepperoni pizza with you."

"I know. Sucks huh?"

"Yes. It does. What the hell do you eat? Tofu?"

"Sometimes."

Monty crinkled his nose in disgust.

"Have you ever tried it?"

"Hell no." Monty finished the water tossing the empty into the trash.

Kellie flinched. "Don't you recycle?"

"Oh. Right." Monty removed the bottle and walked around the kitchen with it, lost.

194

"Man!" Kellie laughed at him. "I need to train you in the ways of the locals."

"You won't get me driving a Prius. Forget it." He slapped the empty bottle on the counter with a bang.

"They have bins to recycle curbside."

"Right." Monty nodded. "I did notice one had a blue top."

"Is it hard being a civilian after so many years in the military?"

"Some things are just a nuisance. Nothing is hard."

Kellie remembered the tattoo on Monty's shoulder. *The only easy day was yesterday.* How true. "Why don't you sit down? Let me make an ice pack for you."

Monty opened the freezer. "I don't have ice. I have steak."

Kellie broke up with laughter. "Fine. We passed a convenience store on the way. Why don't I buy you some ice and painkillers."

"You don't have to do that."

"You sure?"

"I just need to be fucked 'til I scream. Okay?"

Kellie choked on his swallow of water at the comment. He started coughing and laughing at the same time. He composed himself and blinked in amazement. "You crack me up."

Monty took the water bottle from Kellie and put it on the counter, then held Kellie's hand and brought him to the bedroom. The bed was made, and it appeared to Kellie he could bounce a quarter on it, the bedding was so tight. Kellie was swung around in a pirouette, landing in Monty's arms. Monty embraced him, going for his lips.

All the doubt and hesitation Kellie had evaporated. While their lips were connected, Kellie allowed Monty to undress him. Soon his shirt and pants were lying on the floor and Monty was stripping his own clothing off as well. Once they were naked, Monty drew Kellie to his bed, bringing Kellie to lay on top of him. As Monty spread his legs, Kellie fell between them. The kissing was wild, as if the pent up passion between them had been building for weeks, not two days. Kellie opened his eyes to see Monty's closed, his brows knitted close together, his hands digging into Kellie's hair at the back of his head.

At the sight of Monty's passion, Kellie felt his body respond. He reached between them, righting both of their cocks.

Whether Monty was just enduring his back pain or disregarding it, both he and Kellie were humping hot friction against each other, feeding the flames of their steamy coupling.

Monty broke the kiss with a breath. He stared into Kellie's eyes making Kellie shiver from the potency. This man may be a civilian now, but Kellie had no doubt Monty's intensity in combat as a trained Navy SEAL made him the ultimate predator.

Their cocks throbbed in sync. Still mesmerized by Monty's blazing blue irises, Kellie felt Monty straddle, bending his knees in invitation. Monty's hands lowered down Kellie's back to his ass, where he grabbed tight and ground against him.

"Fuck me." Monty snarled, looking like a sex-god.

A sensation as strong as a back-draft of flames rushed over Kellie's skin and he broke out in dewy sweat and chills. Monty threw his head back into the pillows and opened his lips, releasing a breathy gasp.

Kellie looked at the nightstand behind him. "Rubbers?"

"Top drawer." Monty gave Kellie's ass a good squeeze and released him.

Kellie reached to the drawer, seeing what he needed, along with a dildo and a few leather toys and straps. Though the desire to investigate was present, he ignored it and got what they needed for lovemaking.

Meeting Monty's eyes again, Kellie set the items on the bed beside them and went back to kissing Monty. Monty rolled them to their side and picked up the condom. He tore it open, peeking down as he did, and began putting it on Kellie's stiff cock.

Kellie parted their kiss and watched, holding Monty's rounded deltoid muscle over his tattoo.

Monty efficiently sheathed Kellie's cock, reaching for the lubrication next. He nearly made Kellie come as he jacked him off while he applied it over the condom. It was all Kellie could do to hold back and not come from the stimulation.

Monty nudged Kellie to move over and managed to get to his hands and knees. He sank his face against a pillow, raised his butt into the air, and spread his legs.

"Talk about an invitation for pleasure." Kellie knelt behind Monty, holding his waist. He aimed his cock towards Monty's rim and began sinking inside him slowly. "You can start screaming anytime, handsome."

A low moan came from Monty, slightly muffled by the pillows.

Kellie pulled out and then pushed in deeper each time until he felt full penetration. He looked down at the union in delight. Holding Monty's body for support, Kellie eased into a more aggressive love-making position, using his thumbs to rub Monty's low back in tiny swirling motions, just in case it was aching while he was kneeling.

As the tempo increased, Monty breathed out a long exhale and sucked in a deep inhale loudly.

"Good, babe?" Kellie dreaded Monty's back interfering with his pleasure.

"Fuck harder."

Kellie complied, moving faster and squeezing Monty's waist tightly as he did.

Monty braced himself on the bed, raising himself up on his arms so he could thrust backwards as he desired.

And he desired.

197

Kellie heard Monty's grunting sounds and it sent the hair standing on the back of his neck. Before he continued, Kellie took another good look at their act, squirt a blob of lube into his palm, then leaned over Monty's bottom. He reached for his cock and grabbed it. It was semi-erect and seeping pre-cum. Kellie matched his hip movements with his hand, bringing Monty up quickly to heightened arousal.

Monty jammed his cock through Kellie's slick fingers and his groaning became as rhythmic as their actions.

Kellie closed his eyes and focused on making his lover come. He fisted him hard, knowing Monty loved it that way. Monty's thrusting movements came to a halt but his vocalizations were thrilling Kellie. Kellie hammered his cock into Monty, bracing himself with one hand on Monty's back and jerking him off like a machine with the other. It was a workout Kellie was glad he was fit for. Sweat drenched them both and Kellie was about to come from the wonderful sex.

He grimaced to hold back until Monty climaxed. Kellie squeezed and pulled Monty's cock to the point where he would have sworn Monty would tell him to stop. Instead, Monty came.

He did indeed 'scream', choking and huffing air as Kellie felt his palm fill with hot spunk. With his focus on his own pleasure now, Kellie milked Monty's cock and ground hard for that last push over the edge. The deep pulsating began in his balls and radiated outward to the tip of his cock. Kellie inhaled and pushed his hips against Monty so forcefully, Monty had to use his hand to prevent hitting the headboard.

"*Gahhd*!" Kellie gasped for breath, stilling his hips. "Holy shit…" When the throbbing in his dick stopped, he pulled out slowly, sitting on his heels and staring at both the spent condom and his handful of cum.

Monty collapsed to the bed under him, panting.

Kellie staggered off the bed, looking for the bathroom. He found it and rinsed off his hand, removing the condom and soaking a washcloth for Monty.

When he returned to his man, Monty was sound asleep.

Kellie had no doubt the ordeal of his job was sapping the energy out of him. He made a quick wipe of the gel residue on Monty's bottom and tossed the cloth back into the bathroom.

Leaning against the doorway of the bedroom, Kellie smiled at his sleeping prince. He was growing very fond of this man, and there was nothing he could do about it.

Chapter 17

Friday morning Kellie woke with a start.

Monty had sat up like he was on a spring and looked at the clock. "Fuck!" He leapt out of bed, either forgetting he had pulled his back or ignoring it, and a second later Kellie heard the shower running.

"I take it you're late?" Kellie yelled, but had no idea if it was heard.

The phone rang soon after Monty's sprint to get ready. Kellie stared at it, got out of bed, and carried it to the bathroom. "Monty? The phone is ringing."

"Answer it." Monty soaped up, using the razor in the shower to shave his face.

"Hello?" Kellie put the phone to his ear.

"Who is this?"

"It's Kellie. Monty's friend."

"Put Monty on, please."

"He's in the shower."

Monty rolled back the shower door. "Who is it?"

Kellie asked, "Who is this?"

"Brandon!"

Kellie held the phone away from his ear in surprise at the volume. "He just deafened me in one ear. It's Brandon." Kellie offered Monty the phone, remembering Brandon from seeing him speaking to Monty at the salon.

"Tell him I'll be there in ten minutes."

Kellie said, "He'll be there in ten—" He looked at the phone. "He hung up."

"That's Brandon." Monty shut off the water and grabbed a towel.

"How's your back?"

"Tolerable. Thanks to you." Monty stepped out of the tub, rubbing the towel over his head. "I have to get going."

Kellie moved back as Monty left the bathroom. He followed him, placing the phone back into the cradle.

Monty got dressed quickly. "Take your time. Make coffee, breakfast...do what you want. Just make sure the door is locked." Monty filled his pockets with his wallet and keys, looking at his mobile phone as he sat on the bed to put on his shoes.

Kellie didn't know what to think or say. He'd never been in this situation before. All he could do was stare at Monty and blink.

"Bye." Monty kissed him and left.

Kellie heard the door close and then the home became silent. A second later, the door opened and Monty shouted, "Your car is in my way!"

Kellie jumped in reaction, threw on his pants and ran out with his keys. He backed up, allowed Monty to leave, and pulled back into his driveway again. Once he was inside Monty's house, Kellie took a moment to think, which wasn't easy.

It wasn't even seven a.m. yet, and Kellie's first appointment was at ten-thirty. He looked around the barren walls and felt slightly confused. They had hot sex, fell asleep and poof! Monty was gone.

Kellie returned to the bedroom. He folded the clothing Monty had left on the floor and made the bed. When everything was neat and tidy, Kellie picked up the empty condom wrapper to dispose of and the lube to place back into the side table. He opened the nightstand drawer and before he dropped the bottle in he inspected the contents visually. How rude to snoop.

Very rude.

Kellie snooped.

The wrapper set aside, he checked out the dildo, the cock rings, and a few leather straps used to bind. Under the play things was a magazine. Kellie didn't remove it, but he exposed the cover so he could see it. It was a raunchy gay porn magazine with one man on the cover in a precarious position exposing his well-worked ass, and four men dominating him in various poses all wearing hardcore macho outfits.

"Huh." Kellie tried to make the drawer appear as if he hadn't been nosing in it. With his intentions to shower and leave, Kellie spun around towards the hall and stopped. On the dresser he noticed a stack of small frames, one on top of the other, not on display. Which made sense considering the new paint job.

Kellie picked the top one up. It was a shot of a man naked from the waist up, photographed from behind. The background was a locker room with clothing and gear everywhere, and the man was wearing camouflage pants. *This is fucking hot!*

Then Kellie noticed the tattoo. *This is Monty?* He choked and looked closer. It was indeed his lover, but taken when his man was younger. Though Monty was in perfect condition now, this version of Montgomery Gresham had wide flaring shoulders and dark brown hair, cropped very short, wearing a baseball type billed cap.

Kellie quickly checked the others. A photo of a team of men at what appeared to be training camp, in camouflage uniforms, gathered for a group photo—gorgeous, fit, young hunks, all looking wild and pumped for their first mission. Kellie grew hard where he stood. "This is the stuff of gay fantasies. Tell me you could not come out back then? How unfair was that?"

Kellie looked at each photo, getting a feel for the man who seemed just beyond his grasp. He recognized a younger version of Brandon as well. He replaced them where they had been, and right before he moved on to shower, he opened a small wooden box. His eyes widened in surprise. It was filled with ribbons and medals. "Monty! Why won't you talk to me about your life? Look at this!" He picked up colorful ribbon bars and a pin with the same insignia as Monty's tattoo, but in gold.

It occurred to Kellie that Monty had never actually said he had been a Navy SEAL, or did he? Yes, he said he had been one. But of course when he first met Monty it was an assumption Kellie made because of his tattoos. But Monty kept quiet about absolutely every aspect of his past service, the men who he now worked with's backgrounds, or information of any kind.

Kellie's mouth hung open in a comic gesture of shock at the quantity of medals. He shut the lid and made sure the box was as it was left. The condom wrapper finally back in his hand to toss out, and this time he made it all the way to the shower. He stood under the hot spray, trying not to be overwhelmed. Monty seemed way too big to handle. The man wanted to be dominated by muscle men in bondage gear, had a background of being a mega hero, awarded ribbons and medals...

"I'm just a vegetarian who drives a fucking Prius!"

~

Monty passed through the front entrance of his training facility. He spotted Brandon, who appeared to be gearing up for a sarcastic greeting. Monty said, "Shut up," and kept walking to his office.

Brandon followed him. Monty felt his stare boring into his back. "You let him answer your phone?"

"I was in the shower." Monty booted up his computer.

"Is he living with you?"

He looked at Brandon, reading him. He knew the man too well. "What I do with my life does not concern you."

"I'm not telling you what to do. I'm just fucking shocked you'd let a stranger move in with you."

"I'm here. What the hell has to be done?"

"Today is our final inspection from the California board. Without it, we aren't insured."

"Are they here?" Monty waited before he sat down at the computer.

"No." Brandon looked exhausted. "The guys are doing last minute checks."

"Okay. Let me know when they get here." Monty sat in the chair and began sifting through on-line client forms requesting dates for their training session. "We haven't even had our first one and I have nearly seventy emails waiting for us in my request box."

"Good. But most are flakes and wannabes. How many can pass the cut?"

"Who cares? It's our job to open the training to everyone who wants it, not just the elite of the military." Monty started printing the forms so he could follow up on them. When he looked up, Brandon was staring at him. "What? You go nuts when I'm late and now you're just standing here like a zombie."

"I'm dead on my feet."

"Join the fucking club." Monty stacked the papers as they were printed, reading them.

Brandon sat down opposite Monty and rested his head on his arms on the desk.

"Go get a double espresso. And bring me one."

Brandon slouched in the seat, his face red and puffy.

Monty sighed. "Kathy still gone?"

"She won't even take my calls."

"You want me to talk to her?"

"You can, but I doubt it'll help." He got to his feet.

"Up to you." Monty removed his wallet and handed Brandon a five. "Double shot, mocha, no whipped cream."

Brandon took it and left.

Monty glanced at the door, shaking his head. "You wanted this, not me." He looked at his watch and picked up the phone, dialing. "Hello, this is Montgomery Gresham from the SEAL Training Team. Is this Casey?"

"Yes."

"You sent a request for a session. When are you available?"

"Oh! Cool! I can't wait. Any time."

Can't wait? When you're so sore you can't walk, you won't think it's cool. "Two weeks. I'll send you the complete medical forms and waivers, plus what you'll need for your training camp."

"Awesome! You guys rock!"

Monty tapped computer keys as he spoke. "I need a non-refundable down payment because space is limited. Once you sign the contract either snail mail it or send it in a fax. Got it, soldier?"

"Got it, sir!"

"Good. Paypal or credit card?"

"Paypal. How much?"

"Two hundred. Just call if you have any questions." Monty held out the phone as the young man hooted in pleasure. "Bye." He hung up and shook his head. "Enlist if you think it's so fucking cool!"

He shifted on the chair and stretched his back. "Son of a bitch, Kel. Your magic hands helped my back a hellavuh lot."

Monty picked up the phone to call him and thank him when his office door opened. Aaron had his coffee.

205

"That was quick." Monty reached for it.

"Zak already went to get them before you arrived. We know what you want, MG."

"You'd better. You guys need to anticipate my every need." Monty winked at him.

Thomas poked his head in. "Inspector is here."

Monty hopped to his feet and sipped his coffee as he went.

~

Kellie dropped down on the loveseat in the lounge. He had already finished his morning appointment with Lenny, his workout and his yoga session. Tyson made his way across the room and asked, "Share a smoothie?"

"Sure." Kellie touched his crotch lightly as he repositioned on the cushions, waiting for Tyson to join him. He wasn't wearing briefs. He preferred not to. It seemed only Monty caused a crisis in his pants, so why bother when he wasn't going to see him?

Tyson's cheeks drew in as he tried to suck the thick shake through a straw. He plopped down and handed it to Kellie.

"What did you get?"

"Mango-pom."

"Mm." Kellie tasted it and nodded. "Good one." He leaned his head on Tyson's shoulder. "I stayed with him last night."

"Wondered why you didn't text."

"He forgot to set the alarm and literally sprinted out, leaving me behind."

"Did ya snoop?" Tyson took back the shake to sip.

"Yes. Me bad."

"Dish." Tyson wriggled beside him.

"He really likes the BDSM thing. He had a few toys and a mag with a man-hole the size of an airplane hanger, and four boys about to plug it."

"So? You can wear the leather pants in the family."

206

"True. Then I found a bunch of photos with his military brethren, and he's got enough medals and ribbons to make a fruit salad."

"You did spy."

"Didn't get past his dresser top. Still...I feel inadequate. I mean, the guy's like some national hero now with the killing of the Big Bin."

"He killed him?" Tyson sat up.

"No. I don't think so. I mean, I doubt it." Kellie took the shake. "He's larger than life. Me? I'm just a jerk who lost everything on the real estate market and eats tofu."

"You really have yourself pegged right." Tyson elbowed him, rolling his eyes at the sarcasm. "You are an amazing guy. So stop whining."

Kellie drew hard on the straw for a mouthful of fruit and swallowed. "This is good practice for blowjobs. My man most likely wants me to suck him painfully hard."

"Ouch." Tyson covered his crotch.

"I guess once you've known real agony, nothing gets the adrenaline up like more of it."

"I would think the opposite. That he would want to be touched like a kitten."

"Nope." Kellie handed Tyson back the shake. "Fucker wants everything harder and faster. I pulled my shoulder out of the socket jacking him off."

Tyson cracked up on the sip of shake.

Kellie rolled his arm around, pushing on his sore muscles. "I need to work out just to fuck him. I sweat like a pig humping that hard."

Tyson rolled over and went hysterical laughing.

"You say anything and I'll blackmail you." Kellie poked Tyson in the ribs.

"Girl, I wish I was a fly on the wall!" Tyson handed him the shake.

"Huh. You do, believe me. Whoever would have imagined I could play dominatrix for a Navy SEAL. It staggers the mind."

"Oh? You wear a bodice and high heels?"

"You know what I mean. Dom. Okay? See? I don't even know the lingo."

"You don't need the lingo, you just need the dance." Tyson snuggled against Kellie. "Did you please your man?"

Kellie smiled and snuggled back. "He screamed as he came."

"Mm hmm." Tyson nodded smugly.

Kellie sighed. "I want him."

"Then you go get him."

~

By seven-thirty Monty was up to his neck in paperwork. He had nearly three months of sessions scheduled but it wouldn't mean shit if the reviews of the first one, starting tomorrow, were bad. Aaron and Zak were sorting paperwork for Monty as he divided approved client application forms into numbered sessions.

The door opened and Brandon and Thomas brought in pizza boxes. The smell of sausage and pepperoni filled the space.

"Don't put them down here," Monty said, "Go to the cafeteria. We have paperwork all over the place." He rubbed his neck, feeling a headache growing stronger. It made him want Kellie.

"Okay." Brandon tilted his head. "Break time."

As they filed out, Monty picked up his phone, expecting to leave Kellie a voicemail. When he answered Monty surprised. "Well, hello."

"Hello, macho-man," Kellie sounded happy.

"Got a headache. Thought of you." Monty smiled.

"Are you home? The number came in blocked."

"Still at work. Are you done for the day?"

"Just finished my last appointment. Dinner?"

Monty looked out of the open door of his office. "The boys ordered pizza. I have about an hour more to do around here."

"Okay."

"Can you come by?"

"Huh? Me there? With a bunch of macho Navy SEALs? They are all ex-Navy SEALs right?"

"I'm not saying, but," Monty laughed, "there isn't a safer spot to eat dinner in LA at the moment."

"True."

"Maybe I can get you to work your magic on me."

"Oh? Which magic?"

"My head is killing me."

"Did you buy painkillers?"

"See? I need you for things like that."

"On my way. Where are you?"

Monty gave him his address. "Should I save you a slice of pizza?"

"Is it vegetarian?"

"Uh. No. The opposite. Let me order one for you."

"No. I'll pick up something on the way and we can eat together."

"You're a doll."

"See you soon."

Monty hung up and kept working, a smile on his lips.

~

A garden salad along with an assortment of over the counter painkillers in the paper bag in his hand, Kellie walked up the dim front entrance of an unbelievable building. From the outside it was a fortress of steel and glass. Three bold letters rode the top cornice—'STT' in red. A trio of metal flagpoles with banners waving—Old Glory, California State, and the US Navy flag—

whipped in the cool October breeze. The lot was nearly empty when Kellie pulled in, but of course the grand opening was tomorrow. A dozen macho muscle cars, pickup trucks, and even an army Hummer were parked near the wide flaring entrance steps.

His Prius looked silly among the American built monster motors. *He* felt silly. Inhaling deeply, thinking, *I top you!* Kellie made his way up the steps and assumed the door would be locked. It was not. He pushed it back and was stunned at the grandeur of the interior, as if the enormity of a building this close to downtown LA wasn't enough to stun him. In huge block letters the name 'SEAL TRAINING TEAM' was in red, white, and blue on the wall as he stepped inside. It explained the acronym on the exterior of the building.

Kellie couldn't help but be impressed with the enormity of the property. But then again, in a poor economy where foreclosures were plenty, prices of real estate could be negotiated. This was the time to buy and build.

"Kel!"

Hearing Monty's voice was a relief. Kellie hadn't a clue how to find him in this palace. When Monty approached, Kellie exaggerated his astonishment. "Montgomery! You outdid yourself."

Monty hugged him, picking him up off his feet in his excitement. "You like it?"

Monty's smile said it all. Kellie looked around in awe. "I can tell you're going for upscale clients. The fixtures alone must have cost a mint."

"They did. But a lot of them were reclaimed from older buildings. The architect used old columns and the ceiling trim from a theater that had been demolished."

"It's recycled." Kellie put his tongue into his cheek.

"See? I can learn." Monty held Kellie's free hand. "I know you're hungry, but I want to give you a tour and then we'll meet the guys."

Kellie was escorted to a huge gymnasium. Monty turned on the lights. "Wow."

Monty pointed. "Obstacle course there. Calisthenics there. Through that door is the locker room." Monty continued to pull Kellie around like a kid showing off his new toys. "Five star dining area here, through there is the sleeping quarters..."

"Monty! Jesus! I love it."

"Do you?" Monty spun around, his blue eyes red from exhaustion but still full of inner life.

"Yes! I bet you charge a bundle to come here."

"We do. It's obscene. Especially since the military will do it for free." Monty smiled.

"Sure. But here you get gourmet meals and don't have to head out on a tour of duty."

"We will spoil our clients, but they will be sore as hell from the work out." Monty pulled Kellie along. "The boys are in the cafeteria. I waited for you to eat, but they didn't."

"You didn't have to do that."

"I did. Come here."

Kellie was urged through another opened set of double doors. More than a dozen men were sitting around long tables, drinking beer and eating—pizza boxes scattered around with paper plates.

"Men? This is my partner, Kellie Hamilton."

Partner? Kellie gulped and wanted to do a happy dance.

"Hey." Most of the men gave him a tiny tilt of their head as they said, 'hey' with little to no enthusiasm. Of course, they were dead tired. Kellie imagined he and Monty were the only gay men in the room. He had little doubt, but then again—who knew?

"Have a seat." Monty gestured to the end of a table filled with deliciously handsome fit men.

As Kellie set his bag on the table in front of him he asked, "Are all of you former Navy SEALs?"

No one answered. Several men began their own conversations between themselves.

Kellie shut up. He took the food out of the bag and heard the pill vials jingle. Monty placed two bottles of water down for them, taking a plate of meat-laden pizza for himself. "What do you have to eat?" Monty leaned on Kellie's shoulder playfully. "Tofu?"

"No. Garden salad." Kellie unwrapped it and began to eat hungrily. "How's your headache?"

"Don't ask. I'm pretending I'm fine again."

"Here." Kellie opened up each pill bottle. "Two from column A, and two from column B." He shook out two ibuprofen tablets and two acetaminophen tablets.

Monty took them and swallowed them down. "Thanks, doc."

"My pleasure." He kept eating and looked across the table. A man was glaring at him. Kellie stared back, trying not to be intimidated, finally recognizing him. "Hi, Brandon."

Monty took notice. He said, "Brandon, stop flirting."

Kellie coughed at the irony.

"Don't mind him, Kel. His wife left him 'cause he's closet gay."

The few at their table guffawed and enjoyed the joke. Kellie could only speculate on the actual meaning.

"You don't eat meat?" Brandon asked, appearing either exhausted or drunk. Even so, Kellie thought they were all fucking hot and should do a naked calendar for gay men and straight women.

"I eat his meat." Kellie elbowed Monty.

Monty nearly choked on his food he laughed so hard. "Good answer!" Monty said with his cheeks full, trying to chew. "When's the last time you got your cock sucked, Brandon?"

"Shut the fuck up," Brandon said, his lip curling.

"That long?" Monty swallowed his food and winked at Kellie. "He's tired. And seriously bummed because he fucked up his marriage with this monstrosity." Monty gestured to the building.

"I'm sorry, Brandon."

Brandon shrugged, like it didn't matter.

A man stood behind Monty and asked, "What else needs to be done before we go?"

"Just do a walk through. We'll all be here before the clients in the morning, so we can do another last minute check then. Thanks, Aaron."

"Okay, boss." He rubbed Monty's shoulder and left.

Another man walked around resupplying everyone's beer. When he handed one to Monty, Monty asked Kellie, "Want a beer?"

"Sure." Kellie took one from the young man and read the label. "Nice!"

"Told ya," the young man said to Monty.

"Two points for Zak." Monty picked up a bottle opener from the table to open both beers.

"You serve beer here too?" Kellie gulped the microbrew down.

"Not to the clients, no. We don't have a liquor license." Monty took a long swig. "We already spent everything we have."

"Later," another man sitting at their table said. "After the first million."

Kellie noticed Brandon looking at the man who spoke for a moment before he said, "You better be right."

"He is, Brandon. Have another drink. You look like shit," Monty said.

"My head is killing me."

Kellie noticed Monty tilting his head at him to do something, so Kellie dumped more pills onto the table and slid them over. Without a question, Brandon swallowed them with his beer.

"You look bad." Kellie narrowed his eyes in sympathy. "I can help."

"You just did." Brandon sipped his beer.

"Let him help you." Monty brushed off his hands.

"Help me what?" Brandon replied in frustration like he was overwhelmed.

Kellie stood and walked around the table.

"What the hell is he doing?" Brandon asked.

"Shut up for a minute, will ya?" Monty shook his head in exasperation.

Kellie stood behind Brandon and very lightly touched his shoulders. The reaction from Brandon nearly knocked Kellie over. He spun around appearing as if he was going to punch Kellie.

"Brandon!" Monty yelled like an order. "Let the man do his job."

"What? He's going to rub me?" Brandon asked.

"If you're smart." Monty finished his slice of pizza.

"Well?" Kellie asked Brandon.

Brandon faced forward again and rested his elbows on the table.

Kellie felt the attention of a room full of he-men around him. *Look, boys, a little man on man action! Excited?*

As if Monty had read Kellie's mind, he said, "He won't turn you gay by giving you a neck rub, Brandon."

Kellie again rested his hands on Brandon's shoulders, waiting for a second to see if he would just stay still. He did.

Kellie stared directly at Monty while he began massaging Brandon's shoulders. When he saw Monty's sly grin, Kellie knew he was doing good. He increased his pressure and worked

214

the knots in Brandon's neck, shoulders, and digging through his hair to his scalp. Brandon slunk down to rest his head on his arms on the table.

Kellie grinned at Monty who appeared to be loving it.

"Feel good, Brandon?" Thomas asked.

"Mm." Brandon sounded as if he was falling asleep.

"I'm next," Monty said, drinking his beer.

"Can we all try it?" a man asked.

Kellie counted heads and figured ten minutes on each man would be nearly an hour and a half, but he was up for it.

"All?" Monty made a face of disbelief. "Book an hour, you cheapskates!"

Kellie finished up his mini massage with Brandon and petted his hair. "There ya go."

"I can't move."

Monty chuckled. "You have no idea what an hour and a half is like with him. He'll stroke your aura."

The room erupted with laughter.

Kellie walked around the table to his rascal and wagged his finger at him.

"Get over here, beautiful." Monty curled Kellie onto his lap and embraced him.

Brandon sat up slowly, looking groggy. "My fucking headache is gone."

"Magic man." Monty pushed his face into Kellie's body and moaned sensually.

"Do you have a business card?" Brandon asked.

Monty choked with hilarity and slapped the table. "Brandon wants a man's hands on him. I never thought I'd live to see the day."

Kellie smiled at Brandon, fishing his wallet out of his pocket. "It would be my pleasure, Brandon." He handed him a card.

A few of the men close to Kellie reached for one as well. Kellie handed them out. "Half-price for the first session for you guys."

"Nice." Zak nodded, reading the card.

"I'm ready to go home, Kel." Monty met his eyes.

"Okay."

"Come home with me?"

"You got it." Kellie brightened.

"But we have to set the alarm clock. I have to be here and ready to go at oh-six-hundred hours."

"Yes, sir." Kellie saluted, stood off his lap, putting the pill bottles into his pocket and sipping one last gulp of beer.

"Leave it. The boys will clean it up." Monty stopped Kellie from busing the table.

"You recycle?" He held up the bottle.

"We do. We're green. Got solar panels lining the back of the roof."

Kellie was surprised.

Brandon said, "It's about money. Not climate change, Greenpeace."

Monty put his arm around Kellie to walk out with him.

"Bye, fellas. Don't hesitate to call me if you're sore."

Someone yelled, "Monty's the one who'll be sore by morning."

Kellie gave Monty a mischievous grin. He mouthed, 'my bottom boy'.

"See ya o-six-hundred sharp!" Monty waved over his shoulder and they headed to the main entrance to leave.

Kellie looked back at the building as they walked to their cars. "You'll do very well. I know this town, Monty, and this is so perfect for the Hollywood elite. They are into every new fad and exercise craze on the planet."

"I'm hoping to be more than just a craze." Monty used his key fob to unlock his car.

"I'm following you?"

"Is that okay?"

"Yes." Kellie winked and for the first time felt confident in this budding relationship.

Chapter 18

Monty glanced at his rear view mirror. Kellie's headlights were behind him. It was nice to be 'out'. Being able to flirt with Kellie freely—not caring what the rank and file thought, being himself—was like beginning life over again.

Once he pulled close to the house, he signaled for Kellie to park in the driveway first, so he would not be boxed in when he left early in the morning.

He pulled behind Kellie's little Prius and shook his head at the size of it. It was half a car.

They met at the front door of Monty's house.

"How's your back?" Kellie rubbed his hand across it.

"Good enough to fuck all night." Monty pushed open the door and gestured for Kellie to enter first.

"Is that all I'm good for?" Kellie smiled as he spoke.

"Yeah. So? Want to back out?" Monty tossed his car keys on the kitchen counter.

"I can't. You have me trapped.'

"True." Monty stalked Kellie, loving the playful gleam in his eyes. Kellie took off running, trying to close the bedroom door before Monty got his foot inside. Monty shoved back the door and they had a standoff with the bed between them. "You can't win."

Kellie tugged his shirt over his head. "Says you."

Monty licked his lips at the sight of Kellie's cut abs and chest. He opened his zipper and exposed his cock from his clothing, stroking it.

"That's playing dirty."

"Yeah. I do that." Monty pointed his dick at Kellie, flapping it at him.

Kellie shed his lower half of clothing, standing naked in a duel of who would cave first in the war of seduction.

Monty did not strip. Instead he lowered his clothing so his balls and cock lay over it. "You know you want it."

"Yeah, but you want it more." Kellie licked his finger and ran a circle over his nipple.

Monty believed that may be true. He looked down at his stiff cock, trying to distract Kellie's attention, then sprang onto and over the bed until Kellie was in his arms. Kellie's surprise at the attack made him laugh heartily. He surrendered and went limp in Monty's embrace.

Monty ran his hands all over Kellie's skin, up his arms, around his back to the nape of his neck. Then he began chewing on Kellie's jaw and earlobe making Kellie moan. He pressed his lips against Kellie's and asked, "Mind if I take you?"

"Mind?" Kellie laughed softly.

Monty spun around and turned down the bed. He walked to the opposite side of the mattress and undressed, staring at the stack of pictures on his dresser with his eyes unfocused. Once he was naked and Kellie was lying on the bed waiting for him, Monty opened the nightstand drawer. He noticed the lubrication was inside it and met Kellie's eyes. "Did you check out my stuff?"

"Check out?"

Monty removed a large dildo, holding it up. "You couldn't miss this."

"I did notice it, but I didn't dig."

"You can. I have nothing to hide." He tossed the dildo back inside the drawer and tore a condom off the strip. "If you left me alone in your place, I'd do my research."

"What did you want me to find out about you?" Kellie reached for him.

Monty sat beside him on the bed, tossing the condom and lubrication close to them. "I suppose I wanted to you find anything you wanted to know, so you didn't have to ask me."

"Why?"

Monty relaxed alongside Kellie, toying with Kellie's soft cock. "Because I want to feel like I belong back in civilian life without constantly regurgitating my past."

"But isn't our past what makes us who we are?" Kellie caressed Monty's face.

"No. The past is gone. I am me from this day on."

"Okay. Who are you now?"

Monty gazed at Kellie's lips, then his blue eyes. "Your partner?"

"As in, exclusive?"

"Ideally."

Kellie's expression brightened.

"Is that a yes?"

"Yes. Yes with an exclamation point."

"My schedule is grueling. Be prepared for that." Monty stretched Kellie's flaccid cock, trying to bring it to life.

"Mine too. But...if we want this..."

"I want it." Monty fingered Kellie's balls, making Kellie open his legs to give Monty access.

"I want it too."

"So? We have an agreement?"

"We do. No cheating."

"No. No cheating. I don't want you sexually touching another person. Am I clear?"

"And you won't either?"

"No. No way. One man-man. You."

Kellie dove onto Monty, flattening him to the bed.

Monty said, "Now I want you in me...alpha male."

"I'll fuck you any way you want to be fucked." Kellie ran his fingers from Monty's neck to his belly button.

"That's what I love about you."

"Love?"

Monty shut up. It was too early for that. He cupped the back of Kellie's head and brought him to his lips.

~

Yeah, he didn't have to hear it. Kellie knew it already.

He kissed his man, knowing only he would be able to enjoy Monty from now until...until when they decided not to be one any longer. A week? A year? Twenty years? Who knew?

Kellie knew one thing. He wanted his bottom boy to play Dom. He embraced Monty and brought him along when he rolled over, Monty now on top of him. Kellie bent his knees and spread his legs, showing Monty just how flexible he was.

Monty parted from the kiss to look down. Seeing Kellie in nearly a split made Monty whimper in what sounded to Kellie like longing. Whatever it was, Kellie knew it would be good.

Kellie ran his hand down his own chest to his cock, working it to show off for Monty. Monty chewed his lip as he watched, his own dick thick, veiny, and red. Kellie picked the condom up from the bed, tearing it with his teeth and removing it. He reached down and rolled it on Monty's cock. Monty's breathing rate accelerated, his chest beginning to heave. Next Kellie used the lube, but instead of coating Monty, he used it on himself. Spreading his legs wide as Monty leaned back to stare, Kellie probed his own rim and hole, enjoying every expression on Monty's face.

Monty's vision was glued to the act. His cock moved in excitement so Monty held the base, ready to spring into action.

Kellie capped the bottle and set it upright on the nightstand. He held his own shins and opened wide.

"Oh fuck." Monty quickly got to his knees and knelt between Kellie's thighs. Before he drove inside Kellie, Monty swept his gaze from Kellie's eyes to his rim. Monty used one hand to surround Kellie's balls under his stiff cock and pulled them downwards, stretching the sack. Kellie closed his eyes and parted his lips in a breath.

Monty kneaded Kellie's balls until Kellie was about to jack off, he was so excited. But he didn't. Kellie gripped his own legs with white knuckles and let his man do what he wanted.

Monty crouched down and enveloped Kellie's ball into his mouth. As he fingered the left one, he sucked the right one, then switched. After a few moments to play with them, Monty sat up again, staring at Kellie's crotch. As Monty noticed something, he met Kellie's eyes. "You shaved."

"Man, you do take a long time to notice shit." Kellie thought Monty would spot it the moment he removed his pants. Poor Monty was too preoccupied.

Monty immediately scooted closer on the bed, pushing the tip of his cock into Kellie's tight rim. Kellie sighed loudly and relaxed his muscles, splaying to a limp straddle.

With his usual, take-charge manner, Monty spread Kellie's ass cheeks as he glided deeper. Once they were united on a very intimate level, Monty ran his fingers over the freshly shaven pubic area on Kellie's body. It made Kellie smile. Sometime the little things were what meant the most.

You give me a commitment? I gave you my pubic hair. How about that?

Monty closed his eyes and gave Kellie a lovely deep, masculine groan which sent Kellie's cock pulsating.

You are the king of tops. I don't care what you say.

Kellie could not stop staring at Monty—his muscular arms, his square jaw lines and broad chest.

"If I move, I'll blow." Monty stilled his hips and inhaled deeply.

"Blow."

"I want to fuck you more." Monty looked down at Kellie's crotch. "Motherfucker, that looks fantastic." He used both hands to touch all over Kellie's groin, his cock, balls, and inner thighs.

Kellie grabbed his own dick because he too was edging the climax. "Babe, I'm good to go."

Monty pushed Kellie's body backwards, a hand on either one of Kellie's legs, and he stared downwards at their connection as he pumped his hips.

Kellie fisted his cock tightly, filling his senses with Monty's looks, sounds, and the feel of his cock touching intimate places inside his body. The urge to come became a tide Kellie could not hold back. He closed his eyes, fisted himself vigorously, and sprayed cum on his chest and neck.

Monty went wild, snarling and piston-fucking Kellie, shouting, "Fuck! Fuck!" as he jammed his cock inside Kellie's ass.

Kellie wiped at the running perspiration down his face and felt Monty's cock begin to pulsate between his legs. "That's it, baby. Come for me."

Monty gripped Kellie's legs tightly and opened his mouth to choke on his silent gasps. The sight made Kellie's cock thicken again, but it soon softened up in his own grasp. He milked it gently, urging more white drops to the slit.

Monty's head drooped and his body heaved with his recuperating breathes. "I can't fucking move, I'm so spent."

"I got ya." Kellie backed up, allowing Monty to pull out. Knowing Monty had a very important day tomorrow, Kellie climbed off the bed and reached for him. Monty nearly stumbled off the bed and into the bathroom, where they both got ready for bed.

Once Kellie was under the blankets with his man, he held him close. "Now this is what I call a happy ending." Kellie thought about JC's version, just for a second.

Monty nestled against Kellie's chest and replied, "Beats a hand-job."

Kellie laughed and squeezed Monty close. When Monty's breathing grew deep and slow, Kellie knew he was fast asleep. Kellie thought about JC and the 'happy endings' he had with him after his massages. He whispered out loud, "Love is my happy ending. And you are my love. Nothing is happier than that."

The End

About the Author

Award-winning author G.A. Hauser was born in Fair Lawn, New Jersey, USA and attended university in New York City. She moved to Seattle, Washington where she worked as a patrol officer with the Seattle Police Department. In early 2000 G.A. moved to Hertfordshire, England where she began her writing in earnest and published her first book, In the Shadow of Alexander. Now a full-time writer, G.A. has written seventy novels, including several best-sellers of gay fiction and is an Honorary Board Member of Gay American Heroes for her support of the foundation. For more information on other books by G.A., visit the author at her official website. www.authorgahauser.com

G.A. has won awards from All Romance eBooks for Best Author 2010, 2009, Best Novel 2008, *Mile High*, and Best Author 2008, Best Novel 2007, *Secrets and Misdemeanors*, Best Author 2007.

The G.A. Hauser Collection

Single Titles

Unnecessary Roughness

Hot Rod

Mr. Right

Down and Dirty

L.A. Masquerade

Lancelot in Love

The Crush

Living Dangerously

Happy Endings

My Best Friend's Boyfriend

The Diamond Stud

The Hard Way

Games Men Play

Born to Please

Of Wolves and Men

The Order of Wolves

Got Men?

Heart of Steele

All Man

G.A. Hauser

Julian

Black Leather Phoenix

London, Bloody, London

*In The Dark and What Should Never Be, Erotic Short
Stories*

Mark and Sharon (formally titled A Question of Sex)

A Man's Best Friend

It Takes a Man

The Physician and the Actor

For Love and Money

The Kiss

Naked Dragon

Secrets and Misdemeanors

Capital Games

Giving Up the Ghost

To Have and To Hostage

Love you, Loveday

The Boy Next Door

When Adam Met Jack

Exposure

The Vampire and the Man-eater

Murphy's Hero

Happy Endings

Mark Antonious deMontford

Prince of Servitude

Calling Dr Love

The Rape of St. Peter

The Wedding Planner

Going Deep

Double Trouble

Pirates

Miller's Tale

Vampire Nights

Teacher's Pet

In the Shadow of Alexander

The Rise and Fall of the Sacred Band of Thebes

Chasing the Dream an Anthology

The Action Series

Acting Naughty

Playing Dirty

Getting it in the End

Behaving Badly

Dripping Hot

Packing Heat

Being Screwed

Something Sexy

Going Wild

Men in Motion Series

Mile High

Cruising

Driving Hard

Leather Boys

Heroes Series

Man to Man

Two In Two Out

Top Men

G.A. Hauser

Writing as Amanda Winters

Sister Moonshine

Nothing Like Romance

Silent Reign

Butterfly Suicide

Mutley's Crew

If you love Manlove romance, you'll love this recommended read by

Michael Mandrake

A Second Chance

http://xoxopublishing.com

Synopsis:

Hesitant to begin a relationship with someone new, two police officers who have lost their partners in the line of duty try to deal with their obvious attraction to one another. Will one of them accept the other's proposition to start over or remain alone because of their places on the police force?

Excerpt:

While we continued to chat, I noticed DeClerc in my peripheral. I couldn't help but stare at him. I moistened my lips, biting the bottom as he came closer.

Damn…

"Um, hello…" I looked past the chief to take a long gander at Daniel. I stood up, extending my hand. "I'm Farris Beason."

He accepted. "Daniel Declerc. Nice to meet you." The handshake was firm, his hands soft like a female.

Don chuckled, "See Beason, if you would've been in the right frame of mind you could've joined Daniel today."

While we exchanged smiles, I gawked at the pretty face in front of me. Daniel was even more gorgeous up close. The only distraction was the defect on his finger. Who was lucky enough to call him theirs? I had to find out.

"Pity," Daniel said with a grin. "Maybe when you've recovered from your wild night?" He cocked an eyebrow.

I laughed, "Yeah, um…maybe…"

We'd broken our hand gestures but not our gaze. Maybe he did play for my team, but the question remained, who was he married to?

Happy Endings

Also by this author: Binding Justice Part of the Bound for Romance anthology

http://shop.renebooks.com/SearchResults.asp?Cat=26

The Bondage anthology by Sascha Illyvich includes star authors, Em Petrova, Clarissa Clique, Sarah Bella, and Michael Mandrake.

Synopsis:

Binding Justice, the only gay fiction romance story in the anthology is a tale of an older man seeking the assistance after losing his wife to cancer. Throughout his life, he has had the desire to be with another man but due to his strict upbringing as well as his time in the armed forces, Sire Jacobs has suppressed those feelings. At the insistence of his gay friend Gabe, he decides to attend a party to find someone of home he can bring this side out. Enter in Jarvis Densley, a twenty three year old gay male, shunned by his parents and looking for someone to mentor and love him.

Apparently, both have similar interests but will Sire's darker desire be what keeps them apart?

Sample Chapter:

Sire felt like an old man amongst so many young people. It had been years since he'd been in a place like this.

I'm only here in support of Gabriel.

He reminded himself of that several times. Sire was pretty sure no one coming through that door would catch his eye. By the looks of things he was spot on since the clientele looked to be exactly what he *wasn't* looking for.

Did he even know what kind of man he wanted? A young, strong, and pretty one. Not a drag queen or flamer.

It amazed him he was going over this in his mind as he downed the last of his scotch while still taking in the sights. He never thought he'd get the chance to experience another man.

Still gazing, he noticed Gabe pulling someone's hand through a crowd. When Sire locked eyes with Gabe, his friend nodded with a smile as the young man with him was turned to the right. After a couple of seconds, Sire got a glimpse of the guy. He was dressed in leather, looking very appealing even from a distance.

Whoa

Sire sat up on his stool, angling his neck trying to get a good look as the twosome threaded through small throngs of people. Before he knew it, Gabe made his way over with a tall, lanky, gentleman with burgundy hair, brown eyes, chiseled features, and a wry smile. He looked a lot like one of the men on the flyer Gabe had earlier; almost the same outfit, his makeup perfect.

His look was just what Sire wanted.

Gabe grinned, "Sire, this is Jarvis Densley. I been talking with him a few minutes about his choice of clothing. He looks a lot like you asked about, right?"

Sire drew up his lips, stroking his beard.

Jarvis Densley, ugly name for a beautiful man.

G.A. HAUSER

About Michael Mandrake:

Michael Mandrake is an "80's child," happily married with
two lovely, bratty kids. Michael has had several stories accepted
for various anthologies. "Longing For A Normal State of
Vertigo" is in the "Riding the Rocket" anthology and "Only
When I Lose Myself," both from Sizzler/Intoxication. "The
Delicacies: Lust, Liquor, and Cannabis" is in "Rock and Roll
Over" while "Sorry Man, My Bad," is in the Sweeter the Juice
anthology, both from STARbooks Press. "A Different Kind of
Family Portrait," for Tattoo Anthology Volume II, "The Gift of
Myself" for XOXO's Christmas collection as well as, "The True
Meaning of Love," are published by XOXO publishing. "Jude's
Gift for Valentine's Day" is in the Love Tells All VDay
anthology through XOXO. Mandrake's tale "Conserving Energy"
was featured on Everynighterotica.com in 2010.

Also recommended read for October :

My Lieutenant

Coming this Fall 2011 from Rebel Ink Press

Synopsis:

Nathan Ellerby's apartment has been ransacked by his ex who didn't like the fact Nathan dumped him. Trouncing through the debris uttering a string of obscenities, Nathan's shocked to see Lieutenant Bryant Duncan at his door claiming he's already caught the offender. Sensing an instant connection, when Nathan finds out Bryant's divorced and he's straddling the fence between being gay or bisexual, Nathan finds himself in a quandary.

Although the Lieutenant does everything in his power to prove to Nathan he's worthy, Nathan is afraid to lower his defenses which leaves both men wondering if Nathan will allow love into his life even through his doubts.

About this author:

The Triad, otherwise known as Michael Mandrake, Rawiya, and B.L. Morticia are the characters inside the head of Sharita Lira. They're three separate muses that are the driving force behind her small amount of success. Misses Lira sees her own life as one that's very ordinary, so instead of presenting herself out to the world, she created three personalities that continue to haunt her all hours of the night to get several WIP's done at the speed of light, and push her to the brink of sheer exhaustion, but she loves it and that's the reason she hasn't told them to get out of her head.

Other works by G.A. Hauser:

Born to Please (MM-BDSM)

Twenty-nine year old charismatic, Cary 'Colt' St. John, felt almost too confident in himself even before he graduated law school and began working for an LA law firm. Acting out his sexual fantasies as a powerful dom in nightclubs was near perfection. Until he grew bored with that as well. He yearned 'fresh meat', someone he could train. The repetitive 'acting subs' in the same scenarios he played each night no longer excited him.

Straight, masculine, twenty-four year old Ashton Lake, had been through much in his troubled teens. But he was trying to hold down a steady job, stay off drugs and stick to his support meetings.

When Colt lingers one night at his office, he discovers the shy janitor, already submissive to his assertive gaze. Colt knew he had found the perfect slave. He only had to groom him.

What neither Colt nor Ashton could have predicted was the connection that bonded them. Soon Colt had to wonder, who was serving whom? The scorching heat that was created between them convinced both men, they were born to please- *each other*.

Capital Games

Let the games begin…

Former Los Angeles Police officer Steve Miller has gone from walking a beat in the City of Angels to joining the rat race as an advertising executive. He knows how cut-throat the industry can be, so when his boss tells him that he's in direct competition with a newcomer from across the pond for a coveted account he's not surprised…then he meets Mark Richfield.

Born with a silver spoon in his mouth and fashion-model good looks, Mark is used to getting what he wants. About to be married, Mark has just nailed the job of his dreams. If the determined Brit could just steal the firm's biggest account right out from under Steve Miller, his life would be perfect.

When their boss sends them together to the Arizona desert for a team-building retreat the tension between the two dynamic men escalates until in the heat of the moment their uncontrollable passion leads them to a sexual experience that neither can forget.

Will Mark deny his feelings and follow through with marriage to a women he no longer wants, or will he realize in time that in the game of love, sometimes you have to let go and lose yourself in order to *really* win.

Secrets and Misdemeanors

When having to hide your love is a crime…

After losing his wife to his best friend and former law partner, David Thornton couldn't imagine finding love again. With his divorce behind him, he wanted only to focus on his job and two children. But then something happened, making David realize that despite believing he had everything he needed, there was someone he desperately wanted—Lyle Wilson.

Young and determined, Lyle arrived in Los Angeles without a penny in his pocket. Before long, however, the sexy construction worker nailed a job remodeling the old office building that held the prestigious Thornton Law Firm. Little did Lyle realize when he gazed upon the handsome and successful David Thornton for the first time that a door would be opened that neither man could close.

Will the two men succumb to the tangled web of societal pressures placed before them, hiding who they are and whom they love? Or will they reveal the truth and set themselves free?

Naked Dragon

Police Officer Dave Harris has just been assigned to one of the worst serial murder cases in Seattle history: The Dragon is hunting young Asian men. In order to solve the crime it's going to take a bit more than good old-fashioned police work. It's going to take handsome FBI Agent Robbie Taylor.

Robbie is an experienced Federal Agent with psychic abilities that allow him to enter the minds of others. You can't hide your secrets and desires from someone that knows your every thought. Some think what Robbie has is a gift, others a skill, but when the mind you have to enter is that of a madman it can also be a curse.

As the corpses pile up and the tension mounts, so does the sexual attraction between the two men. Then a moment of passion leads to a secret affair. Will their love be the distraction that costs them the case and possibly even their lives? Or will the bond forged between them be the key to their survival?

The Kiss

Twenty-five year old actor Scott Epstein is no stranger to the modeling industry. He's done it himself between acting jobs. So when his sister, Claire, casts him in a chewing-gum commercial with the famous British model, Ian Sullivan, he doesn't ask any questions. He's a professional. He'll show up, hit his mark, say his lines, and collect his paycheck. Right?

Ian Sullivan is used to making heads turn. Stunningly handsome, he's accustomed to provocative photo shoots where sex sells everything from perfume to laundry soap. Ian was thrilled when Claire Epstein cast him in the new Minty gum commercial. He has to kiss his co-star on screen? No problem. Until he finds out Scott is the one he has to kiss!

Never before has a commercial featured two men, kissing on screen. Claire knows that the advertisement will be groundbreaking, and Scott knows that his sister needs his performance to be perfect. As the filming progresses and the media circus begins around the controversial advertisement, the chemistry between Ian and Scott heats up and the two men quite simply burn up the screen. Is it all an act? Or, have Ian and Scott entered into a clandestine affair that will lead them to love?

For Love and Money

Handsome Dr. Jason Philips, the heir to a vast fortune, had followed his heart and pursued his dream of becoming a physician. Ewan P. Gallagher had a different dream. Acting in local theater, the talented twenty-year-old was determined to be a famous success.

As fate would have it, Jason happened to be working in casualty one night when Ewan was admitted as a patient. Jason was more than flattered and surprisingly aroused by the younger man's obvious attraction to him. The two men entered into a steamy affair finding love, until their ambitions pulled them apart.

Now, one year later and stuck in a sham of a marriage that he entered into only to preserve his inheritance, Jason is filled with regret. Caught between obligation and freedom, duty and desire, Jason finds that he can no longer deny his passion. He plans to win Ewan, Hollywood's newest rising star, back!

The Vampire and the Man-eater

Love at first bite!

Stock broker Brock Hart's idea of fun was playing at the local gay nightclub every weekend with someone new. He imagined the Rules of Relationships didn't apply to him, and his best friend thought his nonchalant attitude towards sex was crazy. Until one night his playboy image was put to the test.

Spying Brock in a crowded club, Vampire Daniel Wolf sets his sights on the handsome 'man-eater' businessman. Sparks literally fly, between the two, and with one bite from the sexy vamp Brock is hooked.

Never did Brock ever imagine falling for anyone, especially not a man from Sixteenth Century England! The only problem is, he's a vampire. Can love conquer all? It will be a challenge, but one Brock is up for, in so many ways.

Murphy's Hero

Sometimes...being a hero isn't about putting on a cape.

Alexander Parker has always been painfully shy and his job at the British Museum keeps him busy. Dedicated and serious, no one is more surprised than Alexander when the replica of a Greek warrior's helmet he impulsively places on his head suddenly transforms him from mild-mannered clerk into something else entirely.

Adrian Mackenzie, the editor of a famous erotic gay magazine, is about to get the scoop of the decade. The crime ridden city seems to have a savior, a mysterious man who is righting wrongs, protecting innocents, and as luck would have it… is extremely hot.

When Adrian happens to stumble upon the Good Samaritan in action he falls hard and fast discovering love *and* Alexander's true identity. Now, if he can only get Alexander to come out of the closet. But is the world ready for a gay superhero?

Let bestselling author G.A. Hauser take you on an unforgettable fun-filled adventure and discover the story that inspired Ewan Gallagher's famous movie roll in G.A.'s *For Love and Money*.

Exposure

Exposure…the truth will set you free

In politics for twenty years, Senator Kipp Kensington knows that even a whisper of suspicion about his sexuality could jeopardize his aspirations for the Presidency. Kipp thought he could be content living a lie in a marriage of convenience. Then he met Robin Grant.

Leather-clad, motorcycle riding Robin isn't accustomed to hiding what he is or denying himself who he wants. The instant he meets Kipp, the sparks begin to fly and what started as a chance encounter soon turns into a full-blown affair of sizzling proportions.

When the contract Kipp has had for nine years with his now alcoholic, bitter wife begins to crumble and he's threatened with blackmail, the senator needs to make a decision. Should he hide who he really is in order to avoid losing his career, or reveal the truth and set himself free?

Mile High

Book One in the Men in Motion Series

Divorced accountant Owen Braydon spends his weeks
working in Los Angeles and his weekends in Denver with his
daughter. Straight-laced and mild mannered, he normally looks
at the weekly flight to and from Denver as an opportunity to get
some extra work done. But then he found himself on the same
plane as the luscious Taylor Madison.

Texas-born Taylor is from Denver, but for several months
he's been flying back and forth to Los Angeles where he works
as a project manager on a major construction job. Charismatic
and confident, Taylor is a man who knows what he wants and
isn't afraid to go after it. The second he lays eyes on bi-curious
Owen, he knows he wants him.

What starts out as a smoldering no-strings-attached initiation
into the Mile High Club quickly turns into a weekly ritual that
both men look forward to over all else. Soon their desire for one
another deepens and both men find themselves wanting and
needing more.

When a possible change in work assignments threatens to end
what they have, both men are faced with a decision. Can the
heights they soared together in the air be maintained on the
ground? Only if Owen and Taylor are willing to cast aside their
doubts, open up their hearts, set aside all inhibitions, and go the
extra mile.

Cruising

Book Two in the Men in Motion Series

Brodie Duncan expected to be taking a week-long Alaskan cruise with his girlfriend. But when she ended their relationship just moments before boarding, he ended up on the ship alone. Determined to make the best of a bad situation, Brodie considers a no-strings-attached fling. What he didn't bargain for was a man as appealing as Julian Richards. Trapped in his own bad relationship with a selfish woman he was starting to resent, the charismatic Julian is shocked by his reaction to tall, dark, and handsome Brodie. Instantly attracted to each other, the men create enough heat on their trip to the Inside Passage to melt the Glaciers in the bay.

In the end, on a vacation full of surprises, Julian and Brodie discover that not only do they have strong feelings for one another, by *Cruising* they just might have found their soul mates.

Driving Hard

Book Three in the Men in Motion Series

They met on the highway. It was the beginning of ride they'd never forget...

Texan Jude Rae Clark hit the road in his pride and joy, a jet black International big rig, searching for a new life after his divorce. Unfortunately the long, lonely hauls provided little comfort until just outside Houston on Interstate 10 a blue-eyed stranger asked for a lift.

Yale Law School graduate, Logan Bleau, set out to explore America and escape his past by hitching his way across country to San Francisco. When he meets up with a handsome stranger in his eighteen-wheeler, a physical attraction blooms and the two men end up taking a detour.

When what began as sexual exploration on the open road turns into something deeper, the pair find themselves reevaluating their lives and Jude is faced with a decision. Give up his career of cruising the highways or pass up on the love of a lifetime.

Leather Boys

Book Four in the Men in Motion Series

Start your engines, mount up, and get ready for the ride of a life-time...

Sexy gay fiction author Devlin Young donned his helmet, black leather jacket, and jeans. Then he mounted his Kawasaki and set off for what he anticipated would be a wild ride to Sturgis. There were thousands of motorcycles, thousands of men, but only one Sam Rhodes. When web-designer Sam Rhodes joined a local group called The Leather Boys, he wasn't quite sure what to expect, but he knew what it was he wanted. Amidst the decadence and insanity of the monster event, all Sam could think about was what it would be like to share an erotic experience with the deliciously naughty Dev Young.

Never one to apologize for who he is, or who he desires, Devlin doesn't understand Sam's reluctance to openly explore their relationship or his wish to keep their liaisons confined to the darkness of their tents while at the rally. Then he crosses swords with a tough-as-nails biker who both taunts and tempts him, unleashing a potentially dangerous craving and pushing Dev to make a choice.

The Boy Next Door

Brandon Townsend and Zachary Sherman were best friends and next-door neighbors. Growing up together in a cozy suburban town in New Jersey, they were inseparable and thought nothing could tear them apart. Then one night something happened between them, something that brought them even closer together…

They didn't anticipate that what began as youthful sexual experimentation would lead them into an affair of the heart that would rock them to the core. Nor did they expect the danger of being discovered and separated by their families. At the time, neither Brandon or Zach realized that life would give them another opportunity.

Now, ten years later, a chance meeting brings them together again. Let best-selling gay fiction author G.A. Hauser take you on an unforgettable journey. A coming of age story about faith, about courage, and about trust…you'll never forget The Boy Next Door.

When Adam Met Jack

Attorney Jack Larsen may not have everything he wants, but between his successful career and best friend Mark Richfield, he's content. But when Mark comes out of the closet only to declare his love for ex-LAPD officer Steve Miller, Jack is devastated. Months later and still wounded, he's not looking to be swept off his feet, but it's hard to say no to handsome

Hollywood hotshot Adam Lewis. Adam Lewis has made a name for himself representing some of today's brightest stars. But when his business partner is accused of unethical behavior, he finds himself in need of legal advice. When Adam walks into the law office of Jack Larsen, it's strictly business until he sets eyes on the powerful and sexy hero that's about to rescue his reputation.

When Adam Met Jack is an amazing new novel by Amazon best selling gay fiction author G.A. Hauser featuring characters from Love you Loveday, For Love and Money, and Capital Games. It's got the glamour of the entertainment industry, the drama of the courtroom, and the amazing passion that you've come to expect from every G.A. Hauser book.

Love you, Loveday

Angel Loveday thought he had put his life as a gay soft-porn star of the 1980's behind him. For seventeen years he's hidden his sexuality and sordid past from his teenage son. But when someone threatens Angel's secret and Detective Billy Sharpe is assigned to his case, he finds himself having to once again face them both.

Since his youth Billy Sharpe has had erotic on-screen images of Angel Loveday emblazoned in his mind. Now Angel is there in the flesh, needing his protection and stirring up the passionate fantasies that Billy thought he'd long ago abandoned.

As the harassment continues and the danger grows, Billy and Angel become closer. What began as an instant attraction turns into an undeniable hunger that unlocks Angel's heart. It's a race against time as Billy tries to save the man of his dreams from a life without love and the maniacal stalker hell-bent on destroying him.

G.A. Hauser

To Have and to Hostage

When he was taken hostage by a strange man Michael never expected he'd lose his heart...

Michael Vernon is a rich, spoiled brat with a string of meaningless lovers and an entourage of superficial friends. With no direction in life, he wastes his days spending his father's money and drowning himself in liquor...until he crashes into a man even more desperate than himself, Jarrod Hunter.

Jarrod Hunter grew up on the wrong side of the tracks. Out of work, about to be evicted, and unable to afford his next meal, Jarrod thought he'd reached the end of his rope and was determined to take his life. Then fate intervened delivering him

Michael Vernon. Why not take him home, tie him up, and hold him hostage to get the money he needs?

Two men from two different worlds...one dangerous game. Trapped together in close quarters, Jarrod and Michael find themselves sharing their deepest thoughts and fighting an undeniable attraction for each other. As the hours tick by, the captor becomes captivated by his victim and the victim begins to bond with his abductor. This wakeup call might prove to be just what Michael needs to set himself free. To Have and to Hostage...sometimes you have to hit bottom before realizing that what you need is standing right in front of you.

Giving Up the Ghost

The visit from beyond the grave that changed their lives forever...

Artist Ryan Monroe had everything he wanted and then in a blink of an eye, he lost what mattered most of all, his soul-mate, Victor. Tortured by an overwhelming sense of grief and unable to move on, his pain spills out, reflected in the blood red hues of his paintings.

Paul Goldman thought he'd found the love of his life in Evan, his beloved pianist. Their mutual passion for music was outweighed only by their passion for one another. They were planning a life-time together, but then one fateful night Evan's was taken. Drowning in sorrow, unable to find solace, the heartbroken violinist has resigned himself to a life alone.

Now it's two years later and something, someone, is bringing them together. Two men, two loves, two great losses... and one hot ghost. Giving up the Ghost by G.A. Hauser, you won't be able to put down!

Made in the USA
Lexington, KY
14 February 2012